SAIL

Book Two in The Wake Series

by M. Mabie

Cover Design Copyright © 2015 by Arijana Karcic, Cover It! Designs Book Formatting by Stacey Blake, Champagne Formats Editing by Marion Making Manuscripts, Marion Archer, and Bare Naked Author Services, Claire Allmendinger

ISBN-10: 1502388642
ISBN-13: 9781502388643

Also by the author

Fade In

The Wake Series
Sail, Book One

For my moms,
Linda and Lucille

PROLOGUE

Casey

Friday, January 1, 2010

SHE WAS SO TIGHT.

Concave and convex, we fit together like two praying hands. A prayer that begged for absolution and time. We were both sinners and the truth of that hurt. But having her in my arms, her mouth on mine, I couldn't understand how I'd ever be forgiven. And I didn't want to be.

Her hands met my flesh and searched for something lost. She pulled at my hair and her lips met my neck. Hot and greedy, she sucked and bit at me.

Our sweat mixed. Our breaths shared.

I hovered above her on my elbows, my hands cradling her head to ensure she was really there. Ten fingers scored my back. One pink nose encouraged me. Two clear eyes penetrated mine, conveying everything I knew was true.

Her guilt.

Her pain.

Her love.

And I fucking owned all of it.

"I love you," she said. Or maybe she didn't, but I heard it anyway.

She was terrible at loving me. Never getting it right, but she tried. She fought hard, usually with herself, and that alone gave me hope.

At this point in the game, if she didn't love me, she was plain crazy. The heaven she helped create. The hell she'd put us through. They were one and the same.

Our bodies moved together. Old hat. They knew this dance. We left them to it. The mechanics of fucking like we did came naturally. It was the feelings we had the hardest time navigating.

"Just stay this time," I said, knowing she didn't have a choice. "Don't go."

Her eyes met mine with a fire in them and I recognized the hint of guilt. The ebony-colored irises melted into the deep black as they dilated. Her honest pink nose told me the truth.

My lower back tensed as I pushed into her slowly, a rhythm too intense because it was barely there at all.

Her hands rounded my ass as it clenched, and she pushed against me, inviting me to give her more. Her hands knew more about her heart than she realized.

"I never leave you. Even when I'm gone. I'm *here*." She didn't indicate exactly where *here* was, but the expression on her face told me it was the place where we both belonged.

I buried myself and held still inside her, only rocking my hips a little, creating a friction between us. A move I was well-practiced in, and knew all too well how it affected her. Her legs wrapped around me, and she held on tight, pressing herself against me, building an orgasm that would go off at any second.

She fucked me like it gave her purpose. She always had. Fast. Slow. Gentle. Rough. Standing. Lying down. Bent over. Front. Back. Every way we knew. She loved it all. She responded to soft kisses on her neck as much as she did when I pulled her hair.

I moved my hand in between us and traced the pad of my thumb over her, rubbing Os that matched the one on her face.

"Tell me you love me," she begged. Those precious words were not often shared between us, but who needed words? Not us. Our talk was cheap and sometimes saying them felt like much less than what they really meant. But my honeybee wanted to hear them. From my lips to her ears, I'd wash her body with them and every other word in my meager vocabulary, if it meant she was really mine.

"I've loved you," I whispered, as I pressed into her, deeper than I'd allowed myself until then, "and I've hated you, too."

She flexed around my cock, my words jarring her. It felt so fucking good, and I bowed my head moaning a slur of expletives.

"You've hated me?"

"I had to. Ah." She flexed again, but the look on her face wasn't one for poker; instead it showed amusement. She tightened once more around my dick, and I instinctively rolled my hips. "Ah." I wanted so badly to thrust into her over and over until we were both screaming and satisfied. But I held firm.

"Why? Why'd you have to hate me?"

The small sliver of light from the other room hit her eyes just right and they appeared to be glowing. She was lit up. Cheeks flushed. Fevered skin that matched the heat inside me.

"Because it was too much—too much to figure out. If I didn't hate you at times, I would have hated me, and that wouldn't have done either of us any good."

I wrapped my arms around her and pulled her body to mine as I sat back. Her legs remained curled around me, and when I sat back fully, she sank down on me, allowing me to feel the end of her. Blake's head tipped back, rolling from side to side.

"You feel so good," she said. "Don't hate me."

"I don't want to."

She rode me like she had many times before. I was in heaven.

Then, it was hell.

"I'll never leave you, Grant."

Grant? What the fuck?

Everything got cloudy and warped. I shook my head to clear the words I thought I'd just heard her say and when I did I saw everyone in the room. My family. Her brother, Reggie. My ex, Aly. And Grant.

They all watched.

Grant said, "I know, Betty. When you're finished playing with your toy, let's go home."

Then, I woke up. My stomach tied in knots. Alone.

ONE

Casey

Friday, January 1, 2010

I DIDN'T REST THAT night. Sleep came and went. So, early to rise it was for me on New Year's Day.

As I studied the letter she gave me that was written on a hotel notepad, my mind raced with what happened. I read the words over and over. That tormenting fucking piece of paper. Why had she never mailed it to me? Or better yet, said the words out loud to me? She'd come to me after my mother died and never once told me these things—at least not in so many words.

But did I know them anyway?

It was clear to me she loved me, but simply saying words can't always prove it. Words can be erased or unspoken. Our love never was. Months and years apart didn't fade our love, and all of the things that should've been said, we were never fucking brave enough to, but we'd still heard them in our hearts.

The more I read it, the more power it gave me.

She was still fighting.

I'd fight too. But differently than I had before. I'd be what she wanted—what she was never able to ask of me. I'd be the dependable man she desired. I'd be the stability she craved. I was ready for that. I was ready for whatever it took to have her.

Fuck, if she told me to be a tree, I would've figured out a way to sprout limbs and branches. I'd find a way. I'd be the motherfucking tree of all the other trees if that was what she needed.

I was responsible, not that I'd ever made a point to prove it to her until now. If she was looking for stability, I had full control of my work schedule. I could balance travel and home however I needed to. I was ready for those changes. She wanted a man, and I'd only shown her a boy.

The coffee maker beeped, and I realized I'd been standing there the whole time, watching it fill.

My house didn't feel like a home, not like it had when my mother was alive. Or how it did again while Blake had been here. The sun didn't warm the floors like it had last October. Cooked food didn't linger in the air.

Instead, it felt stale; it even smelled stale. Only glasses, from those select few times I actually took the time to pour my poison of choice into them, filled the sink.

My house wasn't a particularly great place to come back to—not in the state it was. It wasn't somewhere to seek refuge. And by the grace of fucking God himself, if she came back to me, I wanted her to have a warm place to run.

I poured a cup of black coffee and sat at the bar making a mental list.

There were many crimes that I committed against us, too. I couldn't continue blaming only her. I had made my lion's share of mistakes as well. Never telling her how I felt. Never asking her what she wanted from me. Fucking Aly.

I'm not sure how she knew about that, but I guessed a little birdie told her. A hell-bent, blonde birdie. The same fucking birdie I paraded around in front of her to intentionally make her jealous. I didn't think Aly would tell her, but maybe, in the back of my mind, I was glad she did.

I didn't find any pleasure in hurting Blake. Love. Hurts. If we measured our love by the pain we felt, we'd be certified masters in the art. I only hoped that made us stronger.

Another cup of coffee and another thousand missed opportunities to tell her I'd give her anything, all slipped through my fingers.

But the more I thought about the words, the more I felt like a hypocrite.

Words. Words. Words.

It wasn't the words that ever created results. It was our actions that paved the way through this. It would be my actions that would prove to her she could have everything she wanted. *From me.*

I wanted to be the man who provided for her. To build her world around. To rely on. Me.

My cell rang. I prayed it was her.

That prayer went unanswered, but my phone didn't.

"Hey," I said to Troy when I picked up the call, hitting the speakerphone button and letting my cell sit on the counter.

"Dude, what the fuck happened last night? Where'd you go?"

I ran my hand through my hair and leaned against my palm. I ran my thumb around the rim of my coffee.

"What didn't happen?"

"Well, you held your fucking own. That's for sure. I would have beaten the shit out of that drunk bastard. I still can't believe she brought him. I guess that was one way to break it to him," he scoffs, chuckling awkwardly. "Man, she's heartless, isn't she? Good for you for leaving her there. I bet she got the fucking message. You're with Aly. Speaking of Aly, she got pretty torn up after you left. I think Nick had to take her home. But hell, I was pretty tanked too, so I'm not really sure."

Heartless?

"Watch your fucking mouth, dude. You have no idea what you're talking about. I'm not *with* Aly. God. Is that what everyone thinks?"

"Well, you sure did make a show of being there *with* her."

"That's what it was. A fucking show." Trying to make Blake jealous, I'd flaunted Aly in front of her like a trophy. It was wrong, but I was fucking desperate. At the time, bringing her felt like a sure-fire way to make it clear to Blake how I felt seeing her with *him.*

Still, I hadn't thought about what it would look like to outsiders. To my family. To Aly. To anyone else. My judgment was clouded; my focus firmly set on one purpose: Blake and making her crack. I wanted her jealous. I wanted Grant to witness it. I wanted everyone to see her falter. But she was strong and acted like nothing was wrong. I knew her too well. I could see all of the emotions I was trying to force her to admit in her eyes. She only showed them to me—and in the end to Grant, too.

I don't know what happened between them after I left, only that he went back to their room, got his shit and left. When she left Hook, Line and Sinker, I watched from the car. I wanted her to come to me and tell me it was over between them. And in a way she had, but that didn't mean it was all buttoned up and in the past. It was far from that.

Still, he knew. Then, she followed him after being with me in the car. I could still smell her on myself in my kitchen afterward. I could still feel her mouth on my neck, hear her breath in my ear.

"So what?" Troy asked, not following what had actually happened.

"So I took Aly to make Blake jealous, and it worked. I didn't expect Grant to get drunk like he had. I didn't think Aly would talk to Blake. And I sure as fuck didn't think twice about *Aly* after I left."

"Yeah, that was kind of a dick move. What were you thinking?" he said, sounding annoyed.

"I don't know. I was tired of waiting for her. I just thought if I put enough pressure on Blake she'd finally make a move. She'd tell him." I pulled at my hair and I scratched the top of my head. "You know what? It doesn't matter now."

"Oh, it doesn't?" Troy was my friend, like a second brother, but he wasn't one to sugarcoat things. "So let me get this straight. You fucked Aly the other night and brought her to your brother's wedding just to get a rise out of some married chick? Fuck, Casey. Can't you see how messed up that is?"

"Yes! I see that, but I didn't know what to do. Yeah, I fucked Aly, but it wasn't like I went after her. Did she tell you that? Did she tell you she came to *my* house Christmas Eve when I was already fucking trashed? She walked right-fucking-in, Troy. So don't spout off like she's so fucking innocent. If it wasn't for her nosy fucking ass, Blake wouldn't even *be* married." Which was only about half true, but that was just semantics. "Don't judge me, you fucking prick. You. Have. No. Clue."

It was silent on the line and by that time, I had both hands in my hair as I was talking—or shouting—down at my phone on the bar. It was easy for him to criticize what was going on from the outside, but he didn't know. It wasn't fair for me to get pissed at him for trying to set me straight either. He was only trying to look out for a friend—me. He just didn't know everything like he thought he did.

"You only know part of it, dude. So just shut down the sermon, okay?" I said, leveling my tone.

"It must be really fucking lonely in that head of yours," he said, also taking it down a notch.

"I have just as much blame in this as anyone. And don't call Blake heartless."

"Listen, it's going to be a nice day. Let's take a bike ride and you can get some of this shit off your chest. I'm your friend, man. If you want me to quit thinking the worst about this whole thing, then you need to tell me what the hell is going on."

A ride sounded perfect. He was right. I needed to say it all out loud. Lay it out. Own my shit.

And I'd start with him.

My calves burned and the cool January air cleansed my lungs.

Troy and I rode—in almost complete silence—for about two hours before we stopped at a roadside park, up on one of my favorite bluffs.

I used my kickstand while Troy let his bike fall over. Some things never changed. He'd done that since we were kids, and it made me laugh every time he'd hop off, letting his bike fall over.

"You know you wouldn't have to buy new bikes all the time if you'd take better care of them," I commented, as I sat on the bench facing the bay. It was still foggy and the water was hardly visible.

As I took a swig of the water I'd brought, he snapped the sweatband I was wearing, repositioning it over my eyes. Then, climbing up on the bench next to me, he sat on the steel back, resting his feet on the seat.

I pulled the band off my eyes and pushed my hair back with it.

Troy grew up only a few blocks away from me and my family, but he didn't have the same kind of home life we did. I remembered his dad from back in the day, and as the years passed, he began to look more and more like him. Shoulder-length, stringy-blond hair, a lazy beard, and bloodshot eyes. Half-hearted tattoos.

Troy's dad was a musician and had lived a hard life. On the road with bands frequently, he took jobs as a roadie or a guitar tech when there was an opening and a free bunk on the bus. His mother was just as rough as his old man. His parents divorced around the same time as mine did.

Most weekends he'd stay at our house from the time school got out Friday until we went back Monday morning.

True to his family's nature, he worked jobs for cash. He'd pick up a few shifts here and there at Tinnitus Music, where Cory worked, when they needed help, but mostly he'd tend bar or work the door at music venues. He'd play a show here or there when a band needed a fill in, but he didn't play regular shows with just one band.

After we'd sat there longer than his fly-by-night patience allowed, he stole the water bottle from my hands, finished it off, and tossed it toward the nearby trash can. He missed, but instead of picking it up, he tipped his chin up at me. "Start talking, man."

"Where the fuck do I start?" I asked, leaning my head back against the metal surface.

"Start where it started."

Where it started? If I could go back to where it started and do it all differently, I would've. But I didn't have a time machine. Where was Doc with a DeLorean and a clock tower when you needed him?

I began with, "She looked like a drowned cat," and just kept going from there. I told him about that first weekend. Then, about how I looked her up after she started the job with Couture Dining. Aly, Chicago, and how I'd set it up for us to meet in Atlanta.

He listened to me go on and on about city after city, revisiting each chance I had—and missed—at telling her how I felt and what I really wanted. How we talked almost every day, but never really said much. I told him about her wedding, and what happened when she came to me after my mom died.

I told him everything I could remember, and as I listened to myself rehash the past few years, I cringed with every fuck up.

Another few hours passed and we shared a bag of sunflower seeds, taking turns spitting the shells on the ground. He ran across the highway to the park bathrooms and brought back two more bottles of water.

It wasn't like us to have deep conversations about that kind of shit. Every time I thought it was getting too weird or I felt like I was acting like a silly girl, he'd punch my shoulder and urge me to keep going.

By the time I reached the part where she gave me the letter, he'd called me a fucking idiot under his breath ten or two hundred times. As much as I knew the release was cathartic, remembering how *good* we were together brought an achingly familiar pain to my chest. I fucking missed her. And after all the shit we'd been through, I knew it was all worth it.

"What are you going to do now?" he asked, when the story butted against present tense, his knee bobbing up and down. I think I was stressing him out. I knew the feeling.

"I'm not sure. What do you think?" He knew everything and I could finally get some sort of outsider's take on it all. A weight had been lifted. I looked at the water that was not plainly visible and wondered what she was doing, pushing my foot through the dirt over and over until I made a rut.

"I think you have to trust her," he admitted, throwing his hands in the air.

"Trust her?"

"Sounds fucked, huh?" He chuckled and hopped up, stretching his back with his arms in the air.

"No. I do trust her, I'm just sick of fucking waiting."

"Well, if I were you I'd wait. I'd get my shit together and wait my fucking ass off," he said, looking at me as he bent over to touch his toes.

It wasn't at all what I thought he'd say. I imagined him saying something more like, "Well if she comes back, then cool, but don't hold your breath." But he didn't.

I cocked a confused eyebrow at him, silently asking him to elaborate on his grand master plan, which took him all of two hours to figure out. Was it really that easy?

"The way I see it, if you call it quits here, you'll be fucked up forever. She said she was going to fix it? Let her. She has one hell of a mess to clean up, but if she says she's willing to do it, then she's one tough chick. A girl like that is worth waiting a little while for." He chuckled a little under his breath, then said to himself, "Fuck. I know all about waiting."

I didn't know how long it would take her to come back to me, but he was right. She would. I had to trust her and I had to be worth coming back to.

I owed myself that much. Be a man she *couldn't* ever leave again. I'd get her and I'd keep her.

TWO

Blake

Friday, January 1, 2010

I HAD TO COME up with a plan where I got to keep Casey. I needed to think long and hard about how to do it. I owed it to myself to make sure this wasn't one more thing I messed up. My guilt kept piling up by the second.

It was New Year's morning and I'd chosen a later flight, having guessed Grant would take the first one available. I hadn't been far behind him arriving at the airport. I didn't want to see him just yet. I didn't want to see anyone. I needed to sit and process everything that had happened, so after I checked in, I hung out awhile to think before going through security.

The rehearsal dinner.

The wedding.

My chat with Aly in the bathroom. She'd freaking slapped me. *Slapped me.*

Then the fight. Or was it a fight? Maybe it was just a drunk man and a sober man trying to claim what they each thought was theirs. But I wasn't Grant's by any stretch of the imagination. And I wasn't really Casey's yet, either. Hearing them go back and forth, Grant yelling and Casey staying reasonably calm, had been an emotional smack that made the bitch slap I'd taken in the ladies' room look like child's play.

From my vantage during the quarrel, all I could see was the storm in Casey's eyes. I was sick of hurting him.

Maybe Aly was right. Maybe I was bad for Casey. Deep down, I think we both knew what we were doing wasn't good for either of us. So why couldn't we ever just stop? Why didn't he ever just say forget it and be with her?

But he *had* been with her.

Was I allowed to be jealous? Was anyone ever entitled to another person? He had every right to be with her and her with him, but the thought of them together gave me a chill. It was very possible I was going to lose him. To her. And she'd been right. Every time I'd left Casey, it made it that much easier for her to be there for him.

I'd made such a fucking mess.

Sitting in the abandoned terminal, I drank coffee after coffee waiting for my connecting flight out of Reno. But it was good. I needed the minutes.

I needed the quiet. It was peaceful.

My life had just exploded. My husband learned about my affair with the man who I'm really meant for, and once again, I'd left him. Left Casey.

I watched the sun rise over the tarmac.

The planes slowly taxied around the runways, almost as if they were on a leisurely Sunday stroll. They made me question my own patience. A question I wasn't ready to answer, but knew was the root of one of my biggest problems.

They called my flight next and like all the other quiet travelers, I stood in line and waited my turn. Funny how things appear to you all at once.

I sat over the wing on the way to Seattle, watching the low-lying clouds blanket the Earth below me. It was so sunny up there, but the ground couldn't see it. It was covered with grayness when all along the sun shined just above.

At thirty-thousand feet, I accepted that my patience was a bad thing. I was too persistent. At every turn, it was my endurance, my ability to wait for that right moment—that was never going to happen—that had failed me.

Tolerantly, I had waited to fall in love with Grant. My patience had hovered over our relationship like the thick clouds I watched out the window. It wouldn't allow the sun to filter through. Perhaps, in that relationship, there had never been any sun waiting to filter through. Perhaps the wait would have been in vain anyway.

I waited for Casey to tell me what I wanted to hear instead of taking a leap of faith and just asking him. I was so stubborn it had resulted in him not telling me until my wedding day. Then I'd set a timeline of a year. A year? Who does that? What was I waiting for and where in the fuck did I get this sense of fortitude? Because it never felt like I got what I was actually waiting for. It never got me him.

It was when I'd been spontaneous that I'd been the happiest.

The night I'd met Casey in Hook, Line and Sinker, I'd said fuck patience. To hell with waiting. I'd wanted him. That night was almost perfect.

He'd told me what he wanted.

I'd wanted it too.

I sipped cold coffee and vowed to fight my patience. To stop waiting. To move. To appreciate the overcast. After all, the sun wasn't that far away. It was just out of sight for the moment. Not gone all together.

When I landed, it was still very early for New Year's Day. Most people were sleeping it off after a night of partying and celebrating.

Who knew airports could make one reflect so much? I bought a water—another cup of coffee might have made my skin vibrate straight off my bones—and sat by baggage claim after I retrieved my bags, and continued to reflect. I could only imagine what I looked like to the few lonely people in the airport. I had the good sense to at least open a magazine I'd bought so I wasn't just staring off into space. They would have called security. There I was in a dress, trench coat, and last night's makeup and hair. What a hot, pathetic mess.

But my body waited for my head to sort it all out, even though I looked like a single piece of candy in a crystal dish. Forgotten and singular. Regardless, with only the buzz of the suitcase conveyor to hum along with, I could finally hear everything clearly.

I wasn't going back to the house Grant bought for us.

There was no going back. I was never really there anyway.

I'd talk to Grant later, but it was best I either got a hotel room or went to my parents' house. Not just for Casey's and my benefit, but for Grant's as well. This wasn't his fault. I owed it to him to tell him the truth—almost more than anyone. He hadn't deserved his wife cheating on him. No one did. He probably had a major hangover on top of it all.

I reached into my bag for my phone and powered it up for the first time since I'd turned it off before I left the bathroom at the bar. It was late, already early afternoon. I was flooded with messages and missed calls, but the one that stuck out to me was from Casey.

Casey: Happy 2010. Goodbye.

Like hell, *Goodbye.* I wanted to think about my reply thoroughly. I needed to be careful with my words to Casey. How much more could he take? *Would* he take? I had to do better by him. When I'd neglected him, it hurt me worse. That had to stop. There was no mistaking how badly I desired communication with him.

Me: Happy 2010. Don't say goodbye. We're just in a fight. Remember?

He didn't reply right away. I didn't expect him to. I wasn't going to stop reaching out to Casey though, dammit. I needed to think more about what to say to him, but not saying anything to him anymore simply wasn't an option.

I didn't think twice about looking up the number for the Hotel Max. I needed some sleep, even though my mind was still running at full speed.

I took a cab and checked in. I smiled at the door to the room I'd met Casey in so long ago as I walked down the hall to the room I'd been given today. Was there anywhere he hadn't left pieces of himself in my life?

Showering and changing into pajamas, I lay down on the comfortable bed and stared at my phone.

I knew what I needed to do and even though it wasn't going to be easy, it also wasn't going to be that hard. I was going to be with Casey and nothing else mattered. It was where I belonged.

My fingers slid over the screen as I typed to him and hoped his faith in me was still there.

Me: I won't give up on us.

That it wasn't goodbye for us. The light at the end of the tunnel would get brighter and like the sun above the clouds that I couldn't see from the ground, I had to believe it was there.

It was there.

It was there the whole time. I just had to have faith.

THREE

Casey

Friday, January 1, 2010

IT WAS HARD TO have faith when I didn't know how she was or what she was doing.

My phone burned a hole in my pocket all day. I checked the battery. Checked my service. Double-checked I hadn't missed something, scrolling through my missed calls and messages over and over until it was starting to look like a nervous tick.

Troy saw me do it, but had the good sense to leave me alone. I appreciated more as we got older the kind of friendship we had. No bullshit.

When I returned to my quiet home, I didn't have to hide my compulsions.

It was then that something switched in my head and I decided not to look at it anymore. I found the last messages between us and read them again.

I was still doing it. Same as always. I was waiting for her. I always had. Allowing it to be *her* move. How long did I expect her to be the only one going forward when all I ever did was let her muddle through the shit on her own?

Real fucking fair, Casey.

I couldn't hold her responsible time after time, for buckling under the weight of it all, after carrying the burden for both of us. I couldn't expect her to do it alone.

If I wanted to be the man she needed, the man she deserved, I needed to fight too. Hard. I had to quit fighting *her* and fight *with* her.

The night before I'd felt like a man possessed and possessed I was. Territorial even. Like I had control—for maybe the first time—and it was all because I *did* something. I was part of the change I wanted. There was no mistaking the look on her face when she dialed into my assertive behavior. Even worse, or better for me, Grant made a fucking ass of himself.

When I took control, I was a man worthy of her. Composed. Owning my shit. I wanted her; my need was obvious. It felt like lasers shot from every pore on my body, searching for her at all times. She never went undetected.

At the wedding, he fell apart, getting drunk and acting like an ass in front of everyone. I couldn't really blame him. He'd realized a pretty huge thing. But in the bar when he looked weak and pathetic, I stood tall, knowing he was on my turf and I wasn't about to play the part of the fool.

Sure, I could have beaten his foolish ass all over that bar and no one would have stopped me. But I didn't. I was a man deserving of her love.

Then—like a fool—I'd been rough and indifferent with her heart, when all along it was mine feeling vulnerable. Once again, I'd reacted in a way that would have any other woman running for the hills. I'd text her "Goodbye," and she was still fighting for *me*.

I opened my phone to take it back. It was time I *was* the better guy. Me.

The old way didn't work for either of us. If I had any chance of making her mine, I'd have to *be* hers. I'd have to be there for her.

My finger slid the phone open on a mission to retract my shitty message, that I'd only said—once again—to make her feel the hurt I felt. She'd just told me she loved me for the first time and I didn't even look at her.

What a prick.

I wouldn't have been surprised if that was too much. If this time, when I'd pushed her way, she'd really let me go.

Then my phone buzzed and lit up like the night sky on the 4th of July. Many notifications of missed calls and messages flooded it.

Spectacular are those moments—the silent, invisible connections revealed—when you pick up the phone and it chimes. The time for us to be a team in this thing was right in front of us, and it appeared she felt it too.

Honeybee: Happy 2010. Don't say goodbye. We're just in a fight. Remember?

Honeybee: I won't give up on us.

Honeybee: I'm at a hotel, not at Grant's.

I read the last one three hundred fucking times. She couldn't have sent a better text. I'd wondered if she was going back to their house. Finding out she hadn't was like hearing my death-row heart receive a pardon. Even the way she said "Grant's" excited me. Grant's house. Not home. Not their house. *His.* If she wasn't thinking of their house like hers, then maybe she was finally going to make this happen. Us.

We were fantastic at frustrating each other, but we also knew exactly what to offer as a life rope. And that's what she'd done. She tossed me a line and on the end of it was hope.

Admittedly, I'd been rough on her at the party. Parading Aly in front of her. Playing that song. Dancing to it with another woman. Another woman who she'd just learned I'd been with in her absence. I could only imagine how that conversation went down. What had Aly said?

It certainly wasn't a good time to ask, but someday I'd find out. I imagined Aly being callous and Blake not taking her shit. But who knew? I'd put both of them in an ugly situation that night.

I wasn't perfect and hated facing the ugly reality that I'd been with someone other than her—even though I knew she'd been with Grant. And of all people I'd chosen Aly, someone who Blake already had a less than stellar history with. The lines of faithfulness were never clear with us. I wondered if they ever would be.

Actually, no. Going forward, those lines had to be clear.

Would she trust me? Could I trust her? There was no way of knowing. But, shit, I didn't want to find out firsthand if it *was* all possible. Love can make a dude do some messed-up shit.

Me: Are you okay?

Honeybee: I think so. I did a lot of thinking. Took the long way back. Had a layover in Reno, and then hung out at the airport for a while.

Me: Want to talk about it?

Honeybee: I don't know. I'm afraid of being wrong or hurting you any more than I already have.

Me: We hurt each other. It's not just you. It never was.

Honeybee: I don't want us to be like that anymore, Casey. I want this done already. I want to be together.

Me: Me too.

It wasn't like we were talking on the phone, but I muted the television anyway. I'd only been back home for a little while, long enough to order a pizza and take a shower. I lounged on the couch, and it was probably the shock of her sending me the message I'd been dreaming of for a long damn time that made it a mute-worthy moment. I felt like I'd won a battle I'd been fighting alone. Finally, relief.

Me: What are you going to do? Have you told him you're back in Seattle?

Honeybee: I haven't spoken to anyone. Just you.

Just me.

If I were a girl I would've probably made one of those squealy noises, but I'm not. I'm a dude. So instead, I high-fived nothing, midair.

Instantly, I knew it was an opportunity for me to make the right decision and tell her how I felt—spelled out, without any possibility of misinterpretation. Not being completely honest and open about how I was feeling had been my biggest mistake. I leaned back deeper into the soft couch and looked around as I searched my mind for the right words.

I couldn't find them, so I winged it.

Me: Not sure if it's the right thing to say, but I want you to know that what you just texted me makes me happy. You, leaning on ME first. I want that. We can be a team. Me and you.

It was now or never. Literally. And fuck, it was time I showed up for her.

Me: I'm here. All the time, honeybee. I love you. Let's do this.

Honeybee: You love me? You still want me? Want us? What about goodbye?

Me: Yes, I want you. No more messing this up, okay? Either of us. I'm sorry I sent that text. There is no goodbye. I won't lie like that anymore.

Honeybee: Lie?

Me: I lie about how much you mean to me or how bad I miss you. I'm done pretending you're not mine and I'm not yours. Because we are. We always have been. Our hearts just got there before the rest of us.

I sucked my lip into my mouth. The feeling of this text was almost reminiscent of how we started—or how we should have started. How easy it was to talk to her before worry and doubt crept into the equation. All of this could have been different had I just realized she was *it*. End of story. The one for me. I'd felt *it* from the start, I just didn't know what *it* was. Some people probably fall in love as if they've peacefully dropped into a bed of feathers. Falling in love for us was like right before a bike wreck when the front wheel gets all wobbly. Out of control.

Before, when I'd tried to pretend I didn't love her, it was so I didn't have to deal with the reality of her not being mine. And she wasn't mine mostly because I never flat-out fucking told her how I felt about her in clear words from the get-go.

Those days were over. If she needed reassurance, I'd give it to her.

I thought back to Atlanta when I'd left her in the supply closet at the club, about Valentine's Day, and so many other times I should have stayed and laid it all out there but didn't. Instead, I'd tucked my tail between my legs and left like a chump. And like chumps deserve, I lost the girl. Over and over again.

Well, I should have anyway.

Thing is though, by the grace of the god of fucked-up love, she didn't have a damn clue how to *let it go* either. And no matter how I'd beat her down for never knowing what to do, or how to do it, it was my fault for never fighting beside her.

Not anymore. She deserved more from me. I was getting off my poor, pitiful ass and getting this girl. If she was everything I wanted then I had to start being there for her when she was in need.

Everything. If I wanted to be her lover, I needed to be a better friend. If I expected her to talk to me, I had to start being very literal and open with her. This *was* supposed to be a two-way street. I wanted to feel some control over the situation and no one just handed that shit over. I was going to grab it with both hands and take it.

Me: You should call your family though and let them know something.

Honeybee: I will tomorrow.

The clock read five thirty. If she'd been traveling all day, then she was likely tired as hell and probably hadn't even slept.

Me: It's still early.

Honeybee: It's just nice having a little time to think without hearing everyone else's opinions. I'm listening to myself first this time.

That's my fucking girl.

Maybe after everything that went down she was ready to make some changes, too. Big ones, I hoped.

Me: We can do it.

Honeybee: We can.

My doorbell rang and I picked up my wallet on the way to answer it. After paying the delivery guy for the pizza, I almost felt comfortable for the first time in a long time. It was so odd holding my phone and paying for a pizza, all the while reading her next message.

Honeybee: I'm sorry I never believed you'd love me back. I didn't think I could be that lucky.

The shit was getting deep, and after everything I just wanted to make her smile.

Me: No more apologies. Got it?

Honeybee: Ok.

Me: Besides, there's something I need to know.

I typed one-handed as I brought the pizza with me into the living room and flipped the lid open. My hands worked fast, rearranging the pepperoni with the conviction of a frat house jock. Piece after piece, I redecorated my pizza into an abstract phallus, then snapped a quick picture and sent it to her.

Me: Does this dick make your mouth water like it does mine? And should I have penis envy of my pizza?

I pulled a piece, with the lion's share of the balls made of pepperoni, and waited.

Honeybee: I know what you're thinking. How am I going to fit that big cock in my mouth? You get that a lot, huh?

I laughed. We spoke the same language. Equal parts love and diversion. I wanted to hear her. Her laugh. Her voice grow quiet as she got tired. I wanted to hear the gentle humming she did as she drifted off.

We sent each other messages late into the night and it was soul quenching.

I told her about my bike ride with Troy. She explained to me she'd almost overdosed on coffee. She'd spent the past twenty-four hours thinking and figuring out she didn't have to wait for a change anymore. That change was already happening, whether anybody was ready or not. She confessed that it was about time she was honest with everyone, including herself.

Me: This almost feels normal.

Honeybee: I miss you.

Me: You just saw me last night.

Honeybee: Not really. It was more of just a taste. A tease. A mirage.

Me: I miss you too.

My cell lit up a few seconds before it actually rang. The motherfucker rang. Then her name showed on the screen and I knew something had shifted.

"Hey," I answered.

"Hey," she replied. Her voice was low and thick with sleep. It wasn't late, but if she hadn't slept since 2009 it was way past my girl's bedtime.

"How are you still awake? It's almost ten."

"I don't know. I wanted to tell you goodnight. You said you missed me." I heard a rustling and I pictured her lying on her side, pulling the covers up over herself and preparing to pass out.

"You could have just texted me goodnight," I said, but I was more than happy to hear her instead.

"Since you missed me, I thought calling would help." She sounded hesitant, but hopeful.

Hearing her on the other end of the line reassured me it was real. It wasn't just a fantasy. Somehow she knew I'd needed that. Her voice always sunk to the deepest parts of me and filled every crack with her sweet timbre. When had I become such a pussy?

"It does, honeybee. Thank you."

"I was serious. I'm in this. I want to make you feel good more than bad from now on." She yawned. It sounded exaggerated, but it probably wasn't.

"We'll get there," I assured her, yawning too.

"And maybe I wanted to hear your voice."

My eyes closed the same way they would if I'd taken a long drink of a new beer and it was better than I'd imagined. I savored it.

"I hope you want to hear it tomorrow, too."

"I will. I always will," she said and the faintest hum vibrated over the line.

"Goodnight, Blake."

"Goodnight, Casey."

I lay in my bed staring at the ceiling in the dark with only the light from my phone lighting the room. I wasn't content, but I was close. Maybe there wouldn't be any more absences. No more days without calling. Without texts. Without communication.

Maybe it was the end. Or better yet. Maybe it was the beginning.

It had been right to tell her I loved her. Right to tell her I missed her. Right to tell I want her. Us.

Finally.

FOUR

Blake

Saturday, January 2, 2010

I WOKE UP FEELING like the world was spinning in the same direction as I was. It was the beginning of me taking back control of the steering wheel of my life. And knowing that win, lose, or draw, I was going to make the decisions for myself and what I wanted.

Stretching my arms and legs, I felt rested and surprisingly fantastic, considering the shit of a day I knew I might have in front of me. My phone fell on the floor, and it reminded me I'd fallen asleep after talking to Casey. And while my body woke up, my mind informed me of the plans and decisions it had made for me while I slept peacefully, dreaming of big brown curls in my face and his sweet, warm breath in my ear.

It felt like a Sunday even though it was only Saturday. Middle of the week holidays always screwed with me. Days seemed to disappear. I hadn't even made any resolutions and it was already the second day of the New Year.

I used the room phone to call downstairs for some coffee and eggs to be brought up and then I flipped on the television. I hadn't slept in as late as I thought I might, having not had any rest for a few days. But honestly, the sleep I'd been getting in the past few months had been restless anyway. I'd toss and turn and get up for water. Or I'd get up and reread old Casey text messages in the bathroom and check out Twitter to see if there were any new pictures of him.

The unhealthy behavior wasn't normal. I wasn't well. Did I really think I could last a whole year like that? None of it had felt right. It was as if my life was being filmed in front of a live studio audience and no one showed me the script.

That was until New Year's Eve.

Until my layover in Reno.

Until last night.

Everything was so much clearer. I was taking the path of most resistance from everyone and every outside force, except my heart. My heart was pumping in his name, chanting, "Casey. Love. Affection. Forever." Its steady cadence pushed me forward.

I'd been there for him last night. We were there for each other. If this was going to work at all, that was the biggest thing we had to work on. It wasn't so much an honesty thing as much as it was necessary transparency.

We didn't have a flair for lying to each other. We never did. Our missteps were taken with doubt and insecurity. I'd bet on safety and used my happiness as the wager.

After the room service was delivered and I took another quick shower, I picked my phone up off the floor with a mission, and grew a pair of balls.

But first, I wanted to prove I wasn't just talking the talk to Casey, and I sent him a message.

Me: Good morning. I slept really well last night. I'm going to talk to my parents today. How'd you sleep?

After I pressed send, I propelled myself forward and instead of waiting to hear back from him. I dialed my mom and dad's house. On the third ring, my dad picked up.

"Good morning and Happy New Year, Blake," he said. They had caller ID so he knew it was me.

"Hey, Dad. Happy New Year."

"How was San Fran? Are you back home?" His calm and steady

voice fueled me. Reassured me.

For so long I'd been worried about what they would think of me. Of the situation. Of Casey. But there was only one way to truly find out. To throw the cards in the air and let them fall where they may.

"San Francisco was . . . interesting. I'm back in Seattle now. Are you and Mom going to be around today?" I wasn't going to tell them on the phone. I wanted to look them in the eyes and come clean about what I'd been doing. I needed to take responsibility—if for nothing more than to prove I could. I wanted them to see it wasn't easy for me and I hadn't made my decisions spontaneously or without a lot of thought.

"Yeah, I'm going with Shane to the gym. But we'll be around. You and Grant coming over?"

This was the test. The first step. The starting line.

"No. Just me. Grant isn't coming. Something happened at Micah's wedding. I need to talk to you and Mom about it."

"Are you all right? What happened?" Anxiety laced his words.

I made sure my voice held firm and that I sounded confident. If I sounded worried and unsure, that would leave the door open for their opinions and I didn't want the impression I had any doubt. Of course I wanted to like their opinion, but I didn't need it. What I needed was support, one way or another.

"I'm fine. Pretty good, I think. I was thinking about coming over in an hour or two."

"That's fine. You have a key if nobody is here. Mom's at the store, but she shouldn't be that long." He paused. "You know, I can stay here. Shane can go by himself if you want to come now. I'm here."

God, I loved my dad. But I'm sure he probably guessed what it was about, considering I'd told him much of the truth from the start. Well, everything except that I was undeniably in love with Casey, and that I was ending my marriage with Grant as soon as possible. He didn't know any of that.

"No, it's fine. You go with Shane, and I'll be by later."

"If you're sure, all right."

"I'm sure. See you later, Dad."

"Okay, Blake. See you in a bit."

When I hung up, I saw Casey had replied to my text while I was talking to my dad.

Casey: Good morning to you too. I slept pretty damn well. Don't worry about your mom and dad. It'll be okay. I'm here if you need me. Call me later.

Even though I'd been so scared of the coming conversation with my family—and consequently with my husband—for so long, having almost reached it, I wasn't worried it was going to be as bad as I'd made it out to be. I'd just have to see how the rest of the day went.

Pulling up to my parents' house in a cab was a little weird. I'd need to go get my car and figure out what I was going to do for living arrangements soon.

Shit. I was doing the same thing I'd pitied Shane for not so long ago. He'd moved back into my family's house during his separation and subsequent divorce, around the time I'd met Casey.

I could handle staying there for a few nights, but I didn't think I'd be able to move back in with all of them. It'd be too weird, like we were children again. In some ways I still *was* a child, learning how to be in love—real love—for the first time. I'm sure to Mom and Dad, Shane, Reggie, and I would always be just kids. They were good parents and knowing we could always count on them made us trust that, no matter what, we could always come home.

I walked up the steps and instantly knew Mom was home. The volume with which she was listening to her favorite album was the tip off. Clearly my dad was still gone because the Grease soundtrack was cranked. As I opened the door and stood in the foyer of their split-level townhouse, I smiled to myself and listened to her croon. That woman knew every single word. To every single song. On both sides of both records. I'd heard her sing them plenty of times, but never when she thought she was alone.

In her solitude the woman wailed. It wasn't bad; she sang in key. It was just funny because it was *my* mom. Overdramatic was not her gig, but she could've made a damn fine career as a backup singer for the Pink Ladies.

"Mom!" I shouted from the door as I pulled off my coat and tucked my scarf and gloves in the sleeve. "I'm here!"

She popped her head around the staircase wall and smiled at me. She didn't react as if Dad had mentioned to her I wanted to have a come-to-Jesus meeting about my life, like I'd alluded to on the phone. She was happily bee-bopping around in the kitchen like I wasn't about to drop a bomb. That suited me just fine, at the moment anyway.

"Hi, sweetheart. Let me turn this down." She went back into the kitchen for a towel and walked across the living room to the stereo, turning the music down to an almost normal level. "Did you know that a little theater downtown is redoing Grease? I could be Rizzo."

"You totally could, Mom." When I stopped at the stairs, it was evident she'd been in there whipping up something for dinner. By the looks of it, she was making meatloaf. Yuck. I promptly decided it would be a good idea to stay at the hotel for another night. I'd need to grab some food that didn't resemble a flesh pile.

"So how was the wedding? Did you take pictures? Did Grant have a good time?" she asked as she went back to her wad of meat.

Taking a seat at the island, I absentmindedly opened a cooking magazine and began flipping through it, trying to land on what to say and what to hold back. I'd really hoped I could talk to both of them at the same time, but if my dad didn't show up, I'd be spilling it to my mom alone.

"The wedding was beautiful, it was totally Micah. When is Dad supposed to be back?" I asked. My leg was bouncing on the rung of the stool I was perched on. I felt waves of nervousness come and go like an emotional tide in my belly.

She cracked a few eggs and tossed the shells in the trash, but when she did, the face she gave me indicated she'd caught on to my conversation shift.

"Anytime now. Is everything okay, Blake?" she questioned, wiping her hand on a dishtowel tucked into her yoga pants.

"Yeah, I mean, everything is going to be okay. I just sort of wanted to talk to you both. Together." I flipped through the magazine. There was no way she was going to let it drop and my prayers were answered when I heard the shutting of car doors outside.

She cocked her head sideways and then returned to the oven to preset the temperature.

"Just face it, you're old," my brother, Shane, told our dad as they came through the door below in the foyer of their split-level house. "And since there isn't any proof that what you say is true, I'm sticking with my gut and believing your alleged benching stats are nothing more than an old man's fishing tale."

"You're a shithead. When are you moving out?" my dad swiftly argued back, both of them laughing.

"I can't very much leave my feeble parents now. Not when my father is mental and his physical condition is declining so fast."

"Declining? I ran three miles today," Dad countered. "That's more than you ran, son." I watched my dad's chest puff up with pride as the two bickered back and forth.

"I told you. Today wasn't my cardio day. I'm *alternating*."

They squabbled as they filed up the stairs.

"*Alternating* between bullshit and reality as usual," my dad teased. Then, when he noticed us, he said, "*Both* of my girls. Hi, baby girl," he added, just to me, as he rounded the island and went to my mom, wrapping his arms around her.

"You're all sweaty, Phillip." She squirmed, but smiled showing she really didn't protest as much as she tried to let on.

"I know. It's from all the circles I ran around your first-born," he affirmed as he kissed the side of her head. They'd always been loving in front of us—nothing too disturbing—but the older I got, the more I appreciated their affection for one another. I valued seeing the love my parents still had for one another. Sitting there, I was a little jealous of how easy it came for them. I wondered if they'd ever struggled in love. Probably not.

But with my eyes wide open, seeing them together felt like the confirmation I was looking for. I was leaving a *marriage* I wasn't in love with, a *man* I wasn't in love with, and it was the right choice. The only choice I had if I wanted real love. Real intimacy. With Casey.

Preparing to deliver the news with regards to my marriage, I hoped their lack of love trouble didn't affect how they viewed mine.

"Blake wants to talk to us," my mom stated as she skillfully danced out of his arms and rummaged through a drawer for a whisk. Pointing the utensil at him she continued, "Go shower, and we'll all sit down to eat."

I'd be choking down flesh pile with my family. Crow and meatloaf for dinner.

My brother filled a glass with water and turned around to listen when Mom had said I needed to talk, like something major was going on. I suppose there was, but the attention shifting to me like that made me even more nervous on the inside. On the outside, I tried to maintain my cool.

"Are you okay?" Shane asked, concern wrinkling his brow. For the better part of the last few years, Shane had fallen into a sort of life slump. Since moving back in with Mom and Dad, his post-divorce life seemed stalled. Over the past year, he'd drunk more than I was used to seeing from him, became more closed off, and I even worried if he'd suffered a little from depression. But then again, who wouldn't?

Looking at him, I acknowledged he was the one who invited our dad to the gym and I realized he was beginning to look better. Starting to look like pre-Kari Shane. It made me happy seeing him coming out of his love-funk. Hopefully, he was bouncing back from wherever he'd gone.

"I'm fine," I assured quietly and shook my head to dispel his brotherly worry. "I've just made some decisions and want to let you guys know what's going on. You two go shower, and I'll help Mom with dinner. It's fine. Really."

They all sort of looked at each other agreeing, then Shane and Dad left to clean up.

"I'll wash up and help you out," I told my mother, then made my way to the powder room to wash my hands and get a grasp on my nerves. I really missed Casey, but I knew this was the only way I'd ever get him.

These were the steps I had to take. It just sucked I had to take them by myself. Then I realized maybe I didn't have to. I pulled my phone from my pocket and sent him a quick message.

Me: I'm at my parents' house. I'm telling them. I wish you were here.

I didn't know if he'd get it right away or if he'd reply, but just knowing I could message him whenever I wanted filled me with hope. I wasn't afraid of getting caught anymore. I'd already been caught.

It was the first time I'd treated our situation like reality. He was my reality. My truth. When I thought about it like that, I began looking forward to our reality being out there for all to see. Weight seemed to lift off me as I ran my hands under the warm water. When I looked at my reflection, I saw a smile in my eyes. It felt so good knowing I was about to let it all out. Then, it spread to my mouth.

Everything was going to be all right. This was happening. I was doing the right thing and I could feel it throughout my whole body.

My cell chirped at me.

Casey: I'm here, honeybee. You're not alone. You can do this. They love you. Just like me.

That was all I needed. We were in this together. He was with me and knowing that *together* we'd get through this, I felt stronger than I ever had.

Me: Call you in a little while?

Casey: Call me all the time.

I helped my mom cook and she didn't dig for information, like a good mom. When we finally sat down to eat, I began. "I've been keeping a secret for a long time and I've hurt some people. I'm not proud of some of the things I've done over the past couple of years, but I'm in love with a man named Casey. I'm leaving Grant."

They asked questions, but where I'd expected disappointment and disapproval, I'd received understanding and sympathy.

"Sweetie, why did you marry Grant if you didn't love him?" my mother asked as she fought back tears after we discussed my wedding day and how Casey had come there to change my mind.

"I was afraid of what I didn't know. I didn't know if Casey would break my heart or if what I felt for him was even real. It just seemed so overwhelming and crazy to not know what my future would look like. He seemed so wild and unpredictable." My dad sat quietly nodding, his head propped up on his fist as he listened. "I was confused and I thought that you and Dad wanted me to marry Grant." I fought the urge to bite my nails and pictured Casey's smiling face to keep me from breaking down. He was there. "I thought that it would pass. That my feelings for him were just a result of the fun we had together. I didn't know he felt the same way. I do now."

I wasn't ashamed of loving Casey, because I didn't have any control over it. It wasn't a decision to make. It just was. Plain and simple.

We talked for hours. They didn't judge me. Again I was reminded that had I been stronger, had I just a little more faith, there wouldn't be a mess to clean up. I wouldn't be getting a divorce. And I wouldn't be sitting explaining a love that was so hard to put into words. I wouldn't be explaining a love that had been hidden, concealed. Casey would be there *with* me.

If I had been stronger, then there wouldn't be a need to tell them I'll never love anybody the way I loved Casey, because they would have met him and seen it for themselves.

I'd wasted so much time being scared of being wrong. I couldn't see that there *is* no right and wrong with love. It's not debatable. It's not chosen.

Love is true.

I held my composure until I got to the end of my story, until I explained how everything happened at the wedding reception with Grant and Casey.

"I wasn't upset that it was out, Mom, I was relieved. It's so hard acting like you love one man when you're pretending you don't love another. And I'm so in love with Casey."

Hot tears poured over my cheeks.

"Hurting Grant is bad. But knowing I've hurt Casey is the worst pain I'll ever know. That's how I know I love him, because I cannot tolerate the thought of him in pain anymore. I've tortured us for too long trying to do what I *thought* was right." I swiped my face with my dinner napkin and noticed my mom was silently crying.

I smiled through my tears feeling relief, knowing I didn't have to carry the weight of my secrets around anymore.

Shane, who sat beside my mom, rubbed her back as she bit her quivering lip. My dad moved around the table to sit next to me and asked, "How does Casey feel?"

"He loves me too," I affirmed. "He says we'll get through it together."

It wasn't going to be easy, but together we would get through it.

FIVE

Casey

Tuesday, January 5, 2010

ADMITTING YOU'VE BEEN A massive dick isn't the easiest pill to swallow. But together, Blake and I were taking steps to clean up the messes we'd made.

On Tuesday, I finally went into the brewery. I'd worked from home on Monday and set up a few sales calls for the month, but I needed to go in and do some year-end paperwork that I should have done, well before year-end, but it was what it was.

I was apprehensive when I pulled in and saw Aly was there, but something about the way Blake stepped up and laid it all out for her parents and her brother made me feel like I needed to do the same thing. I owed it to her. I owed it to Aly. I owed it to me.

It was a new year and my dick got hard thinking about how, already, so much had changed. It felt fresh and clean and there was so much to look forward to.

In the same spirit as Blake had with coming clean with her family, I wanted to start the year off on the right foot. That began with swallowing my pride and apologizing to Aly.

"I'm not proud of how I treated you," I admitted from behind my desk in my office. I had called her in when I saw her pass by. She looked annoyed and a little smug, which I expected, because deep down she really cared for me. That was the truth. Even though she pretty much took advantage of a really shitty situation when she came to my house, I shouldn't have done what I did. And although I loved how things were turning around, using Aly to make Blake jealous publicly at my brother's wedding, wasn't the coolest thing I'd ever done. But I worked it and—thank fuck for me—it might've all been for the best. But for Aly, it probably wasn't.

She sat cross-legged in the chair facing me and watched me expectantly.

"I owe you an apology for Christmas and New Year's Eve. What it boils down to is, I used you and it was wrong." It was an awkward conversation to have, but a necessary one. I watched the light on my desk phone glow with an incoming call, but I ignored it. What I had to say took precedence over business.

After I began speaking, her mood shifted and she refused to make eye contact with me, but then she finally said, "Don't worry about it." Her posture stiffened, putting up a tougher exterior, having realized I didn't call her in for the reasons she may have thought. Of course, I was speculating, but I'd known her a long time. And unfortunately, it wasn't the first time I'd had to start a conversation I knew she'd rather not be a part of. History had proven she only heard what she wanted anyway, but I continued.

"We work together. We are going to run this business together someday, I think. And most importantly, we're friends. And I'm sorry." Her focus was on the floor in front of my desk. It became too tense and I couldn't take it anymore.

"Aly, please say something. You have to talk to me about this. We need to get it all out. Otherwise, it's just going to fester and get worse." I leaned back in my chair a little. It wasn't the best place for a discussion like that, but I didn't want to lead her on further by asking her to go and meet me somewhere.

"I don't know what you want me to say, Casey." She stood up and it looked like she was going to walk out the door, but it wasn't like her to leave like that. And when she closed my door and then came around my desk, I knew shit was about to get real.

Sitting on the papers I had stacked up in front of me, she leaned toward me. Her blonde hair was pulled back in a tightly pinned bun thing. Like always, she was put together. Makeup. Dress. Heels. The whole nine yards.

"I don't think you understand what I'm trying to say here, Aly," I clarified as I pushed my chair back to get some space.

She leaned in even more. "I'm not sorry about it. Any of it, really. I'm glad you used me. I'm glad you took me to the wedding, and I'm *really* glad you finally came to your senses and left that bitch standing there. Maybe she'll finally learn her lesson and be a good little wife like she should be."

Every hair on my body stood at attention and random muscles throughout my body began to twitch. She was so wrong. How different the night looked from her point of view, just proved how warped the relationship between Blake and I looked on the outside. How it must have always looked to everyone around us.

"You don't know everything, Aly. You only saw part of it."

"What do you mean? You didn't leave with her. She followed her husband. I watched out the window. You left." She smiled like a pageant contestant after answering a question without blunder.

"I came back. Grant left without her. She's leaving him," I said. As soon as the words left my mouth, I thought better, realizing I should have left Blake out of it. The conversation was supposed to be about the things I'd done wrong—with regards to Aly—and seeing if there was a way the friendship between Aly and I could survive or if we'd just be co-workers and partners.

I wasn't sure what I'd do if things couldn't move forward with us professionally, but I'd hoped I wouldn't have to deal with that. However, her sitting in front of me on my desk was a clear indication she still thought there was hope for us in some messed up way.

She laughed as she said, "She's leaving him? And you've thought that *how* many times?" I couldn't sit there anymore. The whole thing was fucked up.

Was eight thirty a.m. too early to start drinking?

"You know what? This was a bad idea," I said as I walked to my door. I wasn't going to participate in this cat and mouse game she liked to play. Not at work and not right then.

"She's never going to leave him, Casey," she announced matter-of-factly as she stood and headed toward me. I swung the door as wide as it would go and propped it open with an empty mini-keg I had in my office.

"I'm not talking about this with you. I wanted to apologize for being a prick. That's all. The rest is none of your business. End of conversation."

"Oh, end of conversation? See, even you know she's just playing you. You just don't want to admit it." Aly was quickly pissing me off. What the hell did she know?

"Well, she already left him," I said, probably a little louder than necessary.

"She did? That's great." Her phony smile reminded me why things with us never worked out. She mocked me with a snotty nodding of her snide face.

"Goodbye, Aly. I'll have the rest of my end-of-year papers done before I leave," I said, my faux professional voice matching her debutant smile.

She paraded out my door a few steps, then turned and probed, "So where is she then? Your *honeybee*. I wonder who she's buzzing around now, because I don't see her. If you've fooled yourself into thinking that her husband is the only one she'd be unfaithful to, you're just as delusional as he was."

What. A. Bitch. Why the fuck did I ever date her?

Propping the door open was a poor choice. I moved the little keg and promptly shut the door.

When do I leave San Francisco again?

I worked on my receipts and expenses until long past business hours. I'd only left for long enough to grab a sandwich down the street and the entire time I wanted to text Blake. I refused to admit that what Aly said had gotten under my skin. She was only trying to be vindictive, and some of that I most likely deserved because of how I'd treated her.

I'd never intentionally hurt her, but she had no problem being a bitch to me on purpose.

It had been Bay Brewing Company's best year ever. We were being served in almost every local pub and our national accounts just seemed to grow and push east through the country. I was proud of the work I'd done over the last few years, but if I ever had to do that much paperwork again, I was quitting and going back to the brewery floor. Projections. Gain reports. Loss business reports—luckily those were few. Travel expenses. Donations. Samples. Write-offs. Blah. Blah. Fucking blah.

I needed a vacation.

It was just after six thirty while I was scanning the last of my account reports to myself, standing by the copier, when I texted her.

Me: I hate paperwork.

Me: My head hurts and I need a beer.

By the time I stapled the hard copies in organized groups and got back into my office, I finally felt my phone vibrate in my pocket.

Honeybee: Work was crazy here, too. I know I was just off for a few weeks, but I need a vacation. That would only make everything worse though.

Or would it? Things were slower around the brewery during January, and with opening up a few new production lines, we were caught up having the holidays behind us.

Maybe a vacation *was* a good idea.

I wondered if she'd go for it. I sat at my desk and immediately began a search. It was winter. So almost anywhere in the US would be cold, which boded well for indoor activities, but I was suffering a bout of cabin fever on top of everything else.

I hastily made a list of priorities: sand, water, Blake in a bikini, taking Blake's bikini off, beers—we must have beers. Then I was sidetracked and opened a bottle—one of the new test brews I had in my mini-fridge—and set back to the task at hand.

Hawaii? No.

Bahamas? No.

Mexico? No.

Then, I saw a picture. It looked like paradise. Beaches. Waterfalls. Private hot tubs near the ocean. Yep. I was fucking sold. I needed that. She needed it just as bad.

She'd told her parents a few nights before. Everything. From the first night through to the wedding, and everything that led to New Year's Eve. She'd called me right after, and I was shocked when she didn't seem too upset. She'd admitted she was relieved. Even though they weren't exactly impressed with how much she'd kept to herself and how she'd treated Grant, they couldn't argue with her not being in love with him. They supported and comforted her, saying that if her heart wasn't there, then it just wasn't. They invited her to stay at their house until she got it all figured out.

She didn't get overly emotional when she retold me how it went down, until she got to the part where her mom said that she'd always wished she'd talked to Blake more before the wedding after what she'd heard us say.

"My mom feels bad she didn't make me talk to her that day. But she thought that since I told you to leave, I wanted to marry Grant. She said she hadn't heard everything we'd said to each other, only the louder parts, but assumed if I really didn't want to get married, I would have called it off," Blake had explained. Looking back, it would have been confusing had she not heard the quieter things we'd confessed to each other that shitty day.

Blake said that had been the hardest part, but it was like a fog had lifted while talking to them and being honest about what she really wanted. They just wanted her happy.

She only talked to Grant via email. Knowing what I did about how they communicated, and how conversations happened more between their inboxes anyway, it was nothing new. Apparently, her message was brief, saying she was moving out and she, her dad, and Shane would be by later in the week to get most of her things.

She told me that finding an apartment was on her shortlist of tasks to do. I wanted her to come here. I said that I'd help her, but she maintained she was going to get an apartment until everything was final.

I didn't like that, but as we'd never really dated publicly, and I hadn't even met her parents, I couldn't really ask her to move in, even though that was what I'd wanted most. The crazy part was, I didn't feel so out of control about any of it. We were talking more than we ever had and calling whenever we wanted.

No hiding. No waiting.

What Aly said couldn't be further from how I felt. She didn't know Blake and she was only trying to cause trouble. I didn't see Blake as a cheater. She was with me. The things we'd both done were because we couldn't fight the pull bringing us together. Over and over. And talking to her as much as I was only confirmed that.

Having the open line of communication made me feel less crazy. It was a revelation going to sleep and not worrying about what she was doing. Not thinking about her next to somebody else while she slept. It was fucked up. With some of that tension and stress gone, it allowed me to think a whole lot clearer about how dead-on she'd been about doing this the *right* way. The right way meant being honest and not rushing, impulsively making decisions that affected more than just *our* lives.

But sitting in my office, after everyone else had left for the day, I just craved to be with her for the first time where we could relax a little. I wondered if our relationship would be different.

I mean, she wasn't divorced yet. *Yet.* But she had an appointment with her family's lawyer next week after he got back from a business trip. Things were moving forward. I could feel it.

But I needed her. I wanted her. I wanted just the two of us to get away. Find a page we could be on together and go from there.

The only thing was convincing her to go. "I need to make her an offer she can't refuse," I thought in my best Godfather inner voice. I was, after all, a godfather.

Me: I have a present for you.

Honeybee: If it's another picture of a guy with a micro-penis again, I'm going to be very disappointed.

Me: No. It's better. It's a real present.

Honeybee: What is it? I want it. I hope it's a one-way ticket to somewhere tropical and they have fruity drinks with umbrellas.

Fuck yeah. It couldn't have gone any better. It was like selling water in the desert.

Me: What if it was?

Honeybee: When do we leave? Ha. Ha.

But it wasn't a joke. I was ready to buy tickets and confirm reservations somewhere precisely like that.

Me: When could you leave?

Honeybee: Don't tease.

Me: Are you at your parents' house yet?

Honeybee: No. I haven't even left work. I'm finishing up the last revisions on a revamped menu, and then I'm heading out.

Me: Anyone there with you?

It was impulsive, and I could've found a much better price had I used a travel agent. I'd become pretty good at arrangements given how much I traveled. I could book a hotel, flight, and car in ten minutes—if push came to shove. I'd figured out the location of the first picture that caught my eye and found the nearest resort. *Costa Rica.*

Honeybee: Just a few chefs in the kitchen, but I'm at my desk.

I dialed her number without hesitation. This was happening.

"So when can you leave?" I asked instead of saying hello when she picked up.

"What's today? Tuesday? I could leave Thursday." Blake laughed. She wasn't going to fight me at all. *Hallelujah.* Then she added, "I have to send this off in the morning. Then I have a phone conference to confirm some transition dates. I think we're going to the house tomorrow night for my stuff."

"Can you really take off work?" I inquired. Her bosses were great. I think they were a lot like Marc had been before I bought into Bay Brewing, with respect to time off. If your shit was done, have at it.

"Yeah, I've got plenty of time. Would I be able to check my email?"

First I thought about telling her no, but then I figured saying yes would buy me a few extra days. So, I caved. Surprisingly, we were full of fucking compromises.

"Sure, whatever you want," I assured her.

"Where are we going?" Finally, a card I could hold.

"I'm not telling you yet. I'll email you your flight info later."

I wanted to make sure we got the same flight out. I had a little travel magic to make happen.

"Okay. I'm excited." And she truly sounded it. It felt so fucking good to hear her sing-song voice, so eager and relaxed. It only confirmed to me that she needed a break as much as I did.

But what I needed more was to feel like *I* was making her happy.

SIX

Blake

Wednesday, January 6, 2010

HE WAS REVVED UP and excited on the phone. I'd made him happy and I loved telling him yes. That could have been my resolution for 2010. Tell Casey yes more. How could I possibly tell him no when he offered me something I needed so much?

The Monday after New Year, I'd immediately started looking for apartments in my old neighborhood where I'd lived before I married. I adored the shops and cafes within walking distance in that part of town. Having parks nearby, even though I rarely went to them, was ideal. There was something calming and invigorating about looking from your window and seeing grass and trees.

Not that staying at my parents' house wasn't great. It was, but it was also strange. I hadn't lived under their roof since before college. It was a peculiar dynamic. I didn't know how Shane had dealt with it for so long, but I had to admit he was finally doing a lot better. Maybe he was just staying because he was lonely.

I got a call back on Tuesday morning about an apartment that was in a different area of Seattle than I was used to, but I thought I'd check it out anyway. The guy on the phone said he was finishing up some renovations and that I'd been the first to call. It seemed lucky and I'd take whatever good fortune that happened my way. He told me it was his retired parents' building and that they'd done a lot of work to freshen it up. It was going on the market as soon as it was completely occupied. Apparently, he informed me, full buildings scll faster than empty ones.

He said he'd give me another call late the next week to set up a walk through and to get my references. It was something I badly needed to get done.

My parents were actually being great about everything. They were disappointed by the way I'd handled, well, everything, but they didn't rub my nose in my mess. Instead, they were helpful and compassionate.

Grant was a totally different animal. I'd called his phone to set up a good time for us to get my belongings, only to get his voicemail. I left a message, but didn't receive a call back. I figured he was upset and angry I hadn't come home. Well, not the way he wanted anyway.

Still, I had to communicate with him somehow and let him know I was coming, so resorted to our tried and true way—email. When I opened my personal account and looked at some of the messages we'd sent to each other over the past months, it kind of made me sad. It wasn't a relationship. It wasn't love. What Grant and I had was a friendship that developed into marriage. No urgency. No need. No playfulness. Only instructions and confirmations. He was loyal and nice enough, but if that's what I'd coveted in a companion, I should have just bought a dog.

I typed out a short message, apologetic in tone, but not in a way that might lead him to think I was coming home or even that I wanted to. I didn't like knowing I'd hurt him, but I had. And for the first time, I was ready to face it. There are things in everyone's life they wish they'd done better. Or just flat out done. Breaking up with Grant, when I didn't dream of or crave a life with him, was at the top of my list.

I had to move forward though, because reverting back into my old ways of trying not to rock the boat only stood to knock me overboard. I was doing him no favors by making light of what had happened and the way the future of our marriage looked. I ended the email telling him I'd like to get my things in the next day or so because I was going out of town. I omitted details of the vacation. Not to be deceiving or dishonest, but because I realized it simply wasn't his business anymore.

Vacation was a crazy idea. From the outside, it may have looked like I was trying to run away from my responsibilities, but that wasn't how it felt. It felt like finally running toward the biggest one. I'd hurt Casey so many times, over and over, and by God if he wanted to fly off somewhere with me for a few days, I saw no reason to deprive him anymore. I'd resisted being with him on so many occasions, most of which never worked out for either of us in the long run. I was breaking that habit. Not just for him, but for me. I wanted to spend time with him. I craved it.

I knew the months ahead would get a little hectic. My job. His job. Everything my impending divorce would bring into the picture would be a challenge. It was going to be nice to start the year off on a good note, though. A better note. A truthful note. A Casey note.

I daydreamed of sandy beaches and relaxation the whole day as I worked.

I'd been working on a new identity for a restaurant called The Clover, a traditional Irish establishment that hadn't done a thing to their menu, or any other part of the place, for over thirty years. My latest version of their menu went through last approvals by the owners without a single hang-up. They loved it and I was glad. I was happy to see months of work finally pay off.

Shane picked me up from the office and we headed to the house. Initially, I'd thought Grant would be at work. It was still early in the evening, and I was shocked seeing his vehicle in the drive at that time of day on a Wednesday. I hadn't been back since everything happened and my car sat there, too. Parked where I'd left it last year.

Had it only been a week?

"You ready for this?" Shane asked.

"I told you, if this is weird, you don't have to come in. I know you're friends." I felt sour about putting Shane in that position, but he'd offered more than once to help. Although I didn't have many things, having him there helped. I wasn't quite so alone.

"You're my sister, Blake. Grant and I got along because you were together. He's an all right guy, but you're what matters here. To me. To Mom. To Dad. Don't worry about it." Then he chuckled under his breath. "It is kinda funny that he helped me move out of *my* house when Kari and I split. Now I'm helping you move out of his. It has a karma-ish feel to it, don't you think?"

"I don't think that's funny," I told him. His attempt at making light of the situation for my benefit didn't go unnoticed, but I really wasn't looking forward to going inside. In terms of karma, I was the one who was in for a double dose.

"Oh, it's funny. Kari was a bitch," he pointed out.

Then he slapped the steering wheel and turned off the ignition just as my dad pulled in behind us. We hopped out and marched up to the door. It was about to get awkward and I silently prayed it would start raining so we'd work even faster. But no. Of all days, it was sunny and mild for January in Seattle.

"Are you sure about this, Blake?" my dad asked, carrying a box full of other boxes and packing materials.

"Yes. I'm sure." I was sure. Sure it was going to suck. I just needed to be kind. After all, I was the adulterer. I'd broken our marriage vows. I was the villain in the situation. The least I could do was be sensitive. "Do you mind if I go in first?" I asked them as we stood on the porch.

"No, that's fine. You go in. Let us in when you're ready," prompted my dad.

Had I mentioned that I love him? I kissed his cheek and fit the key in the lock letting myself in.

The house was quiet, except I faintly heard the shower going upstairs.

What were the rules? Could I go up there? Should I wait outside with them for a few more minutes? One thing was certain, it didn't feel like I lived there. It wasn't my home. I didn't feel loss or like I was making a bad move. I only felt sad I'd wasted a lot of people's time and put them in this position.

I wanted it over with and to get what I needed, at least for the time being. The essentials. Clothes. Sentimental things, although after reflecting, there weren't many. The job probably didn't require both my dad and brother to help me with the few things I wanted. And there wasn't much sense moving everything to a storage unit, just to move them to an apartment a few weeks later. But I had a lot of clothes and shoes—things like that—which I would need in the meantime.

And my mugs.

I trekked into the kitchen at the back of the house, and saw what a mess had become of it. Dishes were piled up. There were take-out boxes on the counter and, above all, the room reeked like a hot trashcan. Compulsion overcame me. The offending receptacle was full, so I emptied it and placed the first bag outside the back door. A second filled up rather quickly and I put it out with the other.

I hurriedly ran the water hot to rinse the dishes and loaded the washer as my family waited outside. In ten short minutes, the state of the wrecked room improved a lot.

Hearing Grant come down the stairs, I shut the dishwasher and started it. Then I waited for him to find me.

"Hi," he announced when he wandered toward the racket I was making in his kitchen. He was freshly showered, but oddly he didn't look clean. His hair was messy, his face had a week's worth of stubble, and dark circles were visible on the undersides of his eyes. I gathered he'd spent his time drinking from the quantity of bottles I'd thrown out. Grant in a crisis was not the Grant I knew.

"Hi," I said. Guilt bubbled inside me and surfaced. How quickly I'd forgotten the sensation of it, but in an instant, its force coursed through me. I'd hurt him. "Are you all right?"

"Are you really leaving me?" he asked point blank.

I tried to be strong, though I didn't feel strong. I felt terrible. "Yes. Did you get my email?"

"No. I haven't checked my *email*."

"Why didn't you call me back?"

"I don't know," he huffed. He was agitated.

"I'm sorry." I leaned against the counter and my hands held onto the stone against my back. "I don't know what to say."

"How about you're done fucking that guy and you're coming home?" He stalked closer to me. "How about you tell me how you could lie to me for so long? How about you tell me why you did it? Huh, Blake. Just tell me!" He'd never raised his voice to me in the past, but to be fair, I hadn't behaved like he expected me to either. He was shouting at that point and only feet from my face.

I bowed my head and took it. I deserved it.

"I can't believe you fucked me over like this. And for that guy? What the hell, *Betty!*"

My lip quivered a little. Then I was comforted by the sound of the front door opening and my dad calling in with, "Blake, are you okay?"

I looked into Grant's eyes and they were red and glassy. Hot tears spilled onto my cheeks and I quickly swiped them away. A cocktail of empathy and anger built in my body. I had no reason to be angry with Grant, but the way he was yelling flooded me with defensive adrenaline.

"I'm fine, Dad," I assured, making sure to speak calmly.

"He's here to help you?" Grant asked, nodding, a sarcastic grin forming on his tempered face. He was shocked and something in his eyes flared to life again. "Ha. This is rich. What lie did you tell him?" He tracked into the dining room, which opened into the front room, where my dad was just inside the door.

"Grant, stop," I urged, but the crazed look on his face told me he wasn't going to.

"Hey, Phil," he said brightly like he was welcoming him into a party. Then Shane came inside too. "Oh, and Shane is here. Is Reggie out there too? Did you all come to help Blake? Did she tell you what's going on? I'd love to know what story she fed you."

I stood in the doorway watching. I knew what he was doing. He was trying to hurt me. And, frankly, that did piss me off. I was so thankful I'd told my family and they were there backing me up, because in that moment I needed it.

Grant wasn't a violent man, well until the last week. And it wasn't like he'd been brutally violent with me, per se. However, the words coming from him were intended to cut me deep, but I was armed with the truth. Finally, that bitch was on my side.

"It's just us. We're here to help Blake pack up a few things. That's all," my dad said as he pulled his arms through his jacket and took it off, laying it over the back of a chair nearest him.

"So what did she tell you? What lie? Was I mean to her? No. That can't be it. Wasn't providing for her? No. I sure as hell bought her this house. Let's see—"

Shane interrupted, "I think that's enough, Grant."

"Oh, maybe she told you I was fucking someone else. Was that it?" He turned to look at me for confirmation of his accusation. It was lucky for him I'd never seen this side of him before we were married. Or maybe not. At least then he wouldn't be going through a divorce. I wouldn't have even considered being his wife had I witnessed how ugly he could be. There never would have been a Blake Kelly.

"I told them the truth," I said. "Everything. They know *every-thing.*"

He laughed. "One should be so lucky. When are you going to tell me *everything?* When is it my turn? When's the next showing of Blake the True Story? I don't want to miss it."

My dad interjected, "Come on, Blake. You wanted to get some of your clothes. Let's go up and get them." He didn't feed into Grant's hostility. I never wanted a fight and the three of us knew that wasn't Grant's normal behavior. He was mad, and rightly so. But my dad was right, that wasn't what we were there for. We were there for my shit and that was all. There was nothing else in that house I wanted. I had never really lived here. I had never really *lived* with Grant. We had . . . co-existed. Yet, he'd been happy with that? How is that possible?

I went back into the kitchen and opened the cabinet to search for my mugs. I couldn't leave them now. Not after almost two years and countless nights of drinking wine from them while dreaming of Casey. Even though their writing had all but weathered away, the words were scored in my mind. I was trouble and he liked it. Those mugs were mine.

When I found them, I wrapped the mismatched pair in a plastic grocery bag. Heading upstairs, I noticed Grant had taken a seat at the table with his head in his hands. It was a miserable sight. I detested seeing what I'd done to someone who I'd sworn to love, but my sympathy couldn't change it. Hell, it couldn't even change the way I felt about him when I'd tried to make it.

Didn't that count for something? Didn't *trying* my best to be with him add up to anything to anyone? It didn't seem like it. So what was it all for? I'd carelessly thrown away so much time.

Packing a closet in a hurry is pretty damn easy. Just grab an armful, lift and drop crap in a box. After we filled what boxes we had and they'd loaded them in the truck, I retrieved some of my things from the office and packed up my laptop bag with items I used when I worked from home.

I reflected as I stepped down the stairs and realized I didn't care about much else within the walls of that house. Would we split up the furniture? Would we divide the flatware and dishes? I didn't give a shit about any of it. He could have it all.

I carried out the last few things I wanted to Shane's truck and told him I'd be right back. I needed to say something to Grant. I wasn't sure what that was, but I hoped by the time I got where he was still sitting, it would be the right thing.

It turns out, the right thing for me was, "I'm sorry I hurt you. I'm seeing a lawyer. We're getting a divorce."

To those words he looked up, but his vision lacked focus. "You don't even want to try?"

"I've been trying for a really long time, Grant. I truly have." Speaking those words, out loud to him, opened a floodgate inside me. He wanted the truth, there it was. Saying it to his face was pivotal.

It felt like my two halves were being stitched back together into one, like I was taking my heart back.

"Am I really that bad? I don't get it," he said, picking at the edge of a place mat my mother had registered for us and we'd received as a wedding gift.

"Grant, it's more that I shouldn't have married you in the first place. That was one of my biggest mistakes, because we should have been friends. Not husband and wife."

I took a heavy breath and smiled through tears that flowed like overfilled ditches during a spring rain. I let them go. In a weird way, I needed him to see them. Deep down I wasn't a monster; I gained no pleasure out of his despair. But I didn't love him, not like I vowed I would.

I reached into my pocket and pulled out my wedding rings and set them on the table. They weren't mine and I hadn't earned them to keep.

"I'm sorry," I whispered. Then I left.

Grant and I were *over* in my mind. More *over* than when I had sex with Casey the first time in the Ashcroft Hotel. More *over* than the countless times I'd prayed Casey would turn up in a city I was working in. More *over* than when I'd cried heartsick tears at our wedding instead of joyous ones. We were done.

The tremendous burden I'd been carrying lessened.

I was closer. I was getting there.

SEVEN

Casey

Thursday, January 7, 2010

INCH BY INCH, MINUTE by minute, she was getting closer. I indescribably felt her nearing.

The previous night, the night before we were to leave for Costa Rica, when we'd talked, she'd been slightly quieter. I attributed that to her going over to their house, her husband's house, her old house, where she used to live. Fuck, I didn't know what the hell to call it, but she'd gone there to get her things.

I was relieved when she'd let me know her dad and brother were going with her, but I'll be damned if I didn't pace the floors all evening. Then I took a walk down to the shed. Then repeated the process hoping it was going all right. It was weird, but I wanted him to be nice to her. I hoped—for her sake—that it went smoothly.

Finally, she sent me a message.

Honeybee: I'm back at Mom and Dad's. I told him we're getting a divorce.

My whole body filled with immeasurable joy.
I tried to keep my excitement at bay, but it was like my birthday,

Christmas, a benign test result, a hundred-dollar bill on the ground, the first sip of beer on a hot day, and that first inch inside her sweet pussy, good. It was a challenge to keep my wits and be sensitive. The awareness I needed to tread lightly was ever present, but I wanted to scream from a mountain, "I'm so fucking proud of you. You did it. You love me!" But, like the good boy I am, I settled on letting her know I was concerned and that I was there for her.

I was an angel. An angel who couldn't wait to show that beautiful girl how happy she'd just made me . . . with my tongue . . . and maybe a finger or two . . . and hell, while I was at it, I'd probably give her the biggest orgasm of her life—if I could. Because—you know—she deserved it.

Twice.

A day.

Forever.

It was only the first full week in January and she was taking big steps. Not pussy-foot Blake steps, but real ones. She'd been nudged—no, shoved—into how it was going down, but I didn't give a rat's ass. It was going down and I was going to go down on her to commemorate the occasion. Thinking back on it, maybe I really just wanted to eat some pussy and she owned my favorite one.

If I was being a girl about it, I could have admitted feeling something like flutter-bugs, or butterflies, or whatever prissy things chicks claim to feel in their stomach, when I read her text. Girls may have a silly way of articulating it, but what they said was dead on. Those fuckers were flapping their light-hearted, winged asses off in there.

However, since it was my story and I'm a man—I'd say it was like someone stuck a power drill in the base of my spine and let the son of a bitch go, full-speed. It wound me up from the inside out. There was an invisible, indefinable feeling she always gave me. It was powerful and punctual, showing up the instant our bodies were in the same room together. Every piece that made up the physical me knew all the places on the physical her where they truly belonged. And those bastards weren't quiet either, every square inch of me wanted to get to her in the worst way, that very second. Every pore screamed her name.

I read her message again. Thought about screen capturing it and emailing it to myself so I could look at the text whenever I wanted. No one likes scrolling through a thousand pictures.

Me: I love you. Are you all right?

My phone rang.

"One more day," I said when I answered.

"One more day," she repeated and exhaled loudly over the line. The breath shook and sputtered uneasily. I wondered how to talk to her. I was in uncharted territory. I didn't know how or what to say. She might be frustrated or excited. Or sad. Or thrilled. The gamut of what she was thinking cluttered my thoughts. I wanted to say the right thing, but fuck, in that moment, I didn't know what that was. I hopped up on the island in the kitchen and sat there cross-legged, waiting for her cue.

She bailed me out when she began, "I didn't really have that much stuff." She was downhearted and I heard it in her voice.

"You've got stuff," I reassured. "It just didn't seem like much because your dad and brother were there, helping you lug it all."

"No, really. I have my office stuff. My clothes. A few pots and pans. Knives. My mugs. That's it."

"What about furniture?" She surely had more things than that. "And there's got to be more kitchen stuff you want."

"I don't want any of it. I only want what I have."

"Isn't half of the house yours?" Like she could just take a half of a house. I pictured a dude with a chainsaw cutting the roof down the center.

Then I reminded myself, this wasn't a joke or a time for celebration.

It was the first time, after all of those months, that it hit me. She was leaving her home and everything. She had to get a divorce. And there I was, all but skipping around my fucking house fantasizing about going down on her. It wasn't an honorable feeling, being elated when someone you care about is going through some major shit. Add that to the Casey-needs-to-get-his-shit-together-for-her list.

I climbed off the counter and sat in a chair like a normal adult and started taking seriously the gravity of her situation as she spoke.

"It's *his* house. I never paid the mortgage. I paid other things, but that's his house." She paused and I waited patiently. "He's been working on it, fixing it up the way he wants it. Does it seem dumb that I don't care about it at all?" Her voice was flat and the lack of emotion showed her unease.

Yeah, I'd play the Devil's advocate.

"Blake, you deserve whatever it is you want. All right? But if you don't want anything else, I don't think there's anything wrong with that either."

"I really don't. How awful am I? I was picking up my things and all I could think about was being with you. It was so bad."

I think she was in shock, like when you are in that buoyant state right before you realize what actually happened. That shit *actually* hit the fan. The few seconds before everything catches up. She was there.

Maybe I was pushing her too hard. I'd wanted things my way, and as fast as possible, but she'd wanted to take her time. I didn't want to cause her any more damage.

People say rip a Band-Aid off quickly and then it's over. But you know what? It still fucking hurts.

If I loved her as much as I claimed, I needed to start being the guy she should be with, not just the dude complaining it wasn't me.

Costa Rica wasn't going anywhere. Of course, it was on the coast and everyone knows that whole side is going to be in the ocean, but not anytime soon.

"Are you sure you want to go tomorrow?" I asked.

"Please don't back out. I really want to go," she pleaded. "I need this trip. I need you."

She. Needed. Me.

Even though the timing was really shitty with everything that was happening, and it was a lot to take in, I wasn't about to tell her no. Not after she'd already made my fucking year only seven days into it.

"I know it isn't any of my business, but I'm kind of proud of you," Morgan said, as she drove me to the airport, after we had lunch.

While we ate, I thought I'd avoided the subject with my youngest sibling—therefore the strangest one for me to talk to about it with—but as she gave me a ride, she brought it up.

"Thanks, but there's a lot more to it than you know," I said not wanting to get into it with her. She was seventeen, what could she know about it? Besides, I wasn't exactly pleased with everything I'd done in those past few years. She only saw pieces. Some of the rougher-for-Casey parts. I didn't want her thinking my behavior was anything to reward. "I've been pretty ass-backward more often than not."

"Yeah, but you held your own," she countered, looking in the mirror to safely change lanes. My little, innocent Morgan was so mature. So by-the-book. If she only knew.

"It's not something that I'm proud of. And regardless, I do feel bad for the guy." Not bad enough to not take his wife on a tropical vacation, but bad enough I didn't need to pound his face in when he touched Blake like an object instead of a woman. His wife. I'd struck that image from my brain on more than one occasion. I saw red every single time it resurfaced. "It was a bad situation."

"I'm not going to pretend to understand what you're doing, or why, or whatever. Obviously, she does it for you."

These were words I'd not heard from her before. Historically, Morgan made it known how she felt about Blake and me together. Her positive sentiment may have cracked my shell a bit. I wasn't sure about what made her change how she perceived us, but I was happy she didn't think I was just some fool. Or maybe she did.

"I can't explain it, but I've never been able to shake her. I'm serious about her, Morgan."

"I know. I've never seen you like that—or you two actually together before. I know that you're serious about your job and that you love it. But I don't think I've ever seen you look so . . . so . . . strong. I'm proud of you and I'm sorry I didn't understand it before. You were just so manly that night." She giggled, like seeing her goofy older brother in that light was preposterous. It meant a lot to me.

I maturely flexed my arm and kissed my bicep like a douchey protein junkie.

"I'm pretty tough, Morgan. I'm offended that you're just now noticing."

We pulled into the departures lane.

I got out and opened the door to the backseat where I'd put my bags.

"Thanks for the ride," I said, as she came around to hug me. I opened my free arm and pulled her in, as I held the luggage handle with my other. We were having a brother-sister moment on the sidewalk at San Francisco International, but it had been a while since our last so I didn't care.

"You're welcome. Have a fun time and get out and see stuff. Don't be a resort tourist," she instructed adamantly as she hugged me. "And Casey, I don't know if this makes any sense, but I think maybe she *is* good for you, so treat her with respect. If you don't want to be the one-night stand guy, then don't *be* the one-night stand guy anymore."

How did she know so much? When in the fuck did she get so damn smart? I kissed the top of her head. Someday there's going to be a guy for her and he better be worthy.

Or I'll kill him.

"Okay. You be careful driving. Tell Dad and Carmen hi for me. I love you."

"I will. Love you, too."

I shrugged into my backpack, ready to get the show going. Ready to see my honeybee. Hell, when wasn't I ready?

After Morgan left, I miraculously whizzed through security and was at our gate in less than twenty minutes. That was a new record for me. I bought a water and a bag of M&M's. I knew what direction she would be coming from. My stalker skills were dangerously close to an all-time high. I waited and people-watched.

I arranged it so I'd meet Blake at our terminal bound for our get-away. She had a little bit of a layover between her flight in and ours out, so I wanted to get through security and to the gate before she got there. I didn't want to waste a minute.

Sitting there I had time to do a little thinking. Preparing. I wasn't going to fuck this up anymore. People talking on their phones and buzzing by as I waited, reminded me of the time I picked her up when Foster was born. God, there'd been so many chances to do better. That time was one of them. I had left her at the hospital, but mostly I'd just left her.

What Morgan said played through my mind—like the proverbial angel on my shoulder she repeated—fueling my desire to be what Blake needed.

Don't be the one-night stand guy.

I'd never been able to hold my shit together when it came to her body and my body, but my kid sister was right. First and foremost, on this trip, I wanted to touch her deeper than just her flesh. Of course, there was no way in hell I wasn't touching her and I'd make her feel good in any way I could. But this time, I was going to give her other things she needed first. The *me* parts that I hadn't given her in the past. The same ones I craved to share with her all along.

I knew we were far from being in the clear. We had a lot of work to do. But my first task was going to be to touch her mind. Touch her heart. I didn't know what the equivalent to an orgasm was in terms of brains and hearts, but I wanted that. I wanted to take those parts of her to that level. Our bodies already trusted each other.

I was thinking the words, "I want her to trust my heart," when I saw her—frazzled traveler that she always was. Bag over her shoulder, lugging that rolling hell-box on wheels and looking at her boarding pass as she walked, probably quadruple checking that she was going to the right gate. I loved watching her before she knew I saw her. Like in Atlanta, I opened my camera and took a picture of her, stopped right in the middle of the walking lane looking at the signs.

Perfect.

She folded the paper and put it in her pocket, and then she wrung nervousness from her hands. Flopping them in front of herself like a fish robbed of water. It was funny, but I did that too. Shake it off. Everyone does that.

Then she saw me.

She smiled and I watched the tension leave her shoulders as she relaxed.

I tried to smile, but because I already was smiling my ass off, it probably looked like I was just showing her every tooth in my head.

I tipped my head.

She tipped too.

I'm not a prick. I could have got up to help her, but she had it on her own. She didn't need help for the last ten feet between herself and me. So I sat there. And enjoyed one of my favorite pastimes, watching that magnificent creature come to me. If I'd propelled myself toward her at that moment, I would've been a runaway train—fucking her at gate G99 for all to watch.

Don't be the one-night stand guy.

I'd be the one-forever man.

EIGHT

Blake

Thursday, January 7, 2010

H E STOLE MY BREATH. It felt like I'd been waiting to see that gorgeous man for forever. It had only been days, but there'd been a huge shift between us.

Finding him, sitting there peeling the plastic label from his water bottle, was almost like the first time I'd seen him. It was crazy how setting my eyes on him reassured me that all of the struggles had been worth it.

He was my fantasy coming true. Head cocked to the side. Hair perfectly messy. Jeans. White button-up shirt, tan army jacket, and a red scarf. How did he get away with looking like that? Like he walked right off the pages of a fashion ad. I didn't know any man, in real life, who dressed like he did. I also didn't know anyone else who I paid that much attention to either. Those curls. That smile. Had I really thought I'd ever *not* want him? I'd been crazy even trying to resist.

I lugged my bag over to the open seat next to him, but didn't say anything.

I wondered why he didn't get up or come over to me, but he was *right there*. The playful look on his handsome face indicated he was riling me up. Poking a friendly stick in my cage to see what I would do. Strangely, that was just his Casey-way of telling me to come to him. To keep taking steps in his direction. Or that was how it felt anyway.

I was a little nervous. It was the first time we'd ever been together. Like this together. We weren't meeting up somewhere randomly. I wasn't going to him or vice versa. We were going in the same direction together and something about that felt fundamentally right in every beautiful way.

"Can I sit here?" I said in my pretend southern voice, and then I second-guessed myself. *Betty.* His smile only fell for a flash of a second. We both wore bruises on the inside. Of all my sins, sharing that intimate secret with someone else—Betty—was one of my biggest offenses. And I just brought it up, the very first thing. I wasn't very smooth.

"I was saving it for you," he said. What he didn't say was, "that still kind of hurts," and what I didn't say back was, "I'm sorry." But through that one look, as I held his gaze, we told each other both.

I smiled even though I was scared I'd already made a mistake. "I like your scarf."

"I bet you do," he said, his genuine good humor shining through, just like it always did.

I sat next to him and put my bag against his on the floor in front of us. It wasn't something I'd normally think about, but having my things and his things there, headed to the same place, was comforting. My healing heart pounded.

Casey wrapped an arm around my shoulder and drew me to him over the armrest and he whispered in my hair, "You look beautiful. And don't worry, I know." I watched as his hand covered his heart, and, therefore, the tattoo underneath his shirt. "Betty's mine," he breathed. My eyes fluttered shut from relief. "She was always mine."

I exhaled and let myself unwind in his words. I let myself relax, feeling his arm around me. It. Felt. Right.

"I'm sorry."

"Me too," he said. "That's old news now though. Okay? Let's talk about something more important," he said as he pulled away, but still leaving his arm around my shoulders. "Do you think there will be a nude beach in Costa Rico?" He'd tried to surprise me with our final destination, but when he sent me my flight information, I sort of figured it out. He got major points for trying.

I laughed and felt at ease, as if he always knew how to make me feel better.

"Well, God I hope so. I only brought shoes." I said a silent prayer that his good humor would always get us through these awkward moments we were bound to have.

I smiled at my joke and what it did to his expression, catching him off guard. He bit his bottom lip. I wanted to kiss him, but quelled the urge with the knowledge that I'd be with him day and night in paradise for almost a week. Plus, we were in an airport and no one else wanted to see all that.

The flight was on time. He'd booked us first class. The funny thing about first class was on some planes it looked really impressive and on others it just looked like nicer seats. That flight was one of the best first classes I'd ever flown in. The bonus? It was my first, first class, with him.

After we were at cruising altitude, Casey unzipped his backpack and produced a pad of paper.

"Doing some writing?" I asked.

"Nope. We're playing Hangman."

"How do you know I'll play with you?" I teased defiantly. I would do whatever he wanted. And, frankly, playing sounded fun, but I wanted to flirt. He brought it out in me.

"Because you'll do whatever I tell you to," he said like the boss he was. Then he winked. He flipped open the notebook and uncapped the marker with his teeth, flipping it and putting the writing end into the cap gracefully without looking. How many days had I squandered away and lost with him? I started to feel like the person who'd been robbed the most, after all the pieces fell, was me. Casey telling me I'd do his bidding was no joke. My instincts always responded to what he'd told me to do. Always. When he told me, outright, what he wanted from me, it killed me to deny him. When things went unsaid, that's when I was unsure, guessing what to do.

What a revelation.

Before I could rethink myself, I told him that. Maybe he needed to know, too.

"I like when you do that."

He stilled, giving me his attention, dropping the pad and marker on his tray table. "What?"

"That. I like when you tell me to do stuff." Initially, I hadn't been thinking about intimate things. Sexual things. But the sentiment was true there, too. I knew that's what he'd taken from my comment because his face flushed and he looked around the cabin, even leaning up to make sure ears and eyes weren't on us.

He chuckled when he knew we were safe from ear-shot, gave me a mischievous grin, then he stowed it—pretending I had a naughty secret to tell. The information wasn't intended like that, but it wasn't confidential how I reacted to him. I'd never been able to hide the physical effects he had on me.

"Exactly what are we talking about here? You like when I suggest Hangman or when I tell you what to do? We need to define *stuff*. I need this to be very clear."

"Both," I said quickly. Then confessed in a more hushed tone, "But I especially like when you tell me what to do when we're alone."

His Adam's apple bobbed when he swallowed. But he hadn't drunk anything and the thought of my statement making his mouth water had my pulse quickening. He cleared his throat. I liked how powerful I felt, which was ironic because I pretty much just told him I liked him taking control.

"May I have an example?" he asked. "For clarity's sake."

My memory scanned over our history and all of my examples weren't really times where we'd been in the best of places, relationship-wise.

"Well, it's a little weird because we were kind of fighting," I admitted, wondering if I should have brought it up. Worrying it might only bring up other unpleasant memories.

"Blake. We've fought a lot, that's just who we are. This is me, telling you what to do. I'm going to need specific details about what you enjoy. It is my new mission in life to do things you like. So, for the love of Hangman, be specific."

I was the worst at talking like that. I didn't have a way with words like he did. However, it was much harder for me on the phone than it was in person, so I went for it.

"I liked the way you," and I paused, looking for the best word. No

I wasn't. I knew the best word. Fucked was the best word. Fucked was the correct verbiage. The look on his expectant face told me he knew what word I was thinking too and he leaned in close so I could whisper it.

". . . Yes?" he sang.

". . . fucked me in Atlanta." I was thankful I didn't have to say it very loud. I barely said it at all. Regardless, the message was received.

"God, I take it back," he said in a low voice and readjusted himself. All of himself.

"Why?" I'd thought that was what he wanted. He'd told me to be specific. What I'd said wasn't graphic, but I was sure he knew which time I was talking about with regards to him telling me what to do. I was confused and it must have shown.

"Come here," he requested. I leaned over, close enough I could smell the original flavored Trident he was chewing. "I know I told you to tell me, but that was a mistake. I forgot we were on a plane. I'd like to pick this line of conversation back up when I have you somewhere I can show you what that just did to me." With his hand still on his lap, he slowly ran it over the impressive bulge he was failing to conceal. His strong hand gripped it through his denim—*and how I'd love to be that hand at the moment*—and I immediately agreed with him. A plane was no place to give my dirty talking another shot, but knowing how well it worked, I'd keep that card in my pocket and try again later.

Before I pulled away from him, he moved his hand from his erection to my chin. And when I thought he was going to kiss my mouth, he kissed my nose instead.

"Your nose is pink, honeybee. We better hang this guy before we get scolded by the flight attendant. She looks like she could whoop my ass." I looked toward the front of the plane where Ruth the six-foot flight attendant manned her post with a watchful eye.

We held hands and played a very vulgar game of Hangman. With him being a lefty and me a righty, we didn't have to let go once. His thumb would rub over my knuckles.

One more thing I loved about Casey. He was fun to travel with.

The poor hangman died at least twenty times no matter how we tried to save him. The last game he died because I didn't get "Dirty Sanchez" before all of his limbs swung from our Sharpie's noose.

First class was nice, but when the driver, who picked us up at the airport, held a sign that read *Honeybee and Lou,* that was a full-swoon moment. When he saw I'd spotted the sharply dressed man in the hat holding the sign, he squeezed my hand. The same hand he'd only let go of a few times in the hours we spent on the plane.

Points for Mr. Moore. Points and more points.

We pulled up to the hotel, the Bella Flechazo, and I immediately realized this wasn't just a quick trip somewhere tropical. Our car pulled into a lane, which wrapped under a huge natural stone hotel front. I realized that—knowing Casey—he probably had many more tricks up his sleeves.

The whole thing felt so dreamlike.

Natural, cream-colored stone covered almost every inch of the hotel lobby, and when we walked into the expansive atrium, my breath caught seeing a huge fountain, which shot water into the air at least twenty feet. Above that hung a spectacular blown-glass chandelier.

My travel companion walked with a strut. He was as proud as a peacock. Still holding my hand, he walked slowly so I could look at everything and didn't rush me in the least, as our bags were carted past us. He looked every part the playboy in his scarf and designer jeans. Unapologetic curly hair, lying where it wanted.

Where I looked road weary and tired, he looked like he could run a mile. I didn't care, because I was there with him and that was all that mattered.

I considered the possibility I'd simply fallen asleep on the plane and I was having a lovely dream, but as long fingers squeezed my hand again, I knew it was wonderfully real.

"It's beautiful, Casey. Look at it." Like a castle on a cliff, the ambiance of the hotel was unlike anywhere I'd ever been. It felt old and regal and fresh and new—at the same time. I was impressed.

Really impressed.

He'd done all of this for me. For us.

Yes, there were hundreds of things I should have been doing and thinking about and debating, but—with him—I was going to just take it all in. What more could I want? I was at a majestic place and finally both halves of my heart were back together. I knew because I felt two pulses in my hand and one was his.

"I'll take care of you," he said with a sexy, crooked grin. There was pride, and the perfect amount of ego, shining in his vibrant blue-green eyes.

"I can see that. You check us in and I'll use the ladies' room." We'd been flying for a long time and I needed to get cleaned up a bit, but really, I just wanted to see what it looked like in there, too.

It was totally awesome—as far as bathrooms go—like I supposed it would be. It had fantastic lighting and great mirrors. The ones that make you look good at every angle and the soap smelled like melted angel kisses. It was divinity in the form of a lavatory.

When I finally came out, Casey was leaning against the back of a white sofa waiting for me. Legs crossed, reading a pamphlet.

Sauntering to him, I thought he was reading it, but when I noticed it was written in Spanish, I knew I'd been fooled.

"Whatcha' reading there, hot stuff?" I queried, feeling much more alive after splashing my face with water, reapplying lip gloss, and re-securing my hair into the hobo-chic up-do I was pulling off at the moment.

"Oh, just some Costa Rican travel rules. Nothing major," he said like it was no big deal, but really he was fishing. Toying with me.

"Rules, huh?" I said playing along as he took his hand in mine and led me to the elevator.

"Yeah, just a few things that we should try to do while we're here," he told me as he pressed the button. Then he kissed my hand. "Your hand smells good," he said. Then kissed it again before letting them hang between us as we waited for the doors to open.

"The bathroom was really nice," I whisper-screamed. The soap smelled better than good. A small thing, true, but there were not enough small things in my life that I took the time to appreciate and I decided I wasn't going to miss all of the tiny things that would surely make this week heaven. I wanted all of the little pieces. They were mine to keep and hopefully add to.

He chuckled a little, but stopped when the doors split, revealing another well-dressed man. The hotel had an elevator operator man?

I mouthed, "Whoa," to Casey as we walked inside.

He winked causing my nether-region to purr.

"Tres," he said to the man. Then handed him some money when we arrived on the third floor. *Fancy.*

I gave him an *Is this for real?* look.

On the third floor and at the back of the hotel, our room was just as impressive. It opened to a large terrace, which had a hot tub, and a set of stairs. I walked around the living room-type furniture to see what else was there. We were up so high, and as I got closer to the floor-to-ceiling glass doors I saw it was the ocean below. The beach was only thirty or so stairs down from our personal veranda. The view of the water below was beautiful, the sun having already set. White-topped waves gently rolling into the sand below glowed in the moonlight.

I was so surprised. I knew he'd take us somewhere nice, but this place was a dream.

"Casey, this is too much. This must have cost a small fortune," I said while turning around to face him. It was all too much. Too perfect. Overwhelming, and I couldn't help but wonder if that meant something bad would happen. In the past, I was always caught off guard when things seemed to be going right.

I was afraid that none of it was real. For all I cared, all of it could disappear, as long as wherever I was left standing I had a good view of him. He was all I wanted.

NINE

Casey

Thursday, January 7, 2010

NOTHING WAS *TOO* MUCH if I got to see her face look like that. It was exactly what I wanted.

Blake stood near the door looking out for a few minutes before she spoke. I felt like I'd finally given her something. Something no one else ever had. And now I knew what it felt like, I wanted to do it again and again forever.

"I'm glad you like it." And I truly was. Seeing the excitement and wonder on her face as we walked through the lobby was almost as breathtaking as seeing that the pretty little finger on her left hand was bare.

No engagement ring. No wedding band. That was my favorite part of the trip so far. If she noticed how much I was holding her hand, she didn't complain, but it was free again and I relished knowing the next ring she wore would be mine.

Permanently.

I also noted that, although they looked short, her fingernails were in relatively good shape compared to how I'd seen them a few times in the past.

All good signs for me.

"Like it? Casey, this is a dream. The hotel. The view. I can't believe you'd spend so much on a little getaway. This is so . . . so startling. It's too much. But thank you." Her thoughts were jumping around. It was a lot to take in—even for me.

I was content she didn't know how much money I had. That fact alone made it so much more fun to spend.

The brewery had done, and continued to do, incredibly well. And to say Marc had been generous with me—even before I bought into Bay Brewing, as an owner—would have been a gross understatement. Aside from that, I bought in at a time when we began making profit hand over fist and we could barely keep up with orders. I didn't have much in the way of bills or free time. I spent a lot of time traveling on business and those expenses were all written off. I'd never been worried about money, even when we'd first met. I wasn't Trump-rich by a long shot, but splurging on a much-needed vacation with my girl wouldn't put a dent in my account.

I could understand why she assumed I only made a fair income and did okay. So it came as no surprise when she thought the Bella Flechazo was out of my price range. It looked that way. Hell, it felt that way—even to me. I'd never stayed anywhere that nice before. One thing was sure though, I would've spent twice as much if I'd known it would guarantee that mesmerized look on her face.

"Why don't you take a shower, put on a little something-something, and then let me take you downstairs for dinner?"

"Why don't you join me?" she replied bouncing up to me on her toes. Her light, carefree steps only proving more how carefree she felt.

Blake's mouth met mine in a leisurely, languid kiss and time finally slowed down for us. Her tongue slid across my bottom lip and I moaned. Her lips were so soft and the only kiss I tasted on them was mine. My hands found hers and I walked us backward to, where I was guessing, the bathroom was through the master suite and around the corner.

Making it to the bathroom, she switched places and pulled me in as I fumbled for the light switch on the wall, trying not to break our kiss. I kicked my shoes off as she unwound the red scarf. *That* I'd only bought to see her blush.

The wicked grin she was flashing charmed me. I had wanted to see her untroubled for so long. So many times when we'd been together there had been *circumstances* looming over us. There were too few precious times when I'd seen her look totally at ease, and this was now one of them. She swayed her hips and pulled her shirt over her head. Then she took a few backward steps to the walk-in shower.

"Why don't you come in here and show me what you brought me here for?" she persuaded. I shrugged out of my jacket and tossed it behind me. My hand reached behind my back and pulled off my shirt. All the while, my mind began debating. I tried to turn the fucker off, but I couldn't. What she'd just said reminded me. Although she was being playful, I didn't want her to have any reason to misinterpret my intentions.

Don't be the one-night stand guy.

I stood before her, sock-footed and only wearing jeans.

By then she only had her panties on and she did something I hadn't seen since the first night we were together. Her right foot rubbed that back of her left leg and her hands clasped politely in front of herself.

Honeybee, I won't make the same mistakes with you twice.

I walked past her to turn on the water, but still didn't take my pants or socks off. She looked at me like I was a perfect stranger, not rushing to take her up on her sexy fucking suggestion. There was nothing I wanted to do more—in the whole world—than fuck her beautiful brains out in that massive fucking shower.

Well, maybe one thing. And it was a big thing. I wanted to actually make her mine this time. If I was getting a second shot at making her mine, I was going to do my best to learn from my mistakes.

I kissed her naked shoulder as I walked back past. She stood still and stared at the floor.

"I'm not going to shower with you. Not this time," I said as gently as I could. I was confusing her, which was understandable. In the past, if there was an opportunity to be inside her, then I was buried eight hard inches in my girl. Cooling things down wasn't something common for me.

If she'd done it intentionally, it most likely wouldn't have been as adorable, but her bottom lip pushed out and her brow wrinkled—just barely. She was literally pouting. Sadly, at that moment, I had to look away.

My ego and my dick wanted to be stroked, but I abstained. An ego that begged to know how disappointed she was I wasn't showering with her. And a dick that really, really wanted to take said shower. I reminded myself she wasn't going anywhere and said, "You look phenomenal. I want that body like my next breath, but I'm going to let you shower and I'll get our bags squared away."

I placed one last kiss on the skin at the crook of her neck and left her there.

I fought the urge to go back in, but it didn't feel the same as when I'd left her in the past. I wasn't leaving her on her own. I was just going into the next room.

Another benefit of taking a flight-risk lover to another country. *Where was she to go?*

I collected my jacket and shirt, deciding if I wasn't going to shower, the least I could do was change. I moved Blake's luggage to her side of the room, or at least that was where I decided her side would be. Where it was in the room was trivial, but the fact our luggage was in the same room was paramount. She could sprinkle her shit over every square inch in the suite and I wouldn't bat an eye. Her shit was with my shit.

I'd made some special arrangements I needed to check on anyway. After booking the room, I called to see what sorts of things there were to do locally. I was only too pleased to encounter Enrique, the perfectly English-speaking concierge. It was a sign.

Enrique and I made fast friends. He was about my age—I surmised—and I immediately won him over when I told him I needed help showing a *very* special girl a *very* good time. After getting a few minor details handled by my new Costa Rican buddy, I felt like I'd chosen the perfect place for us. He was accommodating of my weird requests, but never told me no or that he couldn't help. Enrique—or Ricky, as I liked to call him in my head—had some pretty tall orders to fill.

I called the number I'd saved in my phone for his extension. He picked up and confirmed that, so far, all the things I'd asked for wouldn't be an issue. I only needed to let him know when I wanted them.

Changing and talking to Ricky were good distractions to keep my mind and body from wandering back into the bathroom, where I knew my favorite pussy was wet under steamy water and the most amazing pair of tits were probably soapy and slick with . . . okay, I wasn't completely distracted.

I began unpacking. Staying in a room longer than a weekend merited taking your shit out of a bag and putting it away. That and it just felt good to settle in somewhere.

It wasn't long before Blake came out. In our rush, she hadn't grabbed anything to wear after the great shower-fucking episode of 2010 that didn't happen. *Yet.*

With a big white hotel towel wrapped around her creamy white body, she padded over to her suitcase. I wondered how it was that women's towels always stayed on. Did they know some towel trick? Because every time I did it, either my dick hung out the front or the bastard would fall off as soon as I took one step.

But she sauntered over to her things, like she wouldn't even consider it falling off. I learned at that moment I didn't harbor the power of telekinesis. The damn thing held its own despite my brain's vulgar and explicit damnedest to wish the thing off.

She looked fresh and clean, but she still wore something like disappointment on her face. I lay across the bed and propped my head on my arm to talk to her, while she chose what to wear after opening her largest bag.

"Hey, why the face?" I asked, knowing she didn't understand what had happened in the bathroom and why I didn't take advantage of the moment like I had so many, many, many times before. "Tell me what's on your mind."

"It's nothing. I just thought, we'd . . ." She stopped there, embarrassment claiming her features. Scarlet bloomed under her cheeks. It was different than the turned-on version of her blush. I bet she had tens of blushes yet all this time I'd only concentrated on one. There were so many ways I hadn't been someone who was deserving of leaving a life and a home for.

That all had changed. If she was doing better, then I wanted to, too.

"Go ahead. Tell me," I told her. I was paying attention. She'd said she liked when I told her what to do. I understood; it took so much pressure off knowing what the other wanted.

She pulled a few dresses from her suitcase and laid them on the bed near me. She didn't make eye contact. I think that made it easier for her to spill her thoughts. Still, I wanted her to know what she was doing and acknowledge she was doing it because I'd said so.

I got something out of it too. After all the times we'd fought, all the times that either she or I had left, if I could have just *told* her what I wanted her to do . . . Well, I wasn't completely sure, but our story might have worked out better than the fucked-up way we'd done it.

She took a deep breath as she gathered her words. "I thought we were about to take a shower *together.*" "Together" rolled off her tongue as if spoken in a delicate language. She spoke that, but I spoke me. Good thing for her, I knew both of our languages. Translated, Blake's "together" meant "fuck the marble off the walls" in Casey. I would have loved making her scream my name in there. I bet the acoustics were great. We'd be doing a sound check before we left for home.

"I wanted to, but I'm mixing things up," I admitted. I wanted her to want me like she did and I didn't want her to doubt I wanted her back. It was a fine line. Still, I wasn't about to jump on her the second we were alone again. I was going to take my time, because there wasn't a rush. Not anymore.

As much as my balls throbbed, it gave me pleasure making her squirm a little.

That's right, honeybee. Dangle on my hook.

I needed to make sure she knew where my head was though. I didn't want her dwelling on anything else except how much of a good time she was having.

"What do you mean?" she asked.

I stared up at the ceiling. When I finally had the words, the way I needed them, I spoke to a patiently waiting woman with curious brown eyes.

"Aside from how bad I want to be buried inside of you," I said, and made eye contact while I paused to punctuate what I'd said. I continued when she smiled, "I don't want you to think that's *all* I want from this trip."

She crooked a leg and sat on the bed by my head.

"What else do you want from this trip?"

"I want lots of things." How much did I want to give away? "I want you to relax and know that you're here because I wanted to spend *time* with you."

She grinned, but tried to hide it. "Spend *time* with me? Okay."

"Yes. I'm serious. I want to hang out. Act like we're just a couple on vacation. I want us to unwind and chill-the-fuck-out for a few days. *If* we have some great sex along the way, then that's a bonus. A huge, awesome *bonus.*"

She nodded, getting where I was going. I wondered if she knew what I meant. If I only knew what she was thinking?

"I mean, don't you feel like we've been pulled and stretched so thin over the last few years? I'm ready for some of that pressure to slip away for a minute, even if things are waiting for us when we get back."

Blake ran an open hand over my chest and her fingers rubbed back and forth over my tattoo.

She said, "I know exactly what you mean."

I sat up on my elbows, bringing our faces closer together. "Are you sure? I don't want you thinking anything negative. Got that?"

Her eyes said she did. She appeared relieved, like she'd wanted someone to say that or give her the chance to relax for a few days.

"Got it," she confirmed and then she leaned in and kissed me. "We're taking baby steps. I like it."

I was going to rock her world with this new and improved Casey and then I was going to rock her world with my tongue, my fingers, and my cock.

Baby steps.

TEN

Blake

Thursday, January 7, 2010

*B*ABY STEPS.

For us, the concept was almost comical. We'd either barreled head first, or taken our sweet-ass time. The thought of us taking our time and being cautious was kind of funny. I wasn't exactly sure what he'd meant, but he sounded like he knew what he was talking about. And honestly, if he wanted to put the brakes on things, all it did was make me want him more. Who knew that was even possible?

It wasn't only his body I sought, it was his company. I wanted both, but sadly, time hadn't always been on our side. And when we were against the wall, time wise—well frankly, I was usually against a wall with him inside me. Our chemistry always monopolized our minutes. Here, we didn't have to be desperate. Amongst everything else at the incredibly lavish hotel, we had the beautiful new luxury of time.

Also, this new and improved Casey was showing me he was taking this seriously. Taking steps in our relationship with care, to protect it. Hell if that didn't turn me on, too.

He'd chosen the dress I wore. "I like this one," he said from the bed as I put lotion on in front of him. If he was trying restraint on for size, then I was going to test it. He could tell me to do anything and

I'd do it. It was a paradox: my need for independence and my desire to hand pieces of it over to him. It had almost always been like that; he just never took advantage of my instinctual surrender to him.

My mind.

My body.

My heart.

They were all merely puppets waiting for their turn to be played with by him. I'd never handed more than some of my body and mind over to Grant. Mainly because he didn't understand me. He didn't know where to find the rest and I never had a soul thirsty need to show him. With Casey, he looked for every part of me. I trusted him with all three.

We walked through the restaurant, which was the size of a small ballroom. It was incredible how tall the ceilings were in the Bella Flechazo. Music played quietly, a guitarist and a pianist. The chatter of cheerful conversations soaked into my ears as we walked to a table that was close to the small dance floor.

I'd always loved dancing with him.

The first night. The night in Georgia. The little we danced on the pier in Chicago one hot summer night so long ago. All of those times that once seemed not so long ago, now seemed like eons past.

"Hermosa jovencita," the maître d' said politely to me as he pulled out my chair. Then he tipped his head to Casey and said, "Señor." As soon as I began to sit, so did my date. He had some manners, that guy.

Then I thought about it and realized that this might actually be our first real date. Like a *real* date. My heart almost climbed up my neck and out of my mouth to do cartwheels at the thought. But after a moment, I decided not. We'd had many dates and sweeping them under the rug would be like erasing all the good times too.

It didn't matter. After everything, maybe it was all going to be okay.

The host left us, but it was only a moment until a server came to get our orders. "Nos gustaría dos pintas de cerveza y dos tragos de tequila. Cerveza local, por favor," Casey said slowly. I didn't know everything he was telling the woman, but I could have listened to it all night.

Cerveza. Beer. I knew that. And tequila was easy enough, but had he always known Spanish? *Who was this guy?*

The woman who took his order left to get—what I was guessing were—our drinks.

I leaned in to ask conspiratorially, "Do you know Spanish?" I couldn't help the small laugh that fell out after I asked.

He smiled and said, "No. Not really. I just memorized a few things that I thought we might need." Then he winked at me and took a sip of his water. "I said I'd take care of you."

I sat back, corrected. Shocked and a lot turned on. That wink might soon be the death of me.

I was still revved up from the plane, the almost shower, and then hearing him speak Spanish and ordering for me? I knew *that* Casey, but it was just so different having the man I craved so much in the bedroom act that way while sitting across from me at the table.

"What else did you learn, *Señor* Moore?" I teased. Laughing came easily. My bones poured themselves into the chair and with my legs crossed tightly I relished looking at a miracle. How could he still want me? How could I be that lucky?

His laughs came easily, too. He pointed a serious finger at me. "It's no joke, Blake. We don't speak the language. How did you figure we'd get along?"

"I don't know. I didn't really think about it. People do it all the time."

"Well, I'd just much rather know how to say a few things so I know what we're getting."

"Okay, tell me what you know and I want to guess what you're saying."

Our drinks arrived. A draught and a shot placed before each of us. The server also came armed with a beautiful crystal dish with what looked like candied limes. Then the woman left.

Casey considered the limes and said, in sexy Spanish, with a gleam in his eye, "*Lame. Bebe. Chupa.*"

It was a terrible game. How was I supposed to know what he was saying? "Okay, maybe this wasn't a great idea. I have no clue," I admitted.

"I said lick. Drink. Suck." He was ripe with mischief.

"Ohhh," I breathed and the temperature in the restaurant went up ten degrees.

"Shall we?"

I reached for a piece of lime and his hand slid over mine, giving it a quick, tight squeeze. I caught his eye and saw warmth, fun, adventure, and something so Casey that I'd never been able to put my finger on. Blue-green eyes sparkled brighter than the beautiful glass chandelier in the lobby.

I brought the lime to my lips but waited for his cue.

"*Lame,*" he said and we both licked at our limes. It was a lot of sensations to handle at once. First, watching his masterful tongue sweep over the fruit. *Lucky lime.* Then, the taste of sour, salty, and sweet took over my mouth. I mimicked what he did next, lifting the shot glass to my lips.

"*Bebe,*" he said with a quirked eyebrow and we downed the shots.

My tongue reached out and tasted my briny lips as the tequila touched rock bottom. Alcohol and Casey heated my chest.

He bared his teeth after swallowing the liquor and the tendons strained in his neck as he accepted its burn.

"*Chupa,*" he hissed and our limes once again found our mouths. I was hesitant to bite at first, knowing it was going to be an assault of flavor, and I watched him sink into the green citrus. His eyes squeezed tight and when he opened them, he looked like he'd just come out of water. Alive and ready.

I bit into mine and it tasted remarkably good in contrast to the tequila.

As I stared at him unapologetically, my legs rubbed together under the table, aware of his peculiar brand of seduction playing out. Or maybe I was just really horny from him teasing me the whole day. The strapless, gray dress he'd chosen for me suddenly felt uncomfortable on my skin. I wanted to be naked, disposed of the clothes that kept me from him.

I began to tell him how good the shot was when he stood and stepped around the table grabbing my face. He kissed me there in front of everyone eating and mingling at the bar. His impatient consumption of me took me off guard, but as his bittersweet tongue swept across mine, I no longer cared who watched. And just as suddenly as he'd kissed me, he stopped and said, "Beso." Then he quickly kissed my lips once more before retreating to his side of the table.

I went from overwhelmed with sensation to senseless in seconds.

When he sat down and straightened his dinner jacket, he said, "*Beso*. Kiss. I forgot that part."

I laughed. How could you forget something like that?

Without missing a beat, he told me, "I can also ask where the bathroom is, how to get a taxi, common pleasantries, and I know how to ask for two more of anything. I think there are a few others, but that's mostly it."

I was still a little dizzy from the kiss and the shot, but it was hard to remember when I'd been on a date where I had zero expectations of what would happen. I loved how wild he was at times. He always kept me on my toes.

We ate BLTs, which he'd prearranged to be available for us. There we were at a gourmet restaurant eating bacon, lettuce and tomato sandwiches—one of the best I'd ever had, mind you—and we laughed. We drank beers and shared stories about the funny people we'd met traveling for work.

Then we drank a little more.

Lame. Bebe. Chupa. Beso.

I loved taking shots with him. He was such a good kisser.

After three, I got up and went to him instead. The bartender clapped and gave a little, "woo," catching me. By then the dinner crowd had cleared out, but we stayed as bar-goers began filling the space. Less and less, people were eating and sitting, and more and more were they dancing to the two-piece band.

"Let's dance, *mi abeja*."

That was a new one and tipped my head in question.

"Let's dance, my honeybee."

"Okay," I said, but I was already floating.

We swayed. The alcohol had made our bodies loose. I clung to him and during slower songs I laid my head on his chest and listened to him hum along to music he couldn't possibly know. His deep rumbling, in time to the tiny band, sounded so damn good.

"We need a new song," he said looking down at me.

"No, we don't," I disagreed.

"I shouldn't have danced with her to that. It was a low blow. I ruined our song."

"No. Sheryl Crow ruined it way before you did," I joked. "I only liked it because I danced to it with you."

He pulled away and stopped, shocked. "Are you kidding me?" He smirked.

"It was kinda sad. I mean, I don't think that song has a happy ending. It just sounds sexy with all the ohhhs and ahhhs. It isn't a good *love* song," I explained.

He wrapped his long arms around me and we started to move again.

He kissed the side of my forehead. "Then we needed a new one anyway, didn't we?" he asked.

"I don't want one song, Lou." My feet shuffled parallel to his shoes. My left leg was between his legs. Our bodies coupled naturally, it felt like home. Like my other half was connected. Like Heaven.

"How many do you want? Do I need a pen and paper?" he jested.

"I don't want just *one* song to remind me of you." I tipped my head up, but in my heels I was already closer to his mouth. "I want every song to be our song. I want every song we dance to be ours to keep. I want thousands of songs with you, Casey." Either tequila had magical powers or I was finally learning to talk with my heart. Both stood a good chance of being true.

"I can't deny that I like your logic."

"And *if* every song is *our* song, and we don't dance with anyone else to *our* songs, then we won't ever have to find new ones." I had it all figured out. Me and the *bebe*. I wasn't really jealous of him dancing with Aly, at least not the way I imagined he thought I was. I hated the very thought of her hands touching him, and what was worse, his hands touching her. But more than jealous, I was scared. Scared that I would lose him to her.

It was a damn good thing I didn't allow myself to think about them being *together*. It was wrong of me to feel hurt by it, but maybe not. If it hurt him when I'd been with Grant, it was only fair I'd felt the same pain knowing he turned to her for what I couldn't give him when he needed it most.

But it didn't matter anymore and certainly not at that moment. All that mattered was wrapped around me, in a fairy-tale location where shots came with kisses and every song belonged to us.

That night we kissed without worry of being caught by my guilt and his insecurity. We didn't have to hide. We were Casey and Blake, two people simply trying to figure out the second chance we'd always been fighting for.

"Let's go upstairs," he whispered in my ear and it was almost like we transported there. As if we thought about it and then all of a sudden we were there.

The room was dimly lit with the few lights we'd left on. It was late, and even though I was tired from travel and just life in general, I craved the feel of him.

Our suite was warm, void of chill or worry. In the bedroom, we didn't bother with a light, knowing where everything was by memory. He guided me to bed. He let my hair down and brushed it off my shoulders, and then he held me close and pressed his lips to mine. Casey laid us down so softly I barely knew we were moving until I felt the fluffy pillow under my head.

I deepened our kiss and moaned when his body pressed against mine.

"We're not going to have sex tonight, Blake," he said breathlessly around my lips. Why? I wanted him so badly. Just like that. Slow and easy.

I tried to evict thoughts of uncertainty from my mind, but they snuck in with his words. His behavior was contradictory. He'd shown me nothing but affection and care since we saw each other in the airport. Why wouldn't he make love to me?

Old demons felt the need to speak up.

What if he doesn't want you after the chase? What if he only likes the thrill?

I felt my body begin to tense for the first time since we'd arrived. The hands that had been wandering across his back stilled. The leg I had started to wrap around his waist slowly began falling to the side.

"Hey, where are you going," he said, as he kissed my neck and ran a hand through my hair to the nape of my neck.

"I don't understand," I contested. "I want you." He shifted his weight and I felt how hard he was against my inner thigh. He was definitely turned on. So what was his deal? "Don't you want me, too?"

"Mmmm," he breathed near my ear. "God, I want you." His big right hand hitched my leg back around his hip and he palmed my ass, bringing my dress up to my waist in the process and exposing my pale pink underwear. "I've wanted you day and night for so long now. I don't know how to *not* want you." He spoke between kisses and rubbed his nose along my clavicle. Then he bit me gently at the crook of my neck. "But there've been too many times I've let that need for you cloud my focus."

"But I—"

"No, Blake. Not tonight. Tonight, I'm going to make you come and then I'm going to sleep next to you. I'm going to fall asleep with you in my arms. All those nights I missed out on holding you and feeling you next to me. I stole them from both of us being scared and stubborn. I have to be better this time. I see all that you're doing and I'm so damn proud of you, honeybee," he said calmly. "But I want more than just physical things from you. It isn't that I don't want you. Fuck, do I want you. But I need all of you. Not just this." He moved against my center and I knew I had to change his mind. After hearing those sweet words, I had to have him and I wasn't going to fight fair.

"Please, Casey. Fuck me."

He growled and pressed his forehead to my chest. "You're evil." He laughed. I wished he sounded defeated, but mostly he sounded amused. "You're not making it easy for me to be noble."

"Don't be noble then," I said as I wound my arms around him and pulled him closer to me.

"If you knew what I was thinking about doing to you, you'd know I wasn't." He rolled partially over toward the center of the bed and ran his hand under my dress and up to my breast.

"Then tell me," I shamelessly suggested.

The tips of his fingers roamed down my stomach and my pulse sped up. His fingers slid under the sheer fabric of my underwear and my breaths came in spurts as I mentally begged him to keep going. I was so wound up.

"Don't worry. I told you I'd take care of you."

Casey's hand moved over me and he delicately pressed into the exact spot where I wanted him.

"I love how much you want me, Blake. I can feel it." He kissed my shoulder. "Sit up."

I rose up. There we both sat on a bed I'd hoped we would be messing up by then. I loved that he wanted to show me he appreciated me for more than just sex, but at that point in our relationship, I'd kind of figured. What guy hangs around this long, going sometimes months without any physical contact and keeps coming back?

He wrapped his arms behind me and lowered the zipper on my dress, then pulled it over my head. I wore only my strapless bra, which was on a little sideways from his wandering hands, and my panties.

"Lay down and put your hands together like you're holding them, like I hold your hand."

I interconnected my fingers together and laid them on my stomach while smiling at him expectantly.

"Blake, I want to be someone who gives you more than I take. That's what this is about. Giving to you. But I'm still just a man, so keep your hands together. When you touch me, I lose focus and all I can think about is being buried inside of you. Which is going to happen, just not tonight," he reassured in a matter-of-fact way.

"Okay," I said softly. Just as always when he instructed, I followed. My hands were clasped and they wouldn't part until he said. I loved when he possessed me. I was confident he would give me what I needed. I didn't have to make any decisions. I didn't have to worry about what I was giving him to show him how much I cared. It was freeing.

He sat above me on his knees. The twilight shining through the windows backlit him in the dark room. Tauntingly slow, he unbuttoned his dress shirt and then took off his undershirt letting them both fall on the plush carpet. I felt his eyes on me, but I didn't know how much he could see. Still, his touches were so precise that either he had great night vision or he just knew his way around my body in the dark.

His hands found my breasts and he masterfully removed them from the strapless cups. His thumbs rolled over my nipples. His mouth covered one then the other. Hot and wet, he sucked and gently bit at them until my back began to arch and my ass pushed into the bed wanting more of him.

I always wanted him to declare himself, to show me he actually wanted us. And now he was. I loved him. I loved that he was doing it for us. I knew he was capable of giving more now, and in that, felt a sense of peace and safety. And now, thank God, sexual release at the hands of my sexy man.

It was wonderful receiving all the things he had to give me. I wanted it all.

ELEVEN

Casey

Friday, January 8, 2010

I WANTED TO GIVE her everything. The things she never knew existed, but mostly the things she dared not ask for.

The feel of her in my hands, the taste of her on my lips, it was always more than I could store in my memories. And even when I was with her I wanted more. More minutes. More hours. More places on her body to find and claim for myself.

I touched her breasts and wished I had two extra arms and hands. I loved the shape of her and how she fit perfectly in my palms. I loved how, when she lay on her back, they fell to her sides a little and left a clear path for me to kiss down the middle of her chest. Perfectly, her nipples reacted to my curious touch, growing stiff when I applied even the smallest amount of pressure.

Bending down, I kissed the pair and then my fingers touched over her soft flat belly, which rose and fell shakily as I took my time. She felt like silk or something equally smooth. I always wondered if my hands felt rough moving over her skin. She always seemed to like it, so I wasn't ever going to stop.

My fingers made their way to her panties, but instead of moving under them I teased her by rubbing her over the top. Her arousal made them wet and she lifted into my touch. She squirmed, but her hands stayed clasped together just like I told her to do.

She made me feel incredible and she wasn't even doing anything. Following my requests gave me power, when I used to have none. And hearing her tell me she liked when I told her what to do or what I wanted, well that would keep my dick hard well into my eighties.

"You're making me crazy," she begged. "Please, Casey." Her bare foot dug into the top of the bedspread.

It would have been easy to yank my pants off and push myself into her. Really, really fucking easy. But I owed it to myself—and to her—to be a man who gave without taking.

"What do you want, honeybee?" I asked against her tummy and kissed my way down to her pussy. "Do you want me to touch you with my hands?" I kissed where I knew her clit was through the satin underwear. "Or my mouth?"

"Both," she panted.

I gave her what she needed. My fingers and mouth bringing her to orgasm in only minutes. Then I did it again.

When she was sated and worn out, she curled into my chest and fell asleep. *Had she ever given herself so fully to me? So unguarded? Fearless?* I have loved her for so long, but in submitting so easily to my desire to look after her, she gave me herself. At *that* moment, she gave me everything.

Monday, January 11, 2010

"For a chef, you're kind of a monster when it comes to cracking crabs," I teased.

With her tongue half out, she worked the cracker thing up and down the length of the king crab legs we'd ordered to share. We were on our third order and to say we hadn't been drinking would have been a major lie.

We had barely drunk at all that week, aside from our first night in Costa Rica, and it had probably been the best thing. We talked a lot. I actually listened and it gave me more control than ever in our relationship. And since I'd put the kibosh on jumping right in the sack, it was like we were truly concentrating on reality. Even when we were together at my house in October, there had been something hanging in the air over us.

Maybe it was being on a real vacation.

Maybe it was being there with her and out in the open and seeing new things together, but it all felt peaceful. We were so much closer in lots of different ways. Closer to being a real couple. Closer in distance and communication.

But I hadn't let myself get as close as I wanted. Even though she'd come every day, sometimes twice, and so had I, we still hadn't had sex. Okay. It wasn't like we were celibate; we'd only been there four days. There was a benefit to holding back. Both of us were like live wires. Still, she never pushed, letting me take the lead.

There were a couple of—damn fine—reasons to finally have sex. We were fucking good at it and it felt fucking amazing. But the more time we spent together, the more I was confident that holding off a few days was a good idea.

It just didn't seem right jumping back into our old habits, into the old ways that had never worked out for us. I'm not saying it was always just sex with us, but we had a lot of sex in the past when we could have been building a foundation or just talking. We never expected *us* to be a reality.

Us. A real relationship.

Besides, she'd just moved out of her house. She needed a goddamned minute, and even though her body was ready to go with a few touches or words whispered, I had to make sure her head and her emotions were ready too. It was my job to make sure she was doing okay. Her nerves had to have been shot. She was still reeling from the holidays and then poof, she was in paradise with me? It was enough to make anyone's head spin. Everything back home wasn't magically fixed. She still had a divorce ahead of her and I knew it weighed heavily on her mind.

That night—after not drinking much over the past few days—she was a little loose from the Rum Runners we'd been drinking. She was calm and at ease. Her shoulders were relaxed and sun-kissed beneath the tie of her bikini she still wore. She wore a strapless dress thing that hugged her chest and fell just below her knees. Her hair was swept back in a messy bun, having been wet and then dry, and then wet and dry once more that day. Pieces had fallen free all over. She wouldn't have looked better straight out of a salon.

With one foot up on the extra chair, she sloppily worked at her crab.

We'd stopped at the beachfront restaurant after walking around the little town on the coast, and decided to have a late lunch. Which turned into dinner. And there we still were. Laughing, drinking, and eating. Those seemed to be our three talents.

"I'm on vacation," she said. "And I've been drinking. My hand-eye coordination must be off." She didn't look at me as she pried every last piece of white and orange meat from its shell.

The air was cooler and since we'd been putting down the alcohol, I was going to call a car to pick us up anyway. I didn't want to worry about the long walk we'd have back to the resort. And the ride bought us more time. There was no rush.

The whole trip had been like that. *Easy and carefree.*

I threw my napkin down and leaned back in my chair. There was no way I could eat another bite. I watched her adorably struggle with another leg.

"You look pretty doing it though."

Her eyes finally met mine, having been focused on her food. The compliment got her attention.

"Are you flirting with me?" she asked.

"Maybe. Are you going to eat that piece of crab on your cheek?" It had been there for a while. Her lips glistened from the butter. She was going to taste good. Then again, she always did.

"I was saving it for you," she said, joking, as she faked a seductive voice.

"That was thoughtful." I winked at her playing along.

Her face soured and she snaked her tongue out to find the morsel.

"Hey, I thought you said that was mine."

"Well, that was when I thought you'd earned it by calling me pretty. I've since realized you're just trying to torture me. So, it's mine."

"You're missing it anyway." And she was, but just barely.

I leaned toward her. She leaned toward me. Her eyes blinked slowly meeting mine. I wanted to jump her right there, where she would least expect it. Instead, I used a move that worked well for me once upon a time and pulled her chair closer to mine while I moved in toward her.

"Whoa, hey," she clambered. "I think you *are* flirting with me." The light in her eyes was so much brighter than I ever really knew possible. She just kept getting better.

My voice low, I said, "Give me that." And I kissed the place on her cheek, just out of her reach, and picked up the forgotten seafood.

Her head tipped up to me and she moved in to meet my lips, but I pulled back just out of her reach.

"You are a pain in the ass, *Señor* Moore. Stop teasing me."

I had to admit. I liked taunting her. "I'd never do that."

"Yet here you are, pulling away when I want you."

"You want me, huh?" I asked, knowing we were about to reach the threshold of her comfort with flirty face-to-face talk. I wanted more, too. I always wanted more. "Tell me what you want with me, Ms . . . ." Then I stopped almost calling her Ms. Warren, then concluding it was really Mrs. Kelly. It hurt somewhere in my chest, but I didn't want to let it show. She'd been doing everything I'd asked of her and in my time, not hers. How she got that name bore fault shared by us both.

Almost shyly, she looked up at me through her bare lashes and said, "I *always* want you."

Well, fuck. Those four words were pretty damn sexy. Everything about her was. Deprived looked good on her, or maybe it was my own deprivation playing tricks on me.

"What else?" I was fishing, but we were in new territory for us. Talking, flirting and playing, knowing that it all meant something. Headed somewhere. Somewhere good. Somewhere I'd always wanted it to go, but just didn't have a map.

"I think your face needs a shave." She smiled as she studied me.

"And?"

"Have I ever told you how handsome you are?" Thinking back,

she hadn't that I could remember.

"No? I just thought you liked my moves." I was a little embarrassed and a lot flattered. Turning the tables was a talent she was perfecting and at that moment she was full-out hitting on *me*.

It was the best seafood lunch-dinner I'd ever had.

"Oh, I like those moves, but all this," she said and made a circle in front of my face, "is your secret weapon."

"No, my—" And before I could say cock or dick or whatever other phallic term I could think of, she pressed two fingers to my lips.

"Shhh. Don't ruin it." Her brown eyes looked like amber glass sparkling in the Christmas lights strung around the outdoor dining area where we'd taken up residence.

I didn't say anything, but I gave her a look that said, "Fine. Keep talking."

"I've never met someone who has eyes like yours. Those two green-blue-hazel-whatever eyes can tell me everything I ever need to know. I should have taken them more seriously."

Her chin pushed out. She wanted a kiss, but I was greedy with her thoughts and I wanted her to keep going. Hearing her talk about me like that was medicinal. I was going to lose my man card, but I wasn't telling if she wasn't.

I gave her a swift kiss and pulled away again. She seemed satisfied, for the time being, and then she continued, "Those lips, that mouth. Your tongue. The way they work together. They can make me forget my name and when I remember what it is, they make me want to change it."

Blake Moore sounded about right.

She got another small kiss for that. Maybe dirty talk wasn't all "pussy" and "fuck me harder." The things she was saying were making me hard in my pants and soft and mushy in my heart.

"Sometimes you say such perfect things before I've even told you what I'm thinking about. How thoughtful you are. How romantic. Have you always been this irresistible? And the way you know how to touch me. You got me *good*," she admitted and shook her head a little, bowing it between us.

The tension was growing a little too strong for dinner talk and I wanted to be in private when my resistance failed. I didn't have much left. The only thing I could do was be a wise ass—it would buy me time. Hopefully, we could continue our chat back at the room.

"Did you rehearse this? Do you have all of this written down somewhere? Are you holding out on me? I didn't prepare anything." I grinned at her to show I was only kidding, but seriously, I was so hard that the end of my dick felt like it was about to explode.

"I'm ready to go back to the hotel and talk more about this," I said coolly.

"Okay," she agreed. "Let's get some beers to go." She really was a bright girl. *"Dos mas!"*

"Good plan. You pack up the rest of those legs and I'll go settle up and see if the bar will sell me a few to take back with us."

She nodded and began sorting through the shell ruins for crabs uneaten.

When we got back to the hotel—the heaven we made into our little home—she went to the bathroom to change out of her swimsuit, telling me she didn't want mildew and I went to the kitchen area to put away the leftovers and put the beer in the refrigerator.

When she came back out, her hair was down and brushed out and she wasn't wearing a stitch of clothing.

Oh. Fucking. Hell. That vixen.

"Want to continue our talk outside?" she asked, then slowly walked toward the sliding doors, which opened up to our porch area, above the private stretch of beach that was all ours—for a pretty penny.

What do you say to a question like that? What do you say to a body like that? The answer is nothing. You don't say a damn thing. You grab a bucket of ice, fill it and add the beers you just put in the fridge. Then drop your pants. Of course, she didn't say to do any of that. It was obviously implied.

I watched as she pushed open the tall glass doors. Naked. Then she found a few towels where the staff kept them for quick access.

Did I mention she was naked?

I watched her hips sway as she walked out into the moonlight and she continued until she got to the hammock near the edge of the veranda. I stopped outside the doors and stared. She was stunning.

I was going to do every single thing in my power to have her for myself. Not just her hypnotic body, I'd had that many times. I wanted everything else.

Her desire.

Her heart.

Her smiles.

Her thoughts and dreams.

Her pleasure.

Her laughs.

Her comfort.

Her *future.*

She gave me a look over her shoulders and a light breeze blew through her hair. Maybe I'd had too much to drink. Maybe it was *that* place. Or maybe—just maybe—that look was real and she'd told me the truth. She wanted all of me, too.

My touch.

My ear to listen.

My arms to hold her.

My love.

And I was going to give her those and more.

"You look gorgeous, honeybee," I said barely loud enough for her to hear me over the waves lapping the beach only feet below.

"Can we lay out here for a while?" She sounded like a child, hopeful and wanting.

"We can do whatever you want," I answered as I closed the distance between her and me. I then placed the tub of ice and beer on the ground beside the mesh swing, then she turned to face me.

Hammocks are tricky bastards. One wrong move and the sweet seduction of the moment could be turned into a clumsy topple to the ground. But that didn't matter. We'd flopped in life before and hitting the ground wouldn't hurt nearly as bad.

It came up past her knees, but below her waist, and she leaned back to sit. The oversized hammock lowered with her weight. Where she sat, her head was at just the right height. The urge to touch myself, naked as I was, became too much for me to fight. My hand found my dick, or possibly it was the other way around. I was already as hard as I'd been at the restaurant and my need for her fought all other bodily functions down with one hand tied behind its back.

"Casey, it's so perfect. How did we actually get here? How is this all possible? I never thought we'd get a chance to . . ." and she trailed off looking up at me.

Those were great questions and they demanded attention.

"We're here because how much we want each other is stronger than our fear of being with each other. And it's possible because what we have doesn't give up." For being on the spot, those answers were pretty dead-nuts on point.

After I finished speaking, her eyes trailed down my body. Over my chest where she lingered, studying my tattoo.

Betty Mine. And she was.

My hand continued to knead and pull some of the tension from my cock, but her mouth would have been better.

And then it was.

We traded, her hand for mine. Her fingers curled around me and like they always did, my knees threatened to resign their posts holding me up. She could tell I was less than steady on my feet. I loved watching how excited my lack of control made her.

"Sit with me," she said.

We fell into the netting and faced each other, her hand never leaving my cock.

"I love this," she whispered.

"Which part?" I hardly believed it was the giving a hand-job part.

"Just being here. Having nowhere to go tomorrow. No plans. No one to explain anything to. No one to think about, but *you.*" Either she knew what I'd wanted to hear or we were operating on the same frequency. My wandering hand found her wet as she skillfully slid hers up, around and down my dick. She shifted and opened herself up to me. It was those little things she did that were so fucking hot. I ran my fingers over her heated skin and she lifted into my touch.

It had only been a week or two since that last time we were together—in the back of the car at Cory and Micah's wedding—but everything about this felt new and different and unknown. Felt real. Felt like forever.

"Can we stay out here?" she softly asked, but I knew better with what I had planned.

"We can stay out here for a little while if you want to," I said, my voice gravely and thick with need as I slipped my middle finger inside her and curled it up to the magic spot that only I knew how to find—of that I was confident. Because every time I'd touched it, in all the times and all the places, she'd always looked surprised. "Then we're going inside, because this feels different than before. I want to make love to you like it's our first time. Because it feels like it is."

"Yes," she agreed—or maybe it was the spot talking.

She gripped the cords above her head, beads of sweat running over her face, when my tongue slid across her sex. My toes curled when she hummed while taking all of me into her mouth. Our moans mixed, our bodies speaking to each other intimately. We worshiped each other and took our time at each glorious fucking step.

Long story short, we both came on the hammock.

TWELVE

Blake

Monday, January 11, 2010

IN A NUTSHELL, IT was the best time I'd ever had on a swinging blanket.

The hammock swayed as we touched and kissed each other everywhere. It was a dance of perfectly timed movements, which kept us from tipping. But I wasn't satisfied.

As frustrating at times as it had been—not being fully intimate with Casey while we'd been away together—in the end it was exactly what we needed. We hiked. We took long swims and naps. We talked about our families more and the places we'd like to travel in the future. *The future.* I could hardly believe that was a possibility.

But my marriage wasn't altogether settled. And there was still a chance that Casey might get tired of the situation. However, I had an appointment with a lawyer and I'd already moved out. Two things we both thought would take a lot longer to happen. Despite how uncomfortable it was at first, telling my parents and Grant, I was relieved that process was going quicker than expected.

I was falling even more in love with Casey by the minute. The things I'd always been attracted to only intensified in the sun. His hair, when left to dry and go where it wanted, was out of control, wild and unkempt. His beautiful body hosted a tan I was rightfully jealous of. Golden brown in only a few days. He was cut from a dream list of details that I hadn't even known I'd wished for.

"I hope you're not tired," Casey said from between my legs. We'd mastered a head-to-foot, foot-to-head arrangement that was both balanced on the hammock and which equaled pleasure for both of us. I didn't respond, but I moaned around his cock. I'd never been in that position before—and even though I was hardly doing my best job with the distraction of him licking and sucking at my sex—I loved being able to taste him while he pleasured me.

Still touching me with one hand, he carefully leaned up.

"I think we've hit our limit with luck on this swing, honeybee." He swung his feet out and steadied it. Then he moved my legs and enfolded them around his waist.

I was love drunk. Pliant. Kissing any skin in front of me.

He picked me up and carried me inside. As he walked, I could feel the length of him pressed between us. I ground myself against him, wanton and full of desire.

He didn't put me down when he crawled across the top of the bed, I was still clutching his hard body. When I felt the mattress below me, I let my grip on him go. My hands wandered to his face, where I held him still so I could kiss him. The intimate taste of him, already in my mouth, mixed with the taste of me in his, was erotic and delicious.

He deepened the kiss, his tongue passionately gliding over mine. Then his kiss left my mouth and he licked and sucked down my neck. My hips rolled, wanting him.

He shifted so his cock was sliding over my clit and it was divine. I slid up and down his length loving the friction.

"Is that what you want?" he asked, his husky voice cracked when he spoke.

"Casey, please."

"Why do you want it?"

"Because I love you," I answered without thought or hesitation. He moaned and lowered himself. Before I could catch a breath, he was blissfully inside me. Then he moaned again, but that time it sounded like my name. His hand moved up my side and found my shoulder, then he followed the length of my arm until he found my hand. He laced our fingers together and pushed them over our heads, underneath a pillow that was farther up the bed. He pushed into me with such power and possession that I saw stars. Or maybe Jesus.

He moved with finesse and timing, slowing down and savoring the feeling of our connection. Then each time the intensity raised, the force of him would rock the bed so I bounced back onto him with just as much pressure. It was heaven.

When he'd get close to his orgasm, he'd back off. Slipping a hand between us, he'd make me come. Then he'd reposition us and start the glorious act over again. I didn't know how a man could have so much restraint—we'd been teasing each other for days. Yet, when I felt his stomach muscles tighten against my hand or body, he'd slow down like he wasn't ready for it to end. Silly man, he could have had me as many times as he wanted.

Finally as we lay, my back to his chest, my leg slung over his hip, his hand rubbing mind-blowing circles over my sensitive sex, he sped up and didn't try to control himself.

"I can't stop, honeybee. I'm going to come," he said breathlessly in my ear. Those words sent electricity through me and spurred something deep within me that was waiting for him.

"Yes," I panted. "Oh, Casey. Casey." I repeated his name, over and over it tumbled from my kiss-swollen lips. "Come, Casey. I want to feel you come inside me."

"Oh, fuck, Blake. Ah," he panted.

His hold on me tightened and he pushed so deeply within me, I thought he might touch the other side. I was full of *him* and that thought alone sent me spinning out of control. I pushed back against his body and it was like our bodies were attached. And then I felt him quake and erupt as my sex clenched around him.

He hugged me tightly and told me how much he loved me. He peppered kisses across my shoulders and neck until we were wrung out. Then we lay there for a while catching our breath until I rolled over on top of him.

"I love you, Casey Moore," I said, as I ran my fingers through the hollow space between his perfectly defined stomach muscles.

"I love you, too, Blake."

How many times can a girl get off in one night? I wasn't sure, but I was thinking for me it was at least six. It was like the very first time all over again, along with every other time we'd been together, all rolled into one.

His body reminded mine of the feelings I'd pushed down when I'd had to and of thoughts I'd talked myself out of for so long. Sensations I only thought the lucky people had. Being with him, I *was* one of those lucky people.

I wasn't sure what time it was; it was still dark. I was terribly thirsty—probably because of how much I'd drunk the night before—and I peeked up over his body to see if there was a bottle of water on his side of the table. There had been one earlier, when we were re-hydrating—as he called it. Boy, did I need it.

When we were outside on the hammock, I thought he was going to stick to his *just take our time* bit, which he'd insisted on the first few days. And having that element of our relationship sort of shelved, had felt a little weird—but also it had felt so good. Just to be *with* him in a time and place that wasn't hurried or rushed was eye-opening. I wasn't desperate, thinking it was the last time, like before. It was peaceful and I could finally breathe after months of wanting and denying myself. *Denying us.*

It felt like a true vacation. Lazy and cozy. Warm and relaxing. Sex aside, in those few days, I'd been with him in more ways than I'd ever been with anyone.

I had to admit, I wasn't totally on board with the whole slow down. Of course, we took care of each other in other ways, but after a few days of just kissing and touching, we gained clarity. Our conversations weren't about the future or the past. They were about us. Things we'd done and places we'd love to revisit—together.

However, upon coming inside, after what I'd thought had been the end of our physical activities—not that I would complain—I was pleasantly surprised he wasn't finished with me.

Not by a long shot.

I'd never realized how strong he was before that—the way he carried me into the room from the hammock. He had purpose and didn't stop for anything. The delicate way he took his time. How he moved inside me. And, looking at him sleep, I was reminded of those things as I rolled over to grab the water.

Casey stirred a little, probably from my movement, and mumbled what sounded like, "What are they doing here?"

Who was they? Where was here? And who was he talking to?

I wanted to remember to ask him about it later, but I, too, was delirious. I finished off the room temperature water and accepted I'd probably just forget. I lay back down on my belly and inched my way into the crook of his arm, smelling his scent with huge intakes of air. I fell asleep dreaming of the things we'd done.

It was just as magical the second time.

Tuesday, January 12, 2010

"Wake up."

Two warm lips pressed against my cheek.

I could smell the coffee like it was being waved under my nose. Trying one timid eyelid before both, I found I wasn't too far off. He was holding my new honeybee mug and I could see the steam rising from it.

On our first morning there, he'd somehow arranged for our coffee to come up with mugs he'd bought for us. Mine said *Honeybee is Trouble* and his said *Lou Loves Trouble.*

I would always be his Betty, but I liked honeybee more. It was a name he'd given me and one I'd never shared with anyone else. Just him.

I stretched and felt the repercussions of a night like the one we'd had. I was tender and sore—not only in lady land—but in my sides and abdominals. Sex with him was a workout program I could get used to.

Casey must have seen my wince, because he said, "Are you all right?"

I scooted back on the bed so I could sit up and take the coffee he'd brought just for me. When I was ready, he handed the mug, handle out, for me to take.

"I'm fine. Thank you. I need this," I told him as I leaned into the mug to sip off the first taste. "Mmmm. It's so damn good."

He sat down with his cup and rubbed up and down my leg as we caffeinated ourselves.

"Here's my idea. We leave tomorrow, so we've only got a little over twenty-four hours left." I pouted my lip at him and he pouted back saying, "I know. It sucks."

"Totally sucks," I added.

"Anyway, put that lip up. This is what we're going to do. We're going to order room service and eat it in the hot tub." He sympathetically nodded and said, "That should help your vagina." When he said vagina with a straight face. I giggled and drank my coffee.

"What if there's nothing wrong with my vagina?" I asked.

"Then I didn't do my job," he retorted with a point of his index finger down to the organ in question. "That thing got roughed up last night and we both know it."

I laughed again, but bobbed for him to keep going.

"Then we're going to go down to the beach and lay around, after that we're going to take a shower—*together.* Then we're going to watch Spanish television—I'll translate what I can for you." He was so damn cute.

"And then?"

"Then I'm going to hit that a few more times. Maybe another shower. Maybe not. I haven't worked it all out yet." He smiled that full-tilt Casey grin. "Then I'm going to hit it again."

"Well, it's a good thing you put me off for so long. It would have been a shame to come all this way and not see anything or have any fun." I tried to hide my playfulness by looking into my coffee. "I would have never seen the outside of this room if I'd have had my way on our first night."

"Well, I hope you saw everything you needed to," he said, "because for the next day, you're all mine. And I'm fucking you anywhere and everywhere I want."

Who could argue with that?

Casey made good on his promise.

We ate breakfast in the monstrous Jacuzzi and then we fucked on the side of it. He was right about it making me feel better. Even though my vagina wasn't in as rough a condition as he'd like to have thought, it was tender. By the time we got out of the whirlpool, it was better.

We had sex and laughed and laughed while we had sex, which I didn't know was possible. But when you're getting a lesson in dirty talking, midway through having sex on the floor of your hotel room, and your lover keeps saying, "You take that cock," like a cheesy porn star? Sometimes the only thing you can do is laugh.

It was my favorite twenty-four hours in Costa Rica. It replenished me and was just the fuel I needed to make sure I got back to him as fast as I possibly could.

Not just for the great sex, but because he was such a good friend. My best friend.

THIRTEEN

Casey

Wednesday, January 13, 2010

I FLEW TO COSTA Rica with my lover and left with my best friend, who happened to be the best damn lover I'd ever known.

"I think I'll get a hotel room for the night when we get to San Francisco," she said. Her voice didn't sound as if she'd had a preference one way or the other about it. And I wasn't sure either.

Before responding, I mulled it over. What was the right thing to say? We'd had a fantastic vacation, but here we were flying back to reality—whatever that was—and we weren't sure how to go about it. I hadn't said anything for longer than was cool and it was my fault she had an overnight layover. I'd booked the damn flights.

It really sucked to think about, but maybe it wasn't the worst thing if she stayed in a hotel. Then, I thought maybe I should stay there with her.

Neutral territory.

Somewhere she hadn't left me.

Somewhere I didn't dream nearly every night about having sex with her, while everyone we knew watched. Including her soon-to-be ex-husband.

But I didn't want her to be alone, either. I'd miss her and that was the truth. Having her back in my bed—in my house—then having to sleep there without her, wasn't an option and I knew it would hurt her to hear it.

She sat by the window on our flight back to the States and I watched as she looked at the clouds and the water below us. I searched her expression for nerves. For apprehension. I looked for her many tells.

She wasn't chewing on her lip.

She was quiet, but appeared comfortable with the silence.

Her brow was relaxed and her breaths were long and easy.

The sun had kissed her skin everywhere—thanks to our tiny private beach—and the color made her look refreshed and well. Her cheeks were a little pink, as was her nose, which really fucked me up. Being in the sun so much over the past few days, I couldn't tell whether she was turned on or just getting a burn.

I leaned closer to her so I could look out the window, too. Her hair still held that clean smell of the ocean and since she hadn't blow-dried it in days, it was wavy and natural. Just like the rest of her.

My eyes went to her lap looking at her hand, and when she noticed, she took mine and laced our fingers together. I gazed down at them. I couldn't believe that, until then, I hadn't noticed. Her fingers looked like normal fingers, pretty little unpainted fingernails on every one of her short digits.

"Did you get a hand transplant I didn't know about?" I said, teasing her as I rubbed my free hand over her fingers. Testing to see if what I saw and what I felt were actually the same thing. But it was true. I'd never seen her nails look anything but mauled, sore, and torn to shit. There were no bites taken from the skin around them and the nails had grown out a little with pretty white tips.

"No, why?" She laughed at me and then we studied them together.

"Because, Blake, it's the first time I've ever seen them where they don't look painful." I brought each one to my mouth and kissed them. "They still smell the same, no pungent smell to repel a hungry mouth." I playfully bit at one and talked, with it between my teeth. "They still taste the same."

"Hey, give me those. No biting," she scolded, an easy smile on her tanned face.

"So what gives? Were you hypnotized? Have you been listening to those better yourself while you sleep tapes? Wait . . ." I pulled away from her. "Did you see a witch doctor?"

"Fuck you and no. I just stopped biting them. I don't know why." She splayed her other hand out in front so she could show me all ten. "I just stopped."

"How do you just stop something like that?"

"I guess I'm not that nervous anymore. I think that's why I was doing it. When I'm stressed or freaking out, I bite them. I just haven't felt the need, I guess."

Her eyes were chocolate brown and she looked content.

"Can I have a kiss?" she requested. She could have whatever she wanted. She looked so loveable and pretty leaning toward me. Eyes closed. Lips puckered.

My mouth went of its own accord; I was just along for the ride. Her lips were salty from the pretzels we'd shared earlier and, as I tasted them, she parted her lips for more. Her tongue slipped into my mouth and fooled around with mine. Soft and friendly. Everything in the moment felt right.

We were thirty-five thousand feet above the Earth and at home all at once.

My hand found her cheek. She moaned when I snuck my hand under the hair around the back of her neck to pull her closer. We were seconds from being a little too friendly for company. But as luck had it, we were in the back seat of first class and a barrier separated us from the rest of the passengers.

She pulled away enough to say, "You better stop." Then she kissed me again before adding, "In a minute."

"*You* better stop. Or maybe . . ." and I gave her a pervy grin and waggled my eyebrows. The subtext was blow job. Even though I knew she wouldn't, it was still fun to make her squirm. She pretended to be shocked, and maybe somewhat offended, then she paired our mouths again and spoke into our kiss.

"In the bathroom?" she whispered.

Dirty girl.

She thought I'd meant a quickie in the john. I hadn't, but I liked where her mind was.

"No, right here," I whispered. Even though she was thinking about sex, and I was at first only alluding to a hummer. I was curious if she was serious.

I might have to book us another flight. And soon.

If a gentleman walked a girl to the door for a kiss, I wondered what I could get if I accompanied her back on her flight the next day?

Then, I came to myself and found my mind in the gutter with hers. And by gutter, I meant fantasizing about being smashed up in a tiny airplane bathroom—which was only feet away—pumping her full of Air-cock One and making her scream my name.

"Here?" She flushed in all the right places and confirmed that even a sunburned nose could turn noticeably pinker.

"Well, maybe not *everything* right here, but you could . . ." Then I coughed to avoid saying the rest out loud. I kissed her again like I had ownership of her lips. The slight moaning coming from her propelled my fantasy into a plan. It would have been a messy plan, but shit we always were good at messy.

"Want to stay at the hotel with me?" she asked, as I slowed our kiss so we wouldn't get scolded. I wiped the corners of her mouth with my thumb.

"Yes."

"That was fast."

"Well, I want to stay with you. There's not that much to think about."

Again, she looked out the window as she said, "I know staying at your house isn't right *yet.* I also know we'll get there." She looked back into my eyes. "I don't deserve to be there, but I will soon, Casey." The confidence in her posture and voice sold me. I didn't have to be painfully truthful and tell her I couldn't have her at my house yet. She just knew.

She wasn't fucking around anymore, either.

That week she'd been open and transparent. The part that confused me was how calm she was about all of it. In the past, any time facing what we were, or what we wanted, turned her into a basket-case. She'd think one thing when she was with me and then as soon as I was out of sight, it felt like I was also out of mind. Deep down, I knew that wasn't completely true, but then again she *married* the fucking idiot.

"You're freaking me out a little," I told her. "I don't know this

Blake. So Sure. Decided."

"I know, right?" She beamed, but underneath there was something revealing she hadn't expected it from herself either. "I told you. I'm done with all of that. I'm not *making* a decision anymore. It's *made*. It's *you*. I don't care what I have to do, how long it takes or who doesn't like it. It isn't their life and it—sure as hell—isn't their business."

Her lips chastely touched mine again and the overhead light, indicating we needed to have our seat belts on and our tray tables back to their upright positions, came on with a resounding ding.

We straightened up and Blake put away the magazine she'd had out for the ride. As she tidied the space we'd shared for the last too many hours, and collected the empty water bottles preparing to hand them to the attendant, she said, "I'm not hiding how I feel anymore. I'm not scared of anyone finding out."

She tossed the trash into the bag as the middle-aged flight attendant passed. Then she looked down at her nails.

"I guess I'm not biting these because I'm not worried." She faced me as she said, "What could happen that hasn't already? I'm caught. Red-handed in the cookie jar. I'm getting a divorce. I'm moving into my own place again and I'm getting a second—hell, probably a fifteenth—chance with you. I'm excited. I feel free."

I didn't know what to say, except, "Okay, then. Rock and roll." It was lame, but I felt stunned.

Then she relaxed into the seat and yawned to combat the pressure she was feeling as we descended into San Francisco.

We lay in the hotel bed facing each other, both tired from the travel. Her fingers trailed up and down my arm.

"We should have just gone to my place," I said lazily. "It was stupid getting a hotel room when I live thirty minutes from here." I reached for her, moving my hand to her ass, pulling her naked body closer to mine.

"It's fine. I *get* it."

But did she? I wondered what she thought about me not inviting her over. There was no way she knew about the dream I had almost every night. The one where she says Grant's name while we're having sex in my bed. As stupid and unreasonable as it was, that played a big part of it. Maybe deep down I knew I wouldn't feel safe with her there if she was still married, even as hell bent as she was on following through with the divorce.

"What do you *get*, honeybee?"

"You know. The last time I was there I left you." Blake's fingers trailed up my neck and it caused a shiver to slip down my back. Then she held my cheeks in her hand. "I'm sorry I've hurt you. I hurt me, too. The truth is, *I* don't want to go back until I can stay."

"So you're moving in?" I said as I squeezed her perfectly round butt.

"That's not what I mean and you know it."

"That's what I meant. You can move in," I said and licked her nose. "When you're ready. If you want to."

"You've got all of this planned out then? And don't lick my face."

I went to lick again and she dodged me. "Yep. I can't be one-hundred percent sure, but I like to think I can see where this is headed. And let me tell you what, there's a lot of licking in your future."

Her laugh bellowed and she pulled her face away again, but I got her anyway.

"Stop. No licking my face," she giggled and squirmed.

"Come here. Just one more taste." I reached for her with my tongue and she kissed the tip of it with silly puckered lips.

We both knew where the innuendo was headed and that made it all the more fun. Who would be the one to make it cliché? I couldn't hold out much longer and the fire in her pretty eyes said she couldn't either.

"As much as I'd love to let you *lick me,* I believe I owe you a . . ." then she coughed, omitting the actual words, referring to my unspoken request for a little something-something back on the plane.

"You know? I think you're right," I said, as I rolled onto my back and laced my fingers behind my head. I was ready for the reward for my good behavior.

"Then you'll owe me," she sweetly negotiated on her way down the bed, pulling the sheet down exposing my obvious agreement to her proposal.

"Do you accept frequent flier miles?" I asked.

"Nope."

"Oh. A cash-only girl, huh?"

She playfully slapped the side of my leg with one hand and gripped me tightly with the other, warning, "You're about to ruin this for yourself, Lou."

"Then name your price."

"I'm sure you'll come up with something. It appears you're good for it," she said as she licked the head of my dick.

I could already feel that familiar fullness growing in my balls. Her mouth was a con artist. Looking sweet and innocent, all the while knowing exactly what to do to get what she wanted out of me. The sexy scoundrel took the whole length of me in one sinful dip of her head.

"Take everything I have. You can have it all. Just don't stop," I pleaded. "*Ever.*"

FOURTEEN

Blake

Thursday, January 14, 2010

WOULD LEAVING HIM *EVER* stop feeling so wrong? Casey rode to the airport, and even stood in line with me, while I waited for my turn to print my boarding pass and check my bags at the ticket counter.

"You know, you don't have to stay. I've done this before," I teased.

"You have? Oh, well, in that case . . ." He pretended and acted like he was leaving without saying goodbye. I grabbed the sleeve of his green sweater and pulled him in for a quick kiss. He'd been playful all night and all morning. The last thing I wanted was to leave any minutes behind that I could have shared with him.

I wasn't sure when we'd see each other again, but in the back of my mind I'd silently prayed this was one of the last goodbyes. It wasn't nearly as hard or as emotional as some of them had been, but they all sucked and I was tired of doing it.

I wanted to be with him more. Wherever he was. And although I hadn't thought about moving to San Francisco before, if it was where he wanted to live, then I'd move there when the time came. It only made sense. I had a place to work there. He could probably work from wherever he lived, whether it was there or in Seattle, but it felt easier for me to be the one to relocate.

Only time would tell, but knowing there *was* time made me fill with eagerness and hope for our future. I stood there in line and zoned off a little, thinking about how far we'd come. Casey stood behind me with his arms loosely wrapped around my shoulders. I looked up and back to him, into his greenish-blue eyes and asked, "Are you going back to work tomorrow?"

I had a big week coming up, having been on vacation so soon after the holidays. I was going to have a lot of catching up to do, even though we were pretty slow that time of year. Still, I'd been off the better part of three of the last four weeks.

"Actually, I'm going to swing by there after I go home and shower. I need to make some calls and check on a few of the new brew lines. I leave for Minneapolis tomorrow."

I wish I was going to Minneapolis tomorrow.

"The beer isn't going to sell itself," I said, humoring him.

"Ah, that's where you're wrong. It kind of does sell itself, but they like to keep me away. It's beginning to give me a complex." He kissed the top of my head. "Do you have any trips planned?"

As we moved forward in the line, I thought about the different places I needed to visit in the upcoming weeks.

"Not this week, but next week I think I'm going to Vegas for a day or two to make certain everything is going well for a re-launch. Then I'm going straight to Chicago to do a consult with a new client. I might see Reggie if he's in town. That reminds me, I need to call him."

He whispered in my ear, "I'll get my schedule lined out and email it to you. Maybe we can meet up somewhere soon. You're probably going to start missing me."

Probably? I already missed him and I hadn't even left him to go through security.

"No. You'll be missing me and you still owe me. Remember?" He really didn't though.

The night before, after I'd given probably the best oral of my life, he repaid me twofold. But who was keeping score? He'd gladly pay me again right there in the ticket line if I asked.

"I remember," he said, but looked like he was just going along with what I'd said as he scratched his head.

After I had what I needed to board, we lagged toward the point of no return. I felt the nagging pang in my chest knowing I really *was* going to miss him. The only thing that gave me comfort was knowing he was only a phone call away and I could dial him anytime I damn well pleased.

We stopped and faced each other and I set my carry on down at our feet. If I was going to be without him for a little while, then I was at least getting a real freaking hug first. I wrapped my arms around his neck and he grabbed me around the waist, pulling me near.

My fingers ran through his hair. It was still shorter than I preferred, but was looking more and more like the hair I'd met the first night at Hook, Line and Sinker.

"Don't cut your hair anymore," I requested.

"Don't boss me around."

"Don't argue with me."

"I like arguing with you. You're cute when you're pissed." The hair on his face was less than neatly trimmed. If he wasn't careful, he would easily pass for a lumberjack. All he needed was a little flannel.

I smiled.

He kissed me.

He smiled.

I kissed him harder.

"I'll let you know when I land."

He picked me up so we were face to face. The tightness with which he held me left almost no room for oxygen. Who needed oxygen when Casey Moore held onto you like you were the only thing that mattered in the whole wide world? Sure as hell not me. I could live on Mars, oxygen free, if I had to—and if Casey lived there, too.

He gave me a clever grin and said, "I love you, honeybee. That doesn't really cover it, but it's a start."

Hearing him say those words always had an effect on me, but watching his eyes say them with tenderness and happiness, instead of from fear or hurt, the rest of the air in my lungs turned to blood and overfilled my heart.

"You love me," I repeated as my body melted into his, there in the aggravating way of passers-by. They could eat shit, though. Casey loved me.

"And you love me," he assured.

"And I love you."

"Forever," he said in my mouth. That one word meant more to me than the three he'd said prior. I felt my eyes start to burn. Burn from happiness and burn from the ache I already felt, knowing I'd have to be without him for some unknown amount of time. I pressed my lips tighter and kissed him as hard as I could. My eyes screwed shut to hold back the tears that threatened.

"Okay, I'm going to go," I whispered. Releasing my hold a little from around his neck, he in turn set me down. I straightened out my shirt, which had ridden up my stomach in our public display, then picked up my bag.

"Okay, I'll talk to you later," he said and ran his fingers through his short curls as he stretched his neck from side to side. He grew tense, but so did I in that moment. Our bodies didn't like separation and they proved that by always rejecting our goodbyes.

Goodbyes. Always. Fucking. Sucked.

"This fucking sucks. I'm going to go." Then he laughed, trying to ease the awkwardness and it made me chuckle because I'd just thought the same thing.

He planted one last swift kiss on my lips and one on my forehead. Then he started to walk away.

I headed down the terminal to the security check-point, going through the motions of what I needed to do. Remove shoes. Empty pockets. Take out my liquids.

At that moment, I heard him shout, "Blake, you've got this!"

I twisted to see him standing, not far from where we'd parted only a few seconds prior. People walked around him in a hurry to get where they were going, but all I could see was him—in jeans that looked like they were constructed just for his body and a sweater that was a little too big for him, but they looked sexy because he wore them.

Then he corrected himself shouting, "*We've* got this!"

"We've got this," I said back. I didn't shout, but I didn't have to. He heard.

Wednesday, January 20, 2010

Since my apartment was ready after I got back from my quick trip to Chicago, I took my Dad over to see it and help measure for things I'd need to buy.

I didn't have any furniture. I wasn't sure how long I was going to be living there and my gut wanted to believe it wasn't going to be long, so I'd begged him to swing by the apartment with me. After that, we were going to see about renting furniture.

When I'd mentioned I was going to rent, he'd asked, "Are you planning on moving back in with Grant? Is that an option?"

To that, I promptly answered, "No."

Dave, one of the owners of the building—at least for the time being—met us there to sign papers and give me the keys. As I filled out the last of the papers on the six-month lease we'd agreed on, he studied my face.

"Kelly?" he asked in deep thought. The he snapped his fingers. "That's it. I knew you looked familiar. Do you know Max and Sandy?"

Of course I did, they were Grant's parents. I didn't like where this was going, but my dad was right there so I couldn't just pretend I didn't have a clue who he was talking about.

"Yeah, I know them," I said trying to keep my voice steady. I decided maybe then was a good time to look around and think of something to ask him. My old specialty—changing the subject.

I said, "This place looks great. You did a nice job with the renovation. I love the color on the walls." I gave the conversation deflect a good old college try. The look on my dad's face didn't go unnoticed. He shook his head, seeing right through me.

"You've got the same last name. Are you related? I've known them for a long time. Max is actually my real-estate agent. I do the rentals on my own, but he's actually listing this for me now."

Shit.

I glanced at my dad and he only nodded. It was a dad nod. A tell-him-the-damn-truth, Blake, nod. I'd make him buy me dinner for it and I was going to sit on every couch and lay on every bed when we shopped. I'd get him back.

"I married their son, Grant," I admitted, hoping he would piece together the rest of it on his own without being a nosy bastard.

"Well if you're married, then why do you need an apartment?" asked the nosy bastard.

"We're separated."

I felt a little bad for the guy. He turned a shade of foot-in-the-mouth green that made my annoyance subside.

"I'm sorry. That was none of my business."

"It's okay. Don't worry about it. You have nothing to apologize for. It's still very new to everyone." I wondered if Grant had said anything to his parents yet. Knowing how forthcoming and chatty Grant *wasn't,* I would have bet money he hadn't.

"Actually, Dave, if you don't mind, I don't know if Grant has spoken to his family about our situation. It all happened recently, you see. I hope you don't mind keeping that information to yourself. Discretion would be best, please."

I looked to my dad, who visibly approved of what I'd said. He and my father shared a look. Dave's face showed, not only his embarrassment, but also his sympathy. The messed up part was, here I was the one going through the separation and he looked at my dad like he was the one to feel bad for. All very awkward.

"Of course, it's none of my business. I'm sorry you're going through . . ." he paused looking for the right thing to say, suddenly his filter and common sense showed up, ". . . well, whatever it is you're going through. I hope everything works out. Here are the keys. Two sets. I have a third. You've paid first and last month's rent, so I think that's everything. The place is yours." He offered a small smile and for his benefit I gave one back.

"Thanks. My dad is going to help me measure for furniture. I'll probably start moving things in tomorrow."

He offered my dad a handshake and my dad took it, but my old man gave me a "what's his deal?" kind of look. I supposed some men were old fashioned. I could see where he and Max, and Grant for that matter, would probably be great friends.

When Dave finally left we got down to business.

The apartment was nice and much bigger than the one I'd had before our wedding. It had a great back yard, although I would have appreciated a fence. Most of the other yards around the duplex had them though, so it would be fine. The place had an open concept living area. A large kitchen opened up to the dining and living room. There was a smaller bedroom, a larger one, and a decent sized bath. It would do. It already felt like a place where I'd be comfortable and it didn't even have any of my shit in it yet.

"So what are you thinking, Blake? Table and chairs? Some bar stools? We have your old couch in the storage room in the basement, and I think, your old coffee table. If I'm right, your TV is there, too. What does that leave?"

I hadn't remembered they had kept my couch, so that was one less thing.

"Just a bed, a table and chairs, some kitchen stuff and towels? Maybe a chair?" It was funny how little I needed. There wasn't a thing more I wanted from Grant's. And, even though this was going to be my home for a while, I didn't feel like investing too much into it.

Casey wanted to live together. If I wanted to. When I was ready.

On the way to the furniture place my dad cleared his throat. That usually meant he was about to say something he'd already rehearsed. I'd heard that very same throaty rumble many times.

"Now just because you're on spring break, that doesn't mean you have to be shit-hammered the whole time. Go to a museum or something. You're not an airhead."

"On your first day of classes, introduce yourself to your teachers after class. They like that. I'm a professor. I know these things."

"I know you're not a kid anymore but for God's sake, use birth control. Your mother and I want to enjoy a few years of peace and quiet when you leave."

He was always half kidding and half serious. He said what he had to say and didn't suffer fools. It had been a long time since I'd heard the tell-tale conversation opener by way of his nervous cough intro.

"Out with it dad," I said as I turned on my blinker to pull in the store's parking lot. "Just say what you're working up to say. I can take it."

"I think you should see a doctor. There. That's what I think."

That wasn't what I'd guessed he was going to say at all. A doctor? I felt fine. I put the car in park and turned off the ignition, turning to him to offer my full attention. What the hell was he talking about?

"I'm not sick."

"Not all doctors cure the sick, Blake. Some doctors help you sort through thoughts and feelings," he explained, as he trailed off. His eyebrows warned, "Don't be dumb."

"A shrink?" My dad wanted me to see a psychiatrist?

"It's not a bad idea."

"That's a good reason to do something. It's not a bad idea so why the hell not color my hair purple and get a nose ring?" My sarcasm was thick and I sounded like a petulant teenager who didn't want to do her homework on a Friday night before she left the house.

"Just listen to me before you shoot it down. Your mother and I were talking. You're going through a lot. Even if you don't think of it like that, you are. You had a whirlwind affair. Got married. And now you're separated. You just have a lot going on."

Did they want me to see a counselor to rethink my marriage? I didn't get it.

"But why? I think I'm handling things okay, considering." I slunk back into the driver's seat.

His voice softened and I could hear his obvious concern. "Sweetheart, it's just that you're not that great at talking things out. You never have been. You know you can always talk to your mother and me, but sometimes it's nice to talk to someone who isn't so close. Does that make sense?"

"What do you think they're going to tell me? That I'm stupid and I'm making a mistake by leaving Grant?" I was tiptoeing near defensive.

"No. It's not like that at all. It's more just for *you*." He leaned back in the seat and lifted his ass to get something out of his back pocket. "Here. It's a card. And this is only a suggestion, but think about it. Okay? Don't you want to be the happiest Blake possible? And if you love Casey, as much as you say you do, don't you want to start this with your eyes wide open?"

He had a point. I did owe it to him to be the best version of myself. I owed it to both of us.

"Her name is Dr. Rex. Her first name is Natasha. She has a small practice, but she teaches at the college. I've known her a long time. I didn't go into details with her about anything—it's your story and life to tell—but I think you'll like her."

I looked at the card. It was kind of boring. My business mind instantly wanted to spruce it up. Fix it. Make it better.

It was a little ironic.

It wasn't until my dad had to make almost every decision about the furniture, that I saw how maybe I had something to gain from talking to someone. I believed with my whole heart it was right to leave my marriage and be with the man I love. But I was so fearful she would tell me that was wrong. Just when I was starting to feel I was finally right.

FIFTEEN

Casey

Monday, January 25, 2010

IF I HAD A dollar for how many times I'd been wrong about Blake over the past few years, I'd have loads. *Shit loads.* Scratch that. If I had a blow job for every time I'd been wrong about Blake over the past few years, I'd have a lot *less* loads.

Okay, it wasn't a very good analogy. It sounded better in my head. That went for a lot of things. Sometimes things seemed like a good idea, then weren't. But fuck if this mess didn't teach me a lesson—or a hundred. One being that I'd much rather make a huge goddamned mess trying to get what I wanted, than regret from not doing anything at all.

I had experience with both.

The messes always paid off. *Eventually.*

Except that one time, when I combined the two and my girl married a dick. Maybe he wasn't a dick. Still, I'd made one hell of a mess, but regretfully, I should have done it sooner.

That bitch of a mess hurt like hell.

Even after all of that, she still managed to surprise me.

"I called that doctor I told you about. The one my dad recommended," she'd said the night before on the phone.

Initially, when she'd mentioned it, she wasn't totally sold on the idea. As it turned out, after some thinking about it, she'd come around to it.

Personally, I didn't know what to think about it. My gut lurched at the notion of her getting advice from someone who only saw her side. And Blake's retelling of it all may be mired with her guilt and blame. I had to trust that whatever she decided was what was best for her.

"And what did she say?" I asked while trying to stay neutral.

"She said that she's known my dad for a long time and that she'd be happy to talk with me, if I felt like it was something I could benefit from." Her answer sounded very clinical.

Very Grant.

Very not good for Casey.

"You know I want whatever you want. If you think talking to someone could help in some way . . ." I trailed off. I didn't know what way. She'd seemed fine. More calm about all of it than I'd ever seen her. More sure. More at ease with everything.

One of my fears was that she didn't feel like she could talk to me. That had always been when our relationship—or whatever you call it—ran off the tracks and crashed.

We'd somehow get back on, and then wreck ourselves all over again. Okay. I could see where maybe some professional help might be good for her—and hopefully us, and therefore, me.

I continued, "You know you can talk to me about stuff, right? *I* want to be the one you come to when you've got a problem. Does that make sense?"

"What types of problems are you qualified to handle, Dr. Moore?" She turned on her seductive phone-speak at just the right time. Or the wrong time, because my fucking point was that we could *really* talk, but if this made her feel better—so be it. I'd have to come back to the serious part of where our conversation was going, because she masterfully knew how to distract me

And, Dr. Moore? I liked that.

"Oh, lots of things. Dry nipples. I'm especially good at fixing that. What else?" My back met the bed and I finally started to relax about the psychiatrist subject. In the back of my mind, I heard a voice say I was a failure in the relationship department once again. But loud and clear, right up front, was a voice that said I wanted to chill out and talk some dirty things over with my honeybee. "I have a doctorate in masturbation. I'm pretty much the world's leading mind on the subject. Do any of these things appeal to your needs?"

"I'm sure you're overqualified for my issues." Her laugh was sincere.

We chatted a little about masturbation, which led into a rather lengthy discussion about monkeys at the zoo and then we were right back where we started. Her seeing the doctor. But like usual, after we talked for a while and found our footing, it was easier the second time around.

"I know I was joking before, but I was a little serious too. I want you to talk to me when things are on your mind. I might be okay at it."

"Thank you," she graciously said. "Same for you, if you ever need to talk about stuff. I know I've done a lot and you probably want some answers. I guess I need some too. About myself. Why did I do all that? Why didn't I just do what felt right? That's the part that scares me. I don't want to mess this up again. Not after everything I put you through. Us. Hell, everybody through. I have to do better. I'm going to do better."

Her soft, sleepy voice showed me she was nervous, but okay. And if she continued to tell me things as they were happening, I thought we'd be all right. If she was looking for answers to why she'd made some of the decisions she had in the past, then talking to someone, outside of the situation, just might add some perspective.

"Well, if it's *your* decision and you're doing it *for you*—no one else—then I think it's good. Great actually." And I meant it. I hoped it wasn't something she was doing for anyone else. Just her.

"She's seeing me tomorrow. And I am. I'll let you know how it goes. When do you fly out in the morning?"

I was headed to Boston—more of a stop in and say hello type of trip—and my flight was early.

"My plane leaves at 7:30." It killed me I wasn't flying to her. "I miss you. When do we get to see each other again?" I pulled my phone away from my ear and looked at the date. It was already the end of January. February was close and Valentine's Day would be a good time to meet up.

It was a few weeks away still, but I'd be on the road most of the time. And since Las Vegas had gone so well for Blake, the franchise owner gave Couture Dining another project in Miami. That's where she was headed the following week.

It would almost *have* to be Valentine's Day.

"You just saw me. But I miss you, too. Do you have time to come to Seattle soon?"

I wanted to go that very second.

"Valentine's Day?" I asked.

"It's a date. You can see my new place."

I hoped I could wait that long.

Tuesday, January 26, 2010

"Yeah, I'll have another," I said to the bartender, then swallowed back the last of my third draught. It wasn't *my* beer, but I'll be damned if it wasn't doing the trick. I had a lot of things floating around my head that night. I was in Boston, knowing that Blake was going to see Dr. Rex. And not knowing what the doctor's take on us would be, I felt anxious.

Recently, I had many things to be thankful for. But there were many things, in the past few weeks, I'd realized were *my* shortcomings. I'd spent so much time blaming and pointing my finger, and not nearly enough time thinking about how my actions played into all of it.

There was a ball of guilt the size of Rhode Island in my gut. Yeah, I know Rhode Island isn't really the biggest state, but it's the one that probably gets overlooked the most. That seemed fitting. And regardless of how big it was by comparison, put that fucker in your gut, it felt pretty massive.

Point was: Blake was seeing a counselor and I didn't know how I felt about it.

Yes, I did.

I was scared. I was terrified the doctor would find the pesky spot in her mind that had been doubting us all along. The place where trying for a shot with me was a terrible idea, reminding her of the kind of deal she was making. I was the man she cheated with. Who on the planet would side with me? With us? What the hell was I going to do if I lost her?

I could still lose her.

She had a house. A husband. A planned life.

What did I have to offer other than my love? And that wasn't even something I alone offered her. He loved her too—I assumed, in his weird robotic way.

"Better get me a shot of Jameson, too," I added when I was handed a fresh ale.

The guy, two stools down, asked, "So what are you drinking to?" He wore a sports jacket and the dress shirt underneath was unbuttoned. His tie hung loosely in front of him, as he held all of his weight with his forearms pressed against the countertop. He slouched into the bar.

I tried to come up with a Casey the Sales Guy answer, but all I had was Casey the Fuck-up answers.

"I guess I'm just trying to get my shit together," I answered.

He shook his head understanding.

Standard bar buddy etiquette requires a man to engage in conversation at this point. Speak when spoken to.

"You?" I asked him in turn.

"Bitches."

I glanced at the bartender and he gave a chuckle, before turning to do some bartender-y things.

"I'll drink to bitches. Any particular one or just *them* bitches in general?" I inquired. At least the guy was funny. I'd expected him to be beer bent about work or maybe the economy, which I'd found to be a popular reason to belly up at the watering hole. But bitches was a new one. Not the idea really, just the way he'd said it. He had my attention.

"All the bitches," he confirmed. "Lying, cheating, heartless bitches—the whole lot of 'em."

Oh God.

The Universe was taunting me. Worse than taunting. The Universe was playing let's give Casey early onset heart failure. And just for good measure let's take away his bowel control. Because, I swear, I almost shit my pants sitting in the hotel bar with the bitch hater.

"Okay. Better make it two shots." Bartender showed mercy and poured both of his patrons, me and the bitches-guy, doubles.

"On the house," he said. Then he produced another shot glass, from somewhere under the counter, poured a third and held it high. "To the bitches," he toasted and tossed back the whiskey. So it seemed, I was with two men who had smashing good luck with the ladies.

Maybe we were the three amigos. The bartender. The bitches-guy. And me.

"Yeah, they love to make you into their dream man and then ... then when they've got you by the balls, they fuck you over. Because now you're not exciting anymore or some shit."

I had a hard time believing he'd been someone's dream man. But in solidarity, I had to side with the poor guy. I didn't know his story. I didn't want to know his story. Thick sensation hung in the air that indicated he and I were on opposite aisles of the scenario.

He continued, "Some fucking bitches don't know when they've got a good thing. Am I right?"

"Amen, pal," said the bartender as he rinsed a glass. "Never trust a pretty woman."

"Yeah, the prettier they are the blacker their heart."

Clearly, the two men had some bad luck. I let them rant about how they'd been wronged by the women of their lives. As familiar as some of it was, it didn't sound like my story.

"Who leaves a lawyer for a tire salesman? A fucking tire salesman," he swore. "We had a life. Kids. And she threw it all away for a fucking tire salesman."

I had to sympathize, but then again, I also identified with the tire salesman. I *was* the fucking tire salesman in my scenario.

"But at least I'm getting the house and she's not fighting me on anything," he said, more to his beer than to us. "That makes for a pretty quick divorce." He slugged back half the pint and huffed, "I'm getting a divorce. Fifteen years of marriage and I'm getting a divorce so she can be the Queen of Discount Tires."

Bitches-guy fished out his wallet and threw some money toward our faithful bartender. He swiveled on his stool. All humor had left the building.

Then he said, "You know what the worst part is? I know the guy. I thought he was an all right dude, you know? Why couldn't he just be a man about it? Face to face. Own up to it. Be a fucking man. You want to take away my wife, the woman who loved me through tough times and good times and two daughters? Fine. If she wants you more, then take her. But look me in the face. Not him though. He cowered like a dog, like he was ashamed. The least he could do was be a man for her." Then he stumbled away. I silently prayed he got a cab.

After I finished my beer and settled up with Kevin, the bartender as it turned out, I walked up to my room, showered, and clicked through the TV. Nothing registered, only the poor bastard's words.

Is this what Grant is thinking?

They hadn't built a fifteen-year life together, but was that what I was to him? Just a dick who stole his wife?

Over and over in my head, I replayed the conversation. More specifically, the part about being a man. Blake deserved that. And even though I really didn't like the jackass she shared a last name with, I had to admit I'd wronged him.

I was the tire salesman. I'd stolen his wife. I hadn't been a man about it.

Things needed to change.

SIXTEEN

Blake

Tuesday, February 2, 2010

THINGS WERE CHANGING FAST. I was changing with them. The best part about seeing Dr. Rex was that I didn't fit into her office hours. No uncomfortable waiting rooms. No Scholastic coffee table reads. It didn't smell like a doctor's office, which made sense because that wasn't where we met.

Since I worked long hours, and my office was close to the school, when she had evening classes on Tuesdays and Thursdays, she suggested we meet at her office on campus. That worked great for me, because I could park in my dad's spot since the Psych and the English departments shared a lot.

It was new, but I liked her a lot already. I'd only met her once, and most of that was her telling me about herself. I'm not sure if that was a technique thing or if she could tell I was nervous, and was trying to warm me up.

It hadn't been the best day to start seeing a shrink. Then again, the day you go to a lawyer's office to get a divorce might be a pretty damn good day to go see someone who just lets you sit there, while she goes on and on about herself. I let myself believe she did that for my benefit and not hers.

Dr. Rex was a single mom to a son. He was away at school in Atlanta, a musical engineering student. She told me, with him away, she lived with just her cat. She let me know she only had a cat, because as a psychologist it was good practice—living in a constant state of paranoia. When her son was fifteen he got a cat and named him Dre. The feline hated her very existence. She joked living with such a creature, and fearing for her life on a nightly basis, was good for her professional perspective as a counselor.

She claimed her son, Nathan, loved that cat, but couldn't take him to school. So she made concessions, because she loved him. And that people do that kind of thing all the time. Everything she talked about ended with things like that. Either she was very insightful, or the woman was just damn good at her job.

So walking up to the building's entrance on my second date with the good doctor, I had the impulse to kind of spill my guts. Like, all of the sudden, I was going to burst if I didn't have a chance to tell someone everything. Someone who didn't have a single thing to win or lose in the situation. I felt liberated, and out of somewhere I'd never visited within myself, I felt braver than ever.

The divorce papers, which I'd filed for last week were ready to be picked up the next day and I was seeing Casey in ten days.

I'd had moments of panic—feelings of sheer *what the fuck am I doing-ness?*—but since the New Year, I'd felt like I had a goal. A focus. A purpose.

Walking down the marble hall, I passed the ladies' room as she walked out, startling both of us.

"Oh shit, Blake. You scared me," she gasped and leaned against the door frame. Her crazy half-gray, half-black hair ran wild on her head and down her shoulders. Like a pile of quilt stuffing, it was light and fluffy. She tried to compose herself and straightened her purple bifocals over her light blue eyes.

"I'm sorry. That scared me too," I said, also feeling the startle in my chest, even though I saw her first.

"How's it going?" I panted, bending a little in the hips to catch my breath.

"It's going good. How about you?" she replied, as she stepped away from the lavatory. Together we began walking down the long hall to her office.

Ever want to have a nightmare? Take a walk down the hall in the psychology building in your nearest university, after everyone has left for the day. It made me shiver. I guess brains freak me out.

I spoke as I walked, "I think I'm doing okay." But really, how in the hell was I supposed to know? That's what I was there to see her about.

That's another new thing, or change, that I'd observed about seeing a therapist. Knowing I had a therapist made my mind self-diagnose every decision I made all day. Oh, a bran muffin? What's that say about you, Blake? Are you feeling like you need bran, some stability? Some normalcy—bowel or otherwise? Then, I threw it in the trash. I'd been bested by my breakfast on more than one occasion that week. I won't even go into the theories I came up with concerning my egg choices.

"Well, that's convincing," she countered as we got closer to her office. "Tell you what, Blake. This will go a whole lot better if you just say what *you* feel, in any way *you* choose to. I'm not here to tell you what I think or tell you what my opinion on your life is. I'm here to help you realize how you feel about all of those things. To find the things you think you did well—things that make you *proud* to be you— and maybe, help you implement those behaviors to make you happier in other areas.

"It's not about spilling your guts, then me rummaging through it to see what stuff you messed up. It's more about why you made the choices you did, so *you* understand *yourself.* You don't need my validation, you need yours." She made a lot of sense.

Her office was cozy, inviting. She had books stacked everywhere and instead of using the overhead fluorescent light, she had lamps in every corner. Two comfy chairs sat on the far side of the room by a window, and that's where she led us. It was different from the first time I'd been there, when she sat behind her desk telling me about herself.

"Have you ever talked to a therapist before?" she asked, as she sat and waved a hand for me to do the same.

"No."

"Good. Then I don't have to undo any of their bullshit." She chuckled at the poke she'd made at her profession and, in turn, my sanity.

I was sane. Right?

She continued, "So you know a little bit about me from last week, why don't we get to know you a little. Please, tell me about you."

Where were the numerous anecdotes I'd been dying to talk about on the way in there? On the spot, it felt mildly awkward.

She coaxed, "What do you do for a living? Blake, you're not being graded here. No pass/fail. Just talk to me." She leaned back into her chair and tucked a leg under her butt.

"I'm a trained chef and I work for a company that rejuvenates, or creates themes and menus for restaurants. We work mostly in the hospitality industry."

"That's cool," she said and it didn't sound like fodder. "Do you do only here in the Pacific North West or do you travel?"

"I travel a lot, but I kind of have free reign over that now. I like that part of the job. Most of the time." My finger crept its way to my mouth. I had the urge to bite at the skin I'd been obsessing over for the past minute with my thumb.

"I hope you don't mind me saying this but you look really uncomfortable. Let's go for a walk?"

A walk?

She read the skepticism on my face and added, "Trust me, when you're walking, or doing something trivial, your brain sort of goes onto autopilot. Those easy, routine-like tasks let our minds open up a little. Like singing in the shower."

Just as fast as she walked us over to the chairs, she was up and pulling my hand to follow.

"Come on," she instructed, "your work is fun, but I want to know the good stuff."

She was right. As soon as we started walking, I started talking and it came out almost effortlessly. On and on, I went.

"And then she called me," I recalled, telling her about the day Aly hijacked Casey's phone and I got engaged.

"No. She didn't. Did she?" she asked incredulously, while stopping to sit on a half wall that was home to a makeshift garden in the main entrance of the lecture hall. "What did you do?"

"I denied it. I didn't know what to do. There I was, thinking I needed to find a way to break up with Grant, and then getting those messages from her and realizing that maybe Casey had been misleading me the whole time. I was confused and . . . and sad."

"Not to mention vulnerable, I'm sure. Here you'd fallen in love with a man—through no fault of your own. Love happens sometimes, uninvited and inconvenient. Okay, so then what?"

"I didn't say I was in love with Casey back then," I corrected for accuracy's sake. Had I said that? Surely, not. At that point I'd only met him a few times. I was curious. I liked him. I couldn't stop thinking about him to the point of obsessing, but had I been in love with him then?

"You didn't have to. You were in love with him. I can already tell. When you told me about meeting Grant, you seemed content and your pace was easy and slow. When you told me about meeting Casey, you sped up and became animated with your hands. Casey puts life in you. How could you *not* love that?"

I looked at my watch, I'd already been there for two hours. Weren't therapy appointments supposed to be sixty minutes?

"I'm sorry. It's almost eight o'clock," I said.

"So? I'm an empty nester and I have to know what happens. We'll break for the night in a while. Keep going."

And so I did.

We stopped at a vending machine and she bought us a pack of Starbursts and some bottled water. We sat in the back of a lecture hall, and when I got to the part about Valentine's Day and breaking things off, her eyes went misty and she kindly held my hand.

"Blake, why did you keep doing that? What was your thought process in making the decision to choose Grant over Casey, when you loved Casey so much?"

The black and white of it all was so simple to explain.

"It sounds so stupid now. Living it was different. I didn't know where his head was. He never pushed back or demanded more from me until later. At that time, to me, it seemed like he thought we just had great chemistry. And we got along great . . . and it was fun. I didn't know he wanted more. I didn't let myself see that as a possibility. What I knew was, I was marrying a man my family loved, and who promised to give me things I was used to seeing in a family. Does that make sense?"

"You wanted stability. You wanted your family to be proud. That makes perfect sense, but how did you feel?"

Wretched. Torn apart. Lost. Bereft. Alone.

"I felt commandeered. Like what was *expected* of my life had taken over my real life. I had no idea someone like Casey was even out there when I'd started on that path with Grant. I didn't know it could feel like this."

"So how did you feel, after you told him it was over, and he left you there on Valentine's Day?"

"Lonely. I felt like I'd found and lost these two new, amazing people—me when I was with him, and him. I'm different with him, even I'm aware of it. It feels so much more natural being *that* Blake. Being his Blake."

"What's she like?" she asked, leaning her head on the arm she'd draped over the back of the seat.

I looked at the ceiling and thought about what I was like with Casey. I'd never dissected the two halves of me for anyone before.

"With him, I'm calm and chatty. I say whatever pops into my mind. He's never made me feel stupid or that I'm being ridiculous. He might be thinking it, but Dr. Rex, I think he likes it. We talk about everything. Things that do *not* matter."

"So you're freer in a sense?"

"Yeah, I don't have to filter things with him. I don't have to pretend."

"Why do you pretend with others?"

"You know," I answered, looking for the exact description or reason, "my mom and dad are like the perfect couple."

"They are great together. Your dad has always been very proud of his marriage and family. And for good reasons."

"Yeah, you know them. So, when I was growing up, I thought that was what being happy looked like. Parents home at five for dinner. My mother was home with us all summer, and most of the time my dad was, too. I had two older brothers that tormented me, but they'd murder someone for me in a heartbeat. Kisses goodnight. Board games. Family vacations. That's what I knew. I've never seen divorce. I've never seen a breakup. I've never even really been broken up with. I had a few boyfriends in high school, but those all ended with me just wanting to be friends.

"So when I met Grant, I fell in love with the idea of having *that* life. I knew how happy that life could be. The one I thought I was supposed to have."

"So that kept you tied to him."

"Yeah. Casey is from a divorced family, he knows what that's like. He lives out of a suitcase and I would have only seen him every few weeks at the time—if we were lucky. He's impulsive and reactive. I didn't know if that was him or just him with me."

"You're obviously not a gambler," she teased and bumped her leg against mine. I'd only met the woman twice and I already knew I needed her. It was so comfortable talking to her. I bet her patients loved her.

"You know, talking to you is a lot like talking to him."

"Good. I want you to feel like you're talking to a friend."

"So am I crazy?"

"Yes." Her smile was infectious.

"Then I finally have an excuse."

On the way back to her office she stopped me and asked, "Do you have a picture of Casey. I can almost see him in my head." I laughed, truly laughed.

And there it was. She didn't ask for a picture of Grant and she was a doctor. I wasn't crazy. Or I was crazy in love.

"Yeah, I have a few," I said trying to play off the fact I had many. When I activated my phone, I noticed I had a message.

Casey: Do you know how to cut up an onion so that I don't question my manhood every time I do it?

Casey: If your doctor hypnotizes you, please have her remind you how curious you are about anal.

I felt the smile reach my eyes and the warmth of his silliness light me from the inside out. He was my normal. He was my home. He was everywhere I wanted to be and the place I most wanted to go. I just had to accept that it was good. That we were good. And even though what I'd done was awful and hurtful, I was just learning how to love someone who loved me the way I'd craved. But most surprisingly, I think I was just learning to love myself a little better. The actual *me* that Casey had helped bring to life. The *me* I wanted to be.

I typed back a short message.

Me: I'll call you in a little bit, pussy. I'm not curious about anal. I'm firmly pro-anal. I just never wanted to hurt your delicate ass.

Casey: You're so thoughtful.

I scrolled through the saved pictures on my phone and found one of him I'd taken in Costa Rica. He lay on his belly on a beach towel looking up at me. He'd just told me that I had a huge wedgie and offered to rectify it for me. His face was all ornery and playful. His face was all Casey. And his hair looked rocking, too.

"Son of a bitch, girl. I see where you had your doubts. He looks like trouble."

I looked at my phone with her and we gazed at the photo like two junior high girls gawking over the newest issue of Tiger Beat magazine.

"I like his trouble. I always have."

I supposed, at that moment, trouble was a two-way street. If it took giving more to get more, I'd give him everything.

SEVENTEEN

Casey

Wednesday, February 3, 2010

WE WERE ON COMMON ground. She talked, I listened. When I talked, she understood. We weren't just zooming past everything that we could push off for later anymore. We were meeting things head on.

Days peeled away. Punxsutawney Phil saw his shadow and so it meant we'd have six more weeks of winter. It normally wouldn't matter to me, but I had business on the East Coast that spring and wasn't cool with the longer winter prediction.

She'd seen her therapist a few times. I was so damn relieved that there was no sign of a wind change. We talked on the phone every day. We started making plans for another trip, she wanted to go to Greece. I reveled in the fact we were making plans. Even though we only talked about taking a trip in a vague way, I'd already started looking at places we could visit and bookmarking hotels I thought were cool. For later.

She had her divorce papers back from the lawyer. When she opened up to me and told me she was nervous to call Grant about signing them, my mind didn't go to that insecure place where it used to. Instead, I was happy she was talking to me and letting me share her load.

"I know you don't want to hear this, but I feel really bad for hurting him," she confessed. "In all of the time I've known him, I've never seen him act like he did in San Francisco. Or at the house when I was getting my things."

I couldn't blame the guy. We'd all made mistakes. Thankfully, including him.

To me, he was a shitty husband. Who neglects a wife like that? Maybe not her material needs, but everything else just sort of, slipped past him. How could he have been so blind? How could he marry someone and take such little interest in *her?*

I didn't know everything about their relationship—so I wasn't about to pretend I did—but from the outside, it seemed like he was a dud. Not that I'd ever tell her what to do with her life if I were engaged or married to her, but didn't he miss her when she was traveling? She traveled damn near constantly the year before their marriage. Didn't she miss him? Didn't he ever want to go along? The whole thing was so weird to me.

Maybe that was why I never felt truly awful for the guy. He didn't know how good of a thing he had. He never appreciated her.

I will. I will show her what love is supposed to feel like, even if I'm winging it.

Blake was mine. Not in a possessive-caveman way—okay, sometimes she was. But she was more like an organ. Vital. I have a heart, but the fact that it is *my* heart is redundant. The same went for Blake. She was *my* Blake and she made all of the other parts of me healthier.

Ever since the night with the drunk bastard and the bartender, I kept thinking about Grant. He thought she was his. A thing. A milestone. A check off the life-plan list. A rung higher on a ladder that went where? Retirement? First hand I saw what their love looked like. It was fabricated like the generic photo you get when you purchase a frame. What a waste of passion and life.

Oh, how it must suck for him to be wrong like that.

Obviously he loved her, in his robotic, climate-controlled way.

Therefore, I'd decided I was going to be a man about it. Own up to my shit. I'd helped wreck his marriage. Copy and paste as it was, their union was a falsified duplicate of what they were taught marriage looked like. And as the number I'd found on their real estate website rang, I walked outside to do something that could either be classified as decent or really fucking dumb.

I was calling *my* Blake's almost ex-husband. I was clearing the air, and possibly, if it felt right, apologizing.

"Bowman and Kelly Realty, Janet speaking," answered an elderly lady.

"Hello, may I please speak with Grant Kelly."

"Just a moment, please."

I should have brought a beer outside with me. Day drinking wasn't something I normally did, but I also didn't normally call men and wax poetically about how I'd been fucking their wives for two years. Oh, and that I had no plans to stop. Oh, and I was madly in love with her and I'd fight him tooth and nail if it came down to it. Pacing in the morning sun on the back deck, I waited for her to connect the line. Each time the phone rang, I felt my resolve weaken.

What the hell was I going to say again?

"Grant Kelly," he answered. His voice was level and professional, not that I'd expected anything less.

"Hi, this is Casey Moore."

There was silence. I considered hanging up, but I pulled up my big-boy, big-man pants and took a deep breath. If Blake could face everyone, then so could I.

"Hello," he said after clearing his throat. "What can *I* do for *you?*" He sounded dismissive and a little snide. Again, pretty much what I expected from him. Maybe he would hang up on me.

"I'm sure this call comes as a surprise, but I wanted to call and clear the air," I explained. As I spoke, I straightened my posture and stood to my full height, looking out over my mother's garden.

I tried to summon her strength and wondered what she would think. She'd probably say something about adding insult to injury, but I think she'd be a little proud, too. Carmen avoided my mother like the plague for years and I think that always bothered my mom.

"So you have a conscience now, or something?" His mundane question didn't quite hide his contempt.

I paced.

"Listen, I'm sorry about how everything shook out a few weeks ago. I think I owe it to you to be a man about it and talk about it like adults."

My feet repeatedly marched the same path, back and forth over the cobblestone patio.

"Men? Adults?" Finally, I was hearing emotion. "I'm not sure what you think we have to talk about." There was another long pause. I switched up my routine and began going up and down the stone steps.

"Really? I think we have at least *one* common interest, Grant."

Then he said, "You know, you're right. Let's talk about it. Actually, I have some things I'd like to know."

I was a moron. First, I fucked up his marriage, then I called him at work to ease my own guilt. I was a douche. It was a bad idea. I should have talked to Blake about calling him first, but it was an impulsive thing. It had eaten at me for days.

"Okay, what do you want to know?" I'd let him get out what he needed.

"Is this the first woman you've seduced away from her family?"

Dick.

My hand tightened around my phone, but I reminded myself to stay calm. That was a fair question.

"I didn't seduce her. And I've never been in a relationship with anyone like I am with her."

"And what do you think you can offer her? From what I know, you're a beer peddler who skips from town to town." His monotone voice got louder over the line.

And just how in the hell did he know that?

"Listen, I didn't call to fight with you. I know this isn't normal, or probably even the right thing to do, but she *deserves* a man who's willing to fight for her. To stand up for what *she* wants. As shitty as that is for you, she wants me." As ugly as the conversation was, that felt good. I added, "I thought by calling, I could explain myself, maybe apologize. She never wanted to hurt you."

"How long was it going on?" he fired back.

Here came the painful truth. "Since May of 2008."

"She *married* me. She said *yes* to me. Why do you think she'd do all that if she really wanted to be with you?" The fool tried to rationalize love. Clearly, he didn't know what he was talking about. And it was even clearer, he didn't know Blake.

However, his questions had merit. I had to confess my shortcomings to a man who should own stock in his own shortcomings. "Because I didn't offer her anything. *Not that I can't.* I didn't know what I was doing. We both tried to fight it. And we've told each other goodbye many times, but it never seems to stick."

"Isn't that sweet?" Artificial amusement gave his tone personality and made me want to punch him.

"You know, this isn't easy for her, either. I know she cares about you. Okay? I know that you're a good guy. But I'm a good guy, too."

"Yeah, you're the best."

I pulled my phone away from my ear and silently screamed, while shaking the piss out of it for a second.

"Maybe this *was* a bad idea."

"No. The bad idea was messing around with a married woman. Messing with her head. *That* was a bad idea."

"I'm not messing with her head. And when I first started messing with her—as you like to call it—she wasn't married."

"She's just confused. As soon as she realizes what she's giving up, she'll come around. You'll see."

Like hell I would.

My nostrils flared and I sat down, ready to enlighten him on what I thought of his fucking ass. He needed correcting.

"There's not a goddamned thing you can give her that I can't. Understand me? Maybe you should have paid more attention to her. Ever think of that? How does it feel, knowing all of this was going on right under your damn nose and you didn't see any of it? You don't even know her. Not the *real* her. Hell, her therapist said the same thing."

Why didn't he realize?

Dead silence. I glanced at my phone to see if the call had dropped. And after what I'd just said, letting my temper get the better of me, I sort of wished it had. I called him to ease my guilt, and to possibly feel like I was doing my share of the clean-up. Blake was working her ass off. Fighting for both of us.

Then I heard him question, "The therapist?"

My mouth had no shut off at that point.

"Yeah, the therapist. She's seeing a psychiatrist. I told you, it isn't like she's proud of herself."

The laugh I heard over the line inflamed my already simmering blood. What was so fucking funny?

"I can't believe she told you about that." His tone was condescending and superior. "She's gutsier than I thought."

"What?" I shook my head. What did he say? Did he know she was seeing someone? Had he talked to her family?

I was lost.

"We're seeing a *couples* counselor."

Couples counselor. *Couples* counselor. Couples. Fucking. Counselor?

I didn't believe him.

I couldn't believe him. That wasn't right. She would have told me. She wouldn't have left that out.

"I'm sorry, Casey. I suppose I'm not the only one she hides things from, but we're working on it. I have a client coming in. It's been nice chatting with you." And he hung up.

Suddenly, I didn't feel like daytime drinking was all that bad.

In fact, I drank my lunch. My day off turned into my noon-time drunk and afternoon nap.

I had to talk to her, but I needed a little time. I needed to know the truth.

Here we go again.

EIGHTEEN

Blake

Wednesday, February 3, 2010

"Here we go again," I said sarcastically, as Reggie told me, for the millionth time, he and Nora were only ever just friends.

"Don't you have work to do? How long is your lunch break?" he asked steering the topic away from himself.

"Don't change the subject, Reggie. I liked her. Why don't you ask her out?"

"I told you she moved. I don't even see her anymore. Why don't *you* drop it?" He grew annoyed with me every time I wanted to talk about Nora and him.

I'd never seen my brother like that with a woman. The way he looked at her and her at him. Their chemistry, from what little I saw, was reminiscent of Casey and me. I wanted that for him. That connection. That spark.

"You said you saw her. You brought it up."

"She was with someone. Besides, I have a date tonight," he told me in a clipped tone that implied the discussion was almost closed.

My call waiting beeped and it was Grant, which was unusual. He rarely called before everything fell out, why would he call now?

"Hey Reggie, Grant's on the other line. I better answer it."

"Let it go to voicemail. Did you give him the papers yet?"

"No, but I've been meaning to. I'm procrastinating," I answered truthfully, as I continually clicked the retractable button at the top of my pen.

"What does lover-boy think of that?" *Lover-boy?* That kind of had a nice ring to it, a much better nickname than the robot. I smiled.

"Lover-boy understands." The line beeped again. "I'll call you later. Love you."

"Okay. I love you, too." I switched over to Grant's call. "Hello."

"Hi."

"Hi," I said, even though I'd already said hello. I was still dumbfounded and didn't know what to say.

"Do you have a minute?" Grant asked. There was no distress in his voice and I wished he'd just left a message instead. I didn't want to talk to him.

Something had changed in me.

Maybe it was having everything out in the open with my family. It might have been the talks I'd had with Dr. Rex. I wasn't sure, but where my feelings were always conflicted in the past—where I'd felt obligated to Grant—I didn't feel that anymore.

Sure, he looked like a fool at Micah and Cory's wedding, but so had I. It had been dirty laundry night at HLS. Still, it wasn't like he'd done anything majorly wrong. Even when I'd gone to the house, other than getting a little upset—which was understandable—he didn't yell and scream at me as much as I'd felt I'd deserved at the time.

Yet, there he was calling and I was answering. And it was sad I didn't care to talk to him anymore, but at the same time I felt like I owed it to him—and myself—to not hide.

"Sure. What's up?" I said, as nonchalantly as I could, while my heart thumped powerfully in my chest. I sat at my desk and began doodling mindlessly to stave off the anxiety blooming in my stomach.

Was he going to yell now?

Was he calling to let me have it?

I prepared for the worst.

"We need to get together and talk. Get some things settled."

Things. I had things to settle with him, too. Things like a packet of divorce documents I needed him to sign. It wasn't going to be easy or pleasant, but I had my eye on the goal. *Casey.*

"All right. I can come by the house later. Are you going to be there?"

"No. Let's go out to dinner," he amended.

I didn't want to. I drew a breath and let it out slowly to compose myself. It didn't fucking work, so I did it again. But breathing didn't calm nerves. It just kept you alive.

Grant didn't say anything. He simply waited for me to talk.

I yielded. "Where did you want to go?"

"We could go to Michael's? It a little too cool to sit outside, but you like the food there."

I liked the food there better when I enjoyed the company. My intuition told me nothing I ordered would taste right and it might never taste good there again.

Michael's food. Another casualty.

"I don't know, Grant. Maybe it would be best if I came over and we talked in private," I said, even though I was certain he wouldn't cause a scene. At least, the man I married wouldn't. Who in the hell knew what the one I was divorcing would do?

"You can't have dinner with me now, or something?" His tone was cold, but I absorbed the frigid bite. I reminded myself he was hurting.

I scrambled to smooth it over. "No, it isn't that."

"Are you angry at *me* for something? Last I checked, it was you who had an affair and didn't come home."

Wow.

Being in public wouldn't be so bad, I decided.

He added, "It's the least you could do, Blake. It's just dinner."

It *was* just dinner. Well, dinner with a side of divorce.

"What time do you want me to meet you at Michael's?" I asked, hoping it was sooner than later. I wanted to get it over with and move the hell on.

"I have a showing this evening. Is five too early?"

Perfect.

"Nope, that's fine with me. I'll be there at five."

I finished my work for the day, and since I was the last person in the building to leave, I went through the practice of closing up shop.

I shoved my arms into my coat and searched for my damn keys. I didn't want to go, but the voice inside my head kept telling me, "You can do this. You're almost there. Do it for Casey."

And so I did.

I drove to Michael's and I sat in the parking lot, until it was almost five on the dot. I said a silent prayer it would go well and I slipped the manila envelope into my bag. Then walked inside.

As predicted, it didn't smell as good. Or maybe, it was that my appetite went straight home after work. When I approached the hostess I said, hopefully for the last time, "Kelly for two?"

She scanned the list in front of her and looked over her shoulder to confirm, that yes, he was already seated. Grant sat by the big windows which overlooked the water that was growing darker by the minute— just like my attitude.

I didn't like the way he'd manipulated my emotions, regardless of his right to. The more I'd thought about it all afternoon, the more I should have stood up for myself.

"Right this way," the hostess instructed and I followed her. After leading me to the table, I was left to seat myself, when she quickly pivoted and returned to her post.

Grant didn't even bother to look up when I approached.

He wore a dark blue button-down shirt and dark gray trousers, looking much more together than the last time I saw him. That was an improvement.

"So you have a showing later?" I asked. Small talk would be my saving grace. I took my coat off and hung it on the back of my chair, taking a seat across from him at the table set for two. There was a candle lit in the center, and had it not been under those circumstances, it might have been romantic. But as it was, it annoyed me.

"Yeah, showing a condo. I already ordered some appetizers," he said.

Everything felt forced and difficult, *had it always been that way?*

When the server arrived, I ordered water with lime; Grant ordered a rum and Coke. I noticed he had an empty one in front of him.

Maybe he was as nervous as me?

I fiddled with the table linen and began, "Grant, I owe you an apology." I'd get the hard stuff out of the way. If he didn't respond well to what I had to say, I'd leave. There was no point in waiting for dinner to lay it out there.

The waitress placed the beverages on the table and left without saying a word. The service was awful. I hadn't noticed before.

He leaned back and took a sip of his drink.

I continued, "I know what I've done to you is unforgivable and wrong. And I'm sorry I hurt you."

His gray eyes met mine, but the Grant I knew was dim and hard to find inside of the stare. I'd done that. I'd caused that change to him and then my guilt covered everything within reach.

"Why did you do it?" he asked, running a hand over his face and around the back of his neck.

"I don't know and I know that's a crappy answer, but it's the truth."

"If you'd just tell me what it was that made you go to him, I can give it to you. I can be what you want, if you tell me how, Blake," he negotiated. Did he really think it was that easy? Like I could rattle off a few things and everything would be fine?

"It isn't like that. It isn't something I can describe."

"You've really hurt our marriage and you've broken my trust. How am I supposed to trust you now?"

I processed the question, but it was irrelevant. I didn't want his trust. I wasn't planning on repairing our marriage.

"Grant, I want a divorce." I'd already told him at the house. It made me uncomfortable he didn't acknowledge that was where I saw us headed. He pinched at the bridge of his nose and leaned back farther in his chair. It creaked under his weight and I felt like I was creaking too.

"Just like that? You're giving up? Just like that?" he alleged, with a snap of his fingers.

"Not *just like that.* I've been trying for a long time. *We* aren't what I want."

"Well, what do you want? Let's see if we can get *you* what *you* want, since your feelings are the only ones that matter here."

I leaned in to speak quietly. "I didn't say that. You know I'm not like that, I care about you." My sweaty hands balled into fists in my lap. "I didn't love you like I should have. I shouldn't have married you," I admitted softly. I didn't want anyone to overhear our discussion. "Like I said, I care about you and I'm sorry about how I've treated you. I'm not proud of it."

"Then why'd you do it?" he asked indignantly with his teeth clenched. His jaw ticked and his face lost all color.

"Because I love him. You know? I fought it. I fought for us, but it was wrong. When I met him, I felt all of these things I should have been feeling for you. I didn't know what to do. I didn't expect it, Grant."

"Well, I'm not just rolling over here. I want to see a couples therapist."

My heart sank. I didn't want that. At all. I just wanted out. Out of the conversation. Out of the restaurant. And out of my marriage.

"What? No." I shook my head and looked out the window. "I don't want to work on our marriage, Grant. I want out of it."

"I never pegged you for such a quitter. It turns out I was wrong about a lot of things. But, Blake, I'm not throwing in the towel so easily."

I reached into my purse to get the envelope. Thinking that if he saw it, saw I was serious enough to have the papers drawn up already, maybe he would relent. I placed it on the table and slid it to him.

"What are those?"

"I saw a lawyer. I'm not asking for anything and I'll pay for all of it."

He huffed a fake laugh. "What if I ask for things? What about what I want?" There was an edge in his voice, but it had changed into a more persuading sound when he suggested, "We can work this out. We're just starting out. We just need some help, that's all."

"Help? Grant, I've been seeing Casey since before we were married. I'm in love with *him.*"

We sat there not saying anything when the appetizers arrived. Neither of us touching them or moving to eat. The space between us grew larger and emptier.

"If you want a divorce, then fine. But I want to work on our marriage. We'll see a marriage counselor, if you still feel like that in a few months, then I'll sign. But I'm not just giving up."

Counseling? How much counseling did I need?

I wanted the divorce. I wanted it to happen quickly and with the least amount of resistance, but could I agree to counseling when I was confident it wasn't going to change anything, at least for me?

But he was right. It wasn't *all* about me. I had to consider his feelings.

And Casey's.

I needed Casey that very second.

Just the thought of him eased me. It wasn't a decision I should make on my own. I wanted to share myself with him—be partners—and it was a good time to show him I'd meant what I'd said.

Grant reached over the table, offering me his hand, but I pulled back. Touching him felt wrong now, especially with Casey on my mind. I refused to taint my thoughts of him ever again by touching Grant. Especially when Casey's was the touch I craved.

No substitutions. Not anymore. Not ever again. I got comfort from him and him alone.

"I need to use the ladies' room," I said, excusing myself.

His placed his napkin on his lap and went about eating like everything was fine.

Just having dinner. Nothing to see here.

I couldn't read anything that was going on in his head from his expression. I never could.

With Casey, I saw his emotions. They were conveyed by his body. Even in the past, when his hell-bent mouth would tell me one thing, his truthful body language always told me he cared.

Looking at Grant, as I unhooked my purse from the back of my chair, I saw only superficial things. A handsome face. A man with an expression I couldn't read.

Had it always been like this? And didn't he leave out the biggest reason to stay married? What about love?

The second I was away from the table I pulled out my phone. I didn't have time to wait for a text, and truth be told, I needed to hear his voice.

NINETEEN

Casey

Wednesday, February 3, 2010

I NEEDED TO HEAR it from her lips.

Something about the way he'd said what he did, didn't sound right. Didn't add up.

There were many times where Blake and I hadn't communicated the way we should have. Many times where, if we'd just talked things out, our circumstances could have been different. But it didn't feel like that.

I woke up to my phone ringing beside me.

"Hello," I croaked, sleep heavy in my throat.

"Hey," Blake said hushed. "Can you talk?" Her breathing was labored and her voice warbled.

I sat up on the couch and tried to concentrate through the fog of my nap.

"Yeah, are you okay? What's going on?" It was evening and the sun had almost set. I'd slept away most of the day.

"I'm fine. I need to tell you what's going on. I need you to tell me what to do. I never do the right thing. I never make the right decision. I'm tired of hurting us. Just tell me what to do." She was rambling, and by the sound of it, she was almost in tears. Her tone was high pitched and she spoke in rushed, clipped sentences.

"Hey. Hey. Hey. Shhh. We'll figure it out. What happened?"

The haze that occupied my mind was blown away. She was shaken. The urgency in her voice wasn't something I'd heard many times before. In the past, when we'd fight, I'd leave or she would. We weren't practiced in working through things together.

"Grant called me today. He said that he wanted to talk. And you know how I've been trying to get the courage to give him the divorce papers? Well, I thought it was a good time." She was going so fast, I had to make a real effort to keep up "He wanted to meet for dinner. I offered to meet him at the house, but he insisted on going to dinner."

She spoke like she was confessing. It must have been such a weird place to be. Explaining things, just so I wouldn't jump to the wrong conclusions. She really had changed over the past month, it wasn't all just talk.

Still, feeling like I was missing something, my gut told me I needed more information. I needed to know exactly what he was up to. He'd picked a hell of a time to start fighting for her. That was for sure.

"Okay. Is that where you are? What did he say?"

"Casey, I didn't want to go to dinner with him. This isn't a date or whatever. You know that, right?" Her voice cracked and I wished I could touch her. She was having a difficult time talking through her anxiety and even though she was speaking low, I could hear her agony. She must have either gone outside or to the bathroom to be alone.

Flags rose and alert buzzers went off in my head.

"I know. I know. What's going on?" I sat forward and rested my arms on my knees, running my free hand over the corners of my eyes to rid them of sleep.

"We're at Michael's, a restaurant I like. I drove myself." She just kept confessing. It was painful to hear her sounding so guilty and paranoid. She'd been through a lot for us. Listening to how she was reacting, it killed me I wasn't there to give her relief.

"Just slow down. It's okay," I reassured her.

"Anyway, I gave him the divorce papers and told him I want out of our marriage. I did, Casey. I told him I'm done. I feel bad, but I don't want him and there's no sense in sugarcoating it. I'm not being mean, but he just won't listen. What's the point in dragging everyone through this? It's exhausting, you know?"

Did I ever.

I didn't want Aly, in much the same way, I thought. Good people don't like hurting people, but often that's just life.

"What did he say? Did he get angry?"

"I don't know. Maybe a little, but he said he wants to see a counselor. That if I saw one with him for a while, and still wanted to end things, *then* he'd sign the papers."

That sneaky motherfucker.

He'd lied to me. Then called her to make it the truth.

The fact she was talking about it with me, made me want do a victory lap around my living room. Blake, not keeping it a secret from me, inspired me to get a sky-writer to fly "Betty is mine, Fucker" over Seattle.

But the fact he was fighting for her made me realize, he wasn't going to bow out gracefully. And asking her to tell him to fuck off wasn't the right move. Not for her. Not for him. And, unfortunately, not for me.

Would she wonder, in the years to come, if she'd made the right decision? And even if I didn't give a shit what anyone else thought, she did. Her family's approval meant the world to her and I knew how conflicted she felt telling them she was filing for a divorce.

Since she was freaking, it wouldn't do us any good if I freaked out, too. But inside, the feeling that I'd won huge was already getting squashed by insecurity.

"What do you want to do?" I asked, hoping I already knew the answer. Hoping she didn't want to see a couples counselor with him. Hoping that if she did she wouldn't think I was a mistake.

"I don't want to do anything with him, but I don't want him to fight me in court either. Or make this any worse than it already is."

"How long did he say you'd have to see someone together, before he'd sign?"

"He didn't. I came in here to call you right after he proposed the idea."

I loved that.

"Thank you for confiding in me," I said. If there was such a thing as a pride hard-on, I was in danger of getting one.

"You're very welcome, I needed you. What should I do?"

It was simple. We were both terrible about overthinking things, and where this situation could have been a fucking train wreck, we were doing okay. I just had to stay calm and keep it simple. But we were handling it.

I said, "I love you. Do you love me?"

"Of course I do. *Only you,*" she said purposefully.

If Grant, that bastard, was conniving enough to lie on the phone to me, then he was willing to fight dirty. I didn't want that for her. She liked her doctor and her doctor sympathized with her, from what she'd told me. I had to trust that overnight and just from seeing a shrink a few times, they wouldn't magically grow a great relationship.

"Do you trust me, honeybee?"

"Please, just tell me what to do and I'll do it."

"Then agree to it. Set a limit with him though. However many sessions you feel is enough. Or by a certain date." My chest burned telling her to see a couples counselor—or just a therapist, but whatever—with the man I wanted to throw off a cliff. But it seemed like the best solution for *her.* The easiest. Maybe they would both get closure.

Not that I enjoyed the idea, but maybe they had a chance at being friends.

That fucker.

All right, *friends* was a little too much for me to swallow at that moment. I didn't want them to be friends, but not everything was about me. And after meeting the bitches-guy, in the bar—who was going through some major shit—suggesting a little therapy for them couldn't hurt.

I was being a man about it and that was the man thing to do. God, I hoped it scored me some karma and didn't blow up in my face.

"I don't want to," she objected.

The burning in my chest grew hotter hearing her say that, but I had to focus. "Do you want a divorce?"

"Yes," she said.

"Do you think he'll do what he says?"

"I don't think he'd lie to me." That made one of us.

That fucker.

"Then what are you scared of, honeybee? This seems like the easiest way. It'll be okay. It'll get things over sooner than later."

"I don't want to hurt you." I heard her tears. She cried them for me. I bit my knuckles.

Time wasn't ever our friend, but I'd signed up for a year. She'd been fast-tracking her divorce more than I'd ever dreamed possible. If this made it easier on her, and her family, and that fucking fuck of a fucking robot fucker, then it was the least I could do.

"You're not going to hurt me," I said and I actually believed it. No longer did I think she would hurt me. Not after she'd done everything she said she would. There were many reasons for me to not believe her, but we'd wasted too much time dicking over what the other one was thinking. She'd just poured her heart out, obviously worried about me. She didn't want to hurt me.

Our new way of communicating was foreign, but the simple act of her calling to confer with me about the situation . . . well, I couldn't force her to do something that might bring her more anxiety. More heartache. More guilt. More pain. I couldn't be the bastard that told her no about this. *That* would only bite me in the ass.

"How are you okay with this? Why aren't you freaking out?" She sniffed, but sounded better than when she'd first called. Now, she seemed a little confused.

We were like the love-blind leading the love-blind.

"I'm not glass, Blake. I know what bed I've made. If he thinks seeing someone with you will help, even if it doesn't give him the result he wants, it might help. And you calling me . . ." I had to swallow the sudden swell of emotion I felt bubbling up in my neck. Feeling like she trusted me enough to rely on. It just meant a lot.

Earlier, after I'd spoken to Grant, I knew he was up to something. But sometimes you have to pick your battles. And this was one I was going to let the poor sap have.

I was betting on us.

She came to *me* this time and not just with her body.

"Casey, this is our life. Okay? Not just my life and your life. *Our* life. I'm better with you. I'm stronger with you. I need you. Even if it means I have to call you and tell you things I don't like—and I know you'll hate. I'll prove you can trust me."

My sweet fucking honeybee.

"Well, then we can do this. I *do* trust you, honeybee, and it's because of that trust that I suggest you meet his terms. We'll still have each other. Every. Day," I reassured her.

She sniffed again and asked, "Are we growing up or something?"

"Feels like it, doesn't it?" I replied, as I heard my stomach growl.

"Thanks for being here."

"I'm always here. I won't let you hurt or worry alone ever again. I told you. I like trouble. Fuck. I love the shit. I'm still here, aren't I?" I joked to hear her laugh.

She chuckled and took a deep breath, coming to grips with our plan. "Okay then, but if you change your mind, I'm out. I'll tell him no."

"Just call me when you get home. Be strong. You have the right to want what you want, baby. From me or from him. Got that?"

"Baby?" She laughed at me. I'd never called her that before, but her sweet giggle sounded so fucking good.

"You like that?" I asked. All the muscles that had been tense in my face began to relax. My whole body released the nervousness it had been holding in the whole day.

"No. I'm your honeybee and that's it."

It wasn't twenty minutes later before she called me on her way home.

She'd left the divorce papers with him and told him she would agree to see the therapist on a few conditions. If after a few sessions she still wanted a divorce—which she assured me she would—he had to agree. Under no circumstances was she moving back in. And she could change her mind at any time.

I liked her conditions.

He begrudgingly agreed, she'd said, but he wasn't too happy about her terms.

I mean, what a fucker.

What was there to be happy about though? She was leaving him.

It wasn't like we expected him to bake her a cake and throw a party. But still, you'd think that after she'd lied to him, for so long, he'd be the one wanting a divorce. That's the part that made me the most curious. Why was he still hanging on?

Blake and I talked about that, too. In those next few weeks, we talked about everything.

We were open books.

TWENTY

Blake

Friday, February 12, 2010

I TOLD HIM EVERYTHING and he did the same. It was amazing how we never ran out of things to talk about.

We talked about our trips and often we'd watch the same TV shows at night. It didn't matter where we were, it felt like we were together.

Time didn't seem like our enemy anymore. Being gone was good, but—for the first time—being home wasn't that bad either.

The nice thing about having an apartment that didn't house a lot of stuff, was it was really easy to keep clean. I wasn't there much, but even when I was, I spent most of my time in my bedroom. Sure, I had a couch and a television in the living room, but it still didn't feel that cozy. Which, in the long run, had been my idea of keeping things simple. And let me tell you. They were simple.

There was nothing on my walls. I had a few lamps and a couple of family pictures on a table by the door. As far as decoration went, that was it. The kitchen was simple, too. Only the necessities. It was ironic that I was a professional chef, yet I rarely cooked at home anymore. When I actually went grocery shopping, it was for staples. Cheese. Coffee. Bread. Pop-tarts. Things that a person has to have to survive.

So when I arrived home from Miami, the Thursday before Valentine's Day, it was nice to do real shopping.

Casey was coming to *my* place. Something that had never, ever happened before.

I wasn't sure what he planned, but he told me he wanted to take me out on Saturday, even though Sunday was actually Valentine's Day. The next week, he had an early Monday morning meeting with a distributor in Texas, who by his account, played a major role in having Bay Brew throughout the state. He'd be leaving late Sunday afternoon, which was fine. I guess.

I did what little cleaning needed to be done. Took the trash out, cleaned my hair out of the shower, washed my sheets, and did some laundry on Friday while I waited.

Audrey picked Casey up from the airport. I thought it was sweet he wanted to see his sister. And since he insisted the weekend belonged to just us, I invited her over for dinner.

Hearing a knock at the door, and since I was expecting them, I answered it as fast as my legs could get me there. I opened it to find it wasn't Casey and Audrey, but a delivery man instead. He held a large vase wrapped in green tissue paper. It was the largest bouquet of flowers I'd ever seen.

I signed for the flowers, and set them down on the little table, and in no more time than I could thank the man, my telephone started ringing. I didn't bother unwrapping the delivery, I had to look for my cell. Retrieving it, I saw that it was Dr. Rex.

"Hello," I answered.

"Hi, Blake. I'm sorry to call you on a Friday evening. I know we made plans for Grant to come next week, but I have to reschedule." I didn't like the sound of that. At my last session, I explained what went down with him, and she was very generous in accepting to see us. I hoped she hadn't changed her mind.

"Is everything all right?" I asked.

"Yes, everything is okay, but I have to leave town for a little while. My son just called and he's in the hospital. Now I'm on my way to the airport. It appears he has an appendix that's throwing quite a fit, and they want to do surgery. I told him I'd stick around until he was feeling better. And you don't know my son, but I'll tell you—he's a big baby.

I shouldn't be gone for longer than a week or so. Just until he's feeling better," she explained.

How awful. I remembered my brother Shane having his appendix out his senior year of high school. It wasn't pretty.

"Sure. I'm so sorry. I know how painful that can be. I hope everything goes okay. Do you want to call me when you get back in town? We can reschedule after you get caught up," I suggested.

"Yes, that's perfect. Thanks. And I'm sorry to postpone things for you, Blake. I know how bad you want to get this moving forward. I hope that a few weeks won't cause any trouble. I can always refer you to someone else."

She was right. I didn't want to delay the inevitable any longer than necessary, but I also didn't want to see anyone but her. I had to wait.

"No, don't be silly. We'll wait for you."

"Good. I was hoping you'd say that. Is Casey there yet?" she asked conspiratorially, and quietly laughed into the receiver. I loved her.

"No. I just got flowers though," I told her, like I was chatting with a girlfriend.

"Oh, I'm so excited for you. Now remember, just keep doing what you're doing. Talk. Okay?"

There was another knock and I answered the door with the phone still at my ear. It was them. I held it open and motioned to come inside.

"Hey, Dr. Rex, they're here now. I'm going to let you go. Have a safe flight and I hope your son gets better fast," I said, as Casey walked through the open door and placed a quick kiss on my cheek.

"Ok, sweetie. Thank you. I'll call when I know more. Bye."

"Bye."

I closed the door and spun to see Casey, and his oldest younger sister, Audrey, in my living room.

"Hi," Casey said, looking around and making faces. "I like what you've done with the place. What is this? Minimalist chic?"

"Ha. Ha. I told you, I don't have much stuff," I said to him.

Then I spoke to Audrey. "Was he like this growing up, too? Mouthy and rude?"

She smiled and nodded. "Actually, this is a little tame," she admitted. Casey swung an arm around her neck, like he was bringing her in for a hug, then he wrapped his hand around the other side and covered her mouth.

"You're a liar aren't you, Audrey?" He grinned as he asked. Then he shook her head for her, making her laugh. "I think what you meant was charming and handsome."

Then he shook her head again inciting more laughter. She attempted to kick him from behind, but he dodged her. Just as I suspected, it was easy to see how close they were. Hell, he talked to his siblings more than I talked to either of my mine.

Then, I remembered the flowers.

"And don't forget sweet, Audrey," I added and pointed to the large vase behind me. "You didn't have to send me flowers when you were coming yourself." I turned around to unwrap them, so they'd be proudly displayed. They were just about the only ornamental thing in the place.

"I didn't send those," he stated with a guilty, cheesy grin.

"What?"

I tucked the green crepe paper stuff under my arm and looked for a card. Then the temperature inside me dropped. I prayed they weren't from Grant, but I soon realized my quick prayer went unanswered when I read the card.

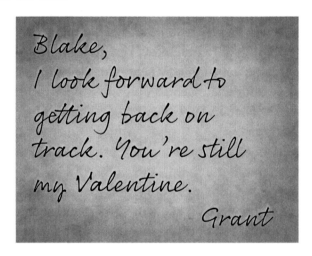

Blake,
I look forward to getting back on track. You're still my Valentine.
Grant

My stomach soured and flipped inside out. He really thought we were going to work things out? Even though when I'd emailed him to tell him about the appointment—that now I'd have to email him, telling him it was off until further notice—I hoped he was going into it knowing I wasn't changing my mind.

That man only ever saw what he wanted. Read what he wanted. Heard what he wanted. My nausea turned to frustration.

I was happy I had planned to cook, because I wanted to cut and chop, and bitch and moan internally. Cooking was a great way to relieve the tension.

"Blake, may I use your bathroom?" Audrey asked.

I mumbled, "Sure," and pointed down the hall. "It's right down there."

I wanted to rip up the card, but first I wanted Casey to read it. If it were me, I'd want to see. I felt him come up behind me and gently kiss the side of my neck, wrapping his arms around my waist.

"They're from Grant," he said already knowing. He didn't sound jealous or suspicious. He sounded like he wasn't surprised at all.

"Yeah, read the card." I held it up so he could read it over my shoulder.

"How do you feel about that?"

"I don't know. I'm annoyed, I guess. I feel bad for feeling like that, but that's what I'm working with." I relaxed as he started rocking us unthinkingly back and forth. It was soothing.

"The dude is oblivious. The *definition* of oblivious." Then he turned me around in his arms. I looped mine around him and just held on for a minute. We continued to almost, but not quite, slow dance in front of flowers from the guy who wouldn't get a clue. "I missed you."

"I missed you too," I said back into his shirt, which smelled of him and Southwest Airlines.

"They're not bad flowers. Roses though? For Valentine's Day?" Casey judged.

"I told you. He's traditional."

He hummed as he thought, and squinted before saying, "I would have got you a tomato and a lettuce plant. And a pig."

"Awww. See? That's romantic." *A BLT-entine.*

"But I didn't get you those things."

"So what? It's the thought that counts. And I like the *thought* of your delicious Valentine better than *real* roses."

Neither of us said anything for a minute or two. I enjoyed that finally, Casey was standing in the same place that my mail came. It was the first time the apartment felt like my home.

"Oh. My. God. He's so damn cute," I squealed, looking at the pictures Audrey had taken of Foster. Some were over Christmas and others were at Micah and Cory's wedding. She was really talented. Her artful eyes looked at things differently than I would have. She'd edited the photos herself and they were amazing, but the ones she'd taken of Foster were especially priceless. "That face is perfect."

"He gets that from me," Casey said, as he stood at my sink washing dishes from dinner. He insisted he do them, since I cooked.

I just liked the way he looked in my kitchen.

Then he looked up, and before he could wink, I beat him to it. He chuckled and said, "I have the same face as his slightly-less-good-looking-than-me father. The kid has good genes."

Audrey and I both rolled our eyes and scrolled on through picture after picture. "Are you sure you don't mind? I can have them printed," I said.

She offered to print my favorite picture of our godson, lying on a blanket with a look that really did remind me of Casey. One eyebrow cocked up like he knew all the secrets to the world.

"No, I want to. We'll call it a house warming gift," she told me and beamed proudly. My little home could definitely use some warming. "I'm getting a lot printed, I know a guy at school who can process them for us. Really."

She was so sweet. Her thick and curly, dirty-blonde hair was tied up in a huge wad atop her head. She had Casey's style. Loose, but trendy. Casual, but she looked like she could walk a runway at any moment. That family did have great genes.

"Okay, thanks."

"Which one did she pick?" Casey asked. He plopped down next to me at the small, bistro-style table in my dining room.

"One of the same ones you did," she answered, and then showed him the one I'd chosen. "I like that one, too."

We talked about the things she was doing in her classes and we had a genuinely great time. It was incredible feeling included—even in a small way—into their family. It made me so hopeful and eager for the future.

The BLT gift would have been nice, but having Casey and Audrey in my apartment, just hanging out, was a fantastic consolation.

"Okay, you two have fun. I'm going to head out. I'm doing a campus tour tomorrow," Audrey told us as she put her jacket on and wrapped her pretty silk scarf around her neck. "I don't need to look tired when I'm walking prospective students and their parents around campus."

Casey hugged his little sister tightly. "Be careful. Drive safe," he instructed. "Text me when you get back to your room."

"Yes, Dad," she mocked as she went out the door.

"Bye, Audrey," I said and she waved. She had one of the most truly perfect smiles.

We closed the door after she pulled away.

"Now, you. Get the fuck over here . . . ," Casey stalked toward me, ". . . with your wink-stealing ass. That's my move." He looked menacing, and fully capable of delivering a wicked punishment for my thievery.

"You don't scare me," I said as I walked backward, retreating through my apartment. He stopped all of a sudden, went back to the front door, locked it and then like a flash he was after me.

"Then why are you running from me?"

"Stop, Casey," I said as I circled my bed.

He paused inside my bedroom, not far from the door, and held up a finger for me to wait a minute. He looked all around, like my bedroom was a fascinating museum exhibit. There wasn't much to see. A closet with shoes all over the place. In retrospect, I could have spent some time in there straightening it up, since I was having bedroom company. Nevertheless, it was my closet and it wasn't *that* bad.

"You have a lot of shoes."

"Yep. And I don't wear half of them. I just put them on for a second and then settle for one of the three pairs that are already broken in." I lay over my bed, but kept my feet on the floor as I allowed him to waltz through my stuff.

Then he saw the picture of us, from Chicago on the Fourth of July, which I'd printed from my phone and framed. I did that the first week I lived there.

"Honeybee, you have a picture of me beside your bed?" he inquired, bending down to look at it on the nightstand. Then, in a much unexpected move, he opened my nightstand drawer. The one with my toy. My special talking on the phone with naughty, dirty, flirty Casey toy. I'd bought that the first week, too.

"You keep a picture of me above your vibrator like a sexual tombstone." He chuckled. "I approve."

I was mortified for about ten seconds. Then he turned the little silver toy on. I can't deny it, I was turned on, too.

TWENTY-ONE

Casey

Friday, February 12, 2010

MY LIST OF TURN-ONS, simplified. She. Had. A. Vibrator. *Happy Valentine's Day to me.* Yes, I had every intention of reinforcing the no one-night stand guy behavior from our trip—at least on the first night—but, fuck if I didn't just find her vibrator.

I have no clue why I looked in the drawer. Okay. I had a clue. Every guy fantasizes about his girl pleasuring herself. Every guy. All of them. That's why I looked. It was predetermined in my chromosomes to find out if my fantasies were true.

Sure, *I* could have used it on her—if she was okay with that. But I'm persuasive as hell, when I need to be. I'm a goddamned salesman. I could talk her into it and she'd believe it was her idea—if it came to that. Just the thought of witnessing that precious sight, *without my participation,* there was a good chance I would embarrass myself. If she used it in front of me, I would come in my pants.

So, even though the rehabilitated one-night stand guy knew better, he still couldn't do anything about the circumstances. Things like that never happened. It was an opportunity I couldn't pass up.

She had to be made aware of the situation.

"Blake, I think we need to have a talk," I said and swallowed the lump in my throat. The sex gods were smiling at me. It was a gift from above. Every man's dream and it had just come true for me.

"About my toy?" She looked slightly embarrassed, but I knew she was excited. She wore the proof of her ramped-up libido on her face. Pink-nose tattletale. God, I loved that girl. "We don't have to talk about it. I know what it does," she challenged.

Thank you, sex toy gods.

"Can you show me?" I tried to keep a serious face, but I was thrilled. I cleared my throat; it was getting hot in her room.

Her eyes were wide, but she didn't say no. She didn't say no. No noes were said. There was a chance. I needed to make my intentions clear, before it went any further.

"Blake, I didn't plan to come here tonight and fuck your brains out like a sex-starved whore-monger. I didn't. I was going to be good, show some restraint." As she dutifully listened, she sucked her lips in and bit her teeth down around them to hide her smile, stopping herself from laughing at me. I continued anyway. "But. *But!* This is a game changer."

I brought the vibrator to the top of the bed, and then mirrored her stance. My feet on the floor, I lay down and met her in the middle.

I accidentally turned it on.

"Whoa, fella. Hold up." The damn thing was more eager than I was. It had a hair trigger. I pressed a button to turn it off, but it just got stronger.

Blake possessively took it from me and with instructional eyes demonstrated how to *off* the little devil. Then a silent, laughter-deprived tear rolled down her cheek as she handed it back.

"Thank you. As I was saying, I didn't come over here tonight with the intention of knocking the bottom out of your pretty little ass and blowing your mind with *this* little thing—and thanks for keeping him a reasonably competitive size, by the way. But I just can't see any way around it."

"You didn't want to knock the bottom out of *all* this before?" Her voice shook as she tried to rein in her composure. It filled my heart seeing her light up with glee. Who knew sex toys could bring so much pleasure? On second thought, that bears no need for answering.

"That's not exactly what I said. I just meant it wasn't my intention."

"And now?"

"Well, hell. Do I have a choice? You're looking so girl-next-door-sexy and you have a picture of us by your bed, that—and I'm only assuming—you look at when you . . ." I waggled my eyebrows. She could fill in the blanks.

"Maybe."

"Maybe? Good answer. I like a little mystery." I stole my wink move back, and gave it to her. She leaned in and kissed me, tasting like the chocolate ice cream we had after dinner.

"Now, knowing what you do, about my pure intentions, can I please see what you can do with this thing?"

"I don't know." She blushed. "I can't just do it. You know? Can you just jack off?"

"Yes," I deadpanned.

"Oh." She put her head down on the bed, shaking it with embarrassment. Then she looked up at me with mischief swimming in her deep brown eyes.

"You first then," she dared.

This girl had game. Well played, honeybee. Well played.

She crawled up on the mattress, her ass in the air and turned around laying perpendicular to me, the way one should lay on a bed. She didn't say anything, but her body told me everything I wanted to know. She was breathing heavier, her back against the fluffy tan comforter. The look on her face telling me she'd do any damn thing I wanted.

If I had to choose, it was one of my favorite looks. Her lips were red from biting at them to stave off a laugh, full and totally kissable. A blush on her cheeks. Her dark brown eyes, dreamy and heavy-lidded. It was sensational and right up there with my other favorites. Her sleepy, satisfied, after climax face. One I planned on seeing a few times that weekend. The way she looked when she came. Totally a contender for favorite. Right next to the way she looked when I told her I loved her and the way she looked when she said it back.

If I were hard pressed, I wouldn't be able to choose, but didn't have to. Because there she was, waiting for me, like a kite in the breeze. Waiting for me to put up or shut up.

I stood to unbuckle my pants. If she wanted to watch, I'd show her. She studied every move I made with hungry eyes.

It wasn't a challenge for me; I'd been hard most of the night. So when I pulled myself free of my boxers, dick in hand, I began a time-honored Casey ritual. I clutched my cock tightly and her eyes widened at the sight of me man-handling my manhood.

She licked her lips and I kept going.

"Is this what you wanted to see?" I asked and slid my palm up and down my dick. Slack-jawed, she nodded her head, yes. I propped one knee up on the bed. If *I* expected a good show, *I* had to give one.

First, her cautious hand found its way to the button fly of her jeans and opened them. Then her slow, shy fingers dipped below her panties where I couldn't see and her head fell deeper into the pillow. Her eyes full of lust and wonder as she watched, never taking her eyes off my cock.

"Take your pants off, Blake," I instructed. She wasted no time heeding my request.

Good girl, the panties, too.

After her bottom half was as naked as mine, she roamed the bed for her toy. I peered down at my stiff dick and saw a drip of pre-come glazing the tip. I slowed my hand at the head, and ran my thumb over its slickness, just as I heard the vibrator turn on.

I stood mesmerized, watching as she gingerly ran it through the lips of her pussy a few times and then, when she found just the right spot, she dialed up the intensity. She pressed herself against it, her hips grinding seductively along the length of it, as a pleasure-filled moan left her lips.

When our eyes finally found each other she mouthed, "I want you."

I couldn't take any more. I dropped my dick and climbed onto her bed, it was softer than the one I had at home and my knee sunk into both the plush bedding and the mattress.

I took her toy away, and tossed it aside, saying, "It's my turn."

My hand wandered under her shirt and over her warm skin. Her breath hitched and she shivered as my fingers lightly danced over her stomach.

She rose and lifted her arms above her head, telling me she didn't need or want her shirt anymore. I grabbed it by the hem and pulled it off, and then she lay back down.

I straddled her, putting a knee on either side of her thighs, and I closed my legs as much as I could so her legs were tightly pressed together. My hands found her sides and I leaned forward to reach behind her and unclasp her bra, but I couldn't find it.

She chuckled a little, and then performed her next trick. With a flick of her wrist, she unhooked it in the front, her breasts softly bouncing free. For someone who didn't think she was sexy, she was doing a damn fine job proving herself wrong.

I moved the fabric to the sides, and with both palms, cupped her, loving the feel of her in my hands. Her tits were gallery-worthy. Perky, but natural and full. Her nipples were almost the same color as her lips and they tasted just as good.

I don't know what it was, but the sight of my hands on her body turned me on even more. The contrast of my big hands and her perfectly delicate skin seemed so erotic.

She puckered her lips requesting a kiss. Another look on my favorites list.

When our mouths met, she tugged at the only piece of clothing left between us. My shirt. I urgently took it off and tossed it, getting back to her mouth as fast as possible.

Her warm hand gripped my shaft tightly, like she'd watched me do to myself. Then she caressed me to the point of almost weakness. Even though I was much more practiced at it, when she did it, I felt so much more.

Somehow, the human body lets you split into two sets of feelings whilst enjoying incredible fucking moments like that. Both the sensations she gave me with her touches, and the ones I took pleasure feeling while exploring her.

My mouth made its way past all of my favorite hang-outs. Stopping behind her ear, where I heard a sigh slip past her lips. I painted a thin stripe up her neck with my tongue and felt her shift under me as her body came alive, rocking into her own hand as she gripped my cock.

I spread my legs to give her more room and I encouraged her to roll over.

Her beautiful ass looked like a picture-perfect heart. I kissed it and ran my teeth over her, wanting to bite, but holding back.

"Ahhh," she quietly panted, but lifted her ass more.

"You like that, don't you?"

"Mmmm," she purred.

I raked my teeth across her, a little harder that time, and she whimpered. Would I ever get bored discovering this woman? It wasn't likely.

I inched forward on the bed behind her, lifting her hips higher to meet mine. She looked back at me, over her shoulder. The sight of her dark hair flowing down her back was stunning. And I could have come right there, as she waved her ass, side to side, over my cock.

"Do you want this?" I asked and gripped myself, running the tip of my erection against her. Back and forth, front to back, teasing her.

Then, out of nowhere, my open hand met her ass. It was a move I hadn't even seen coming. I only knew it happened when I heard the quick pop of my palm meeting her backside.

"Yes," she breathed. Her mouth hung open in surprise, as her tongue wet her lips.

I pushed straight into her and she bowed under the pressure I applied. Wet and ready, she accepted me.

"Yes," she said again and pushed back. Loving the reaction the slap gave her, I let everything primal possess me. I pulled slowly out of her, bent forward, and kissed between her shoulder blades. Then my hand, from no farther away than from my side, swatted her again, as I pushed deeper into her.

I watched her hands ball the pillowcase as she said my name.

It was a new thing. It was exciting as hell. I fucked her like I craved and she responded by fucking me right back. I reached down and pulled her up with me, my front against her back as we both got closer to orgasm. My fingers roamed the top of the bed for her toy, and her head lulled on my chest as she rode me from the front.

I found the vibrator and gently brought it around to her clit, then turned it on.

She became a woman unleashed. Taking what she wanted, as I gave her everything I had. I leaned back, holding her to me, as she talked to God and me alike.

When I came, just after her, with my mouth open, pressed against her neck, I told her I loved her. Because even at my most primal, barbaric and dominant, I did—and it was because of her I was that strong.

TWENTY-TWO

Blake

Saturday, February 13, 2010

I DREAMT OF STRONG arms holding me. And while I slept, I felt protected and cherished, because he was there with me.

When I awoke the next morning, sprawled out with my head at the foot of my bed, I listened to Casey sing in the shower. He had some pretty good moments where he nailed it. But my favorite parts were when he ad-libbed the words through the parts he didn't. I learned a lot of peculiar things about Beyoncé from his lyrics. Listening, I smiled and laughed into my sheets. He was ridiculous.

Entering the steamy bathroom, it felt surreal stepping into a shower—in my home—that hosted a singing Casey Moore. It was my new favorite way to wake up. I wrapped my arms around his wet body from behind, as he rinsed his hair under the hot stream of water.

"Good morning," he said, as the turned around in my arms, slipping easily through my loose hug.

"Great morning," I corrected.

With both hands, he pulled his hair back away from his face so he could see me. He placed a sweet kiss on my forehead, after ridding the stream of water coming from his nose with a shake.

"I didn't know you were such a Beyoncé fan," I said sarcastically, swapping spots to wet my hair.

"I didn't know I had an audience." He squeezed his soap into a washcloth.

I loved watching him shower. Naked. Wet. Soapy. Stretching. Rubbing.

In the times we'd showered together, I'd often lost track of what I was supposed to be doing. He'd remind me, by handing me shampoo or body wash. It was a good thing he did that for me or I would stand there and watch him like a pervert the whole time.

I also liked when he knew I was totally useless and washed my hair for me. He did a great job, his big hands reaching everywhere on my head all at once.

"I'm hungry," I admitted.

He washed his underarms with something that smelled fresh and a little exotic. Casey's hand reached the ceiling, he was tall and seemed so big like that.

"Me too. Hey, I saw the for sale sign out front when I got here last night. Will you have to move if they sell it?"

"I'm not sure. Dave—the guy who owns the place with his parents—said occupied places, like this, sell faster. So I don't think so. That reminds me, he left a message saying that someone was looking at it on Monday around five. I need to write that down."

"Oh," he said. "That's a shame."

"What? You don't like it? It's pretty bare in here, huh?"

"No, that's not it. I just think it would be awful if you needed a place to live."

Wink.

Oh. I saw where he was going with that. It was the second time he'd alluded to me moving in with him. The water in the shower was hot, but a different kind of warmth spread through and around my heart.

I couldn't wait until my divorce was final. Until all of this was just some stuff we went through in the beginning. Until I could actually think about possibly moving.

I balanced myself on the tips of my toes and kissed him for his cute way of thinking.

"I don't think I'd ever have to worry about that. I'll always have a place to go."

"That's right," he said with his head high. "I think the circus takes just about anyone these days." He laughed. "Hurry up. My girlfriend's hungry." He stepped out and started drying off. And, more importantly, letting all of the warm air out of the shower stall in the process.

Girlfriend. Was I his girlfriend?

"What did you call me?" I asked, as I followed him out and took the towel he offered me.

"I called you my girlfriend," he answered, but he kept moving like the whole world hadn't just shifted.

Was that where we were? Was it even possible?

After all this time, after everything, I was overwhelmed by that one tiny word. I felt myself getting choked up and tried not to get silly emotional over it. But it really hit me at that moment.

We'd been given another shot. No. We'd earned our shot.

Where other couples were lucky to have met and effortlessly moved from strangers into such trivial roles as boyfriend and girlfriend, we had to fight like hell—just for the titles. It wasn't a huge thing, and I was sure I was overreacting, but I didn't stand a chance at quelling the happiness that surged through me.

I wrapped an extra towel around my hair. When I stood up, eyes beginning to sting from the first happy tears I'd cried, in I didn't know how long, he caught me. My chin quivered, but I smiled brightly.

"Now, what's this? Are you crying?" He ran a thumb under my eye, which only intensified the moment. He was so . . . so . . . exactly what I wanted.

"No," I disputed, but nodded my head yes. I'd never cried from pride, but that was how I felt. Proud. I was proud to be claimed like that by him.

Then the thought hit me, I couldn't be all-the-way his.

Regardless of not wearing the ring, or parking in the same driveway after work, the truth was, I was still married to Grant. Accepting the precious title of Casey's girlfriend didn't seem right yet.

My happy tears mixed with my frustrated tears. It was a lucky thing both kinds were clear. He couldn't tell them apart.

"Why are you *not* crying then?" he asked, humoring me.

"I'm *not* crying because you called me your girlfriend." I sat down on top of the toilet lid. "And I'm *not* crying because you're so sweet and just wiped a tear—that wasn't really there, by the way—off my cheek. But mostly, I'm *not* crying because I'm sick of waiting to actually deserve being called that." I tucked my chin onto my chest and sat there feeling foolish and hyper-emotional, maybe a little hormonal—as it was about that time of the month.

"Well, I'm glad you're *not* crying." He squatted in front of me.

"Don't look at me. I'm being stupid."

"Hey, come on," he cajoled.

"I'm sorry," I said and took a big breath through my nose and blew a raspberry out my mouth. "I just want it so bad. You know?"

Then my chin shook again. Damn chin.

"Tell me something, do I deserve to be your boyfriend?"

I raised my head to look at him, finding compassion and humor in his expression.

I answered, "Yes, you deserve more than that."

"Why?"

"Because you make me feel so cared for and you never let me down."

"Those are good reasons—a little off—but I'll take them. And when you look into the future, what do you see?"

My knee bounced and I fought the urge to say so many things. I'd never really allowed myself to picture specifics. I mostly wished for him. "I see you."

"And?" He steadied my leg and then took my hands in his. "What else?"

"I don't know? What do you see?"

"Oh, I see lots of things," he confirmed. "Maybe it's weird, but I've always imagined a future with you."

"Like what?"

"It changes," he said. "Where we live. What you'll look like when you're old. The places we'll travel to. Sometimes I wonder what kind of mother you'll be, like when I see pictures of you and Foster." He kissed my knuckles.

"Really?"

"Yep. When I was with Micah on the way to the hospital, I thought about what you'd be like in labor, too. I've pictured what you'd look like in a wedding gown. And I've pictured you naked almost everywhere."

"You've already seen me in a wedding gown," I reminded him. The truth hurt, but it was our truth and we were learning to deal with the pain.

He shrugged. "Depends on what you call a wedding."

Damn, if that wasn't a good point. I nodded in agreement.

"In my mind, you don't wear white when we get married. God, I sound like a woman."

"Kind of," I teased and bumped my knee into him in jest. "But I like it. White's a little predictable. And I'm not really eligible for white anyway. It would be my second wedding."

"Not to me."

Even though I'd love to be Casey's wife, I didn't know if I could ever go through another wedding. Not that any of my first wedding felt like mine; my mom planned almost all of it and I didn't pay attention to any of the details. I was too distracted.

Thinking back about the planning of my wedding, I could see my lack of participation in the planning of it matched my lack of participation in my relationship with Grant. *Distracted?* I wasn't even involved. I hadn't been invested in a future with Grant. Yet a future with Casey was more appealing than I ever thought possible.

"I like the way your future looks," I said anyway.

"Good. Then I'll share it with you. But for now, you're my girlfriend. Now give me a kiss and get up." His lips brushed against mine and once again, he'd eased my mind.

We dressed and he made us grilled cheese sandwiches for an early lunch. It rained all day, and since he was taking me out that night, we hung out and watched the Discovery Channel and napped.

It was an excellent way to spend a rainy Saturday in Seattle.

My mom called just as I was putting in my earrings, and was almost ready leave for our night out.

"Hey, Mom."

"Hi, sweetie. How's your day?" Her greeting was becoming the normal way we started our phones calls. She was worried.

I gave my commonplace answer. "I'm good." Then I gave it a little more thought. I didn't have to hide that I was with Casey anymore. "No, actually, I'm really good. Casey's here for Valentine's Day."

Again it was strange, but wonderful telling the truth—or maybe it was the affirmation of saying it to somebody out loud.

"He is? Okay, well then I won't keep you. I was just calling to see what you were doing for Valentine's Day anyhow and invite you to dinner with us."

"Oh, thank you." I laughed. "I appreciate the invitation, Mom. But you and Dad go have some fun."

"You too, Blake." She paused for a second like she wanted to say something more. Then she simply said, "Happy Valentine's day, sweetheart."

What a difference a year truly made. At the same time the year before, I thought I was saying goodbye to Casey forever. Thank goodness things don't always turn out like you predict they will.

Life's crazy like that, and even more so with a man like Casey. He let me spend all that time getting dolled up, and then ended up taking me to a skating rink.

"Are you kidding me?" I asked as we stood in line at the skate counter to rent pairs for both of us.

"I am absolutely not kidding. Can you skate?"

"As a kid I could, but as an adult? Hell, I have no idea," I admitted. I didn't feel that confident.

I glanced around and saw young, teenage couples, who'd no doubt met there for a sweethearts rendezvous. It was pretty charming. So many young couples holding hands and awkwardly fumbling around on eight wheels.

It was actually kind of perfect.

"What made you think of this?" I asked, as we sat on a bench near the side of the rink.

"When I was younger we used to go almost every Saturday night. My friends always had girlfriends, but I never really got into them at that age. So I thought, it's never too late. You're my new girlfriend and we're both kinda fumbling our way through this thing. Just like these little fuckers."

He tied his laces and when he was finished, I propped my skate up on his knee for him to tie mine.

He said, "This morning got me thinking. We're both so unsure. So are all of them." He nodded to the junior high aged kids doing laps, hand in hand to awful pop music. "We don't know much more than they do, as I see it. Rolling around trying not to fall down and look dumb. Boyfriends and girlfriends. Young love. Making out in dark corners at the end of the night. Which we won't do here. They don't need to see that—we've got that part down to an art form."

I switched legs, crossing my left one over my right and onto his jean-clad lap. As he worked on my other skate, he added, "We're going to fall down most likely. It might hurt. That's nothing new for us. But we'll help each other up from here out."

I full-on swooned, and I, just like the tween girls going round-and-round with their boyfriends, felt the nervous excitement only a beginning can give you.

"I like you," I confessed and batted my eyes at him.

"Blake, officially, will you go out with me?" he requested and bobbed his head around like a shy, squeaky voice boy. "I think you're hot and funny and I was just kinda hoping you'd want to be my girl-friend. *Officially.*" It was hilarious and I loved him even more.

"Gee, Casey, I think you're hot and funny, too." I brought my mouth to his, and before I kissed him I said, "Yes, I'll be your girl-friend. I love you." I sealed the promise with our first official kiss as a couple. And in true junior high fashion there was gratuitous tongue.

We skated and laughed at ourselves. I did better than he did, which was very surprising. Maybe he was doing it on purpose to make all the young dudes look cool, as they sped by the hot older guy, flat on his ass. Maybe he just liked looking up my skirt, which he did every single time. It didn't matter though, because when he fell I helped him up.

And wasn't that what relationships were all about? Helping the other be their best, and seeing them through when they weren't? Well, and letting your boyfriend look up your skirt.

Although it wasn't what I'd expected for our Valentine's date, we had a great time. We acted like we were thirteen, eating pizza and drinking soda. We shut the place down. I loved how it was unexpected and quirky, because it was memorable and totally all us.

Casey left as planned on Sunday and flew to Houston.

I hated watching the cab pull away with him, but he insisted I didn't take him to the airport. After he left, I was pleased to find his scent on my couch and I lay there thinking of him and watched sappy romantic comedies all evening.

Before I went to bed, I emailed Grant about the situation with Dr. Rex. And I made a note to remind myself I needed to be out of the apartment by five the next day for the showing.

I lay in my bed, thinking about the weekend and how comfortable it was having Casey in my space. I couldn't wait until he came back.

He text when he got settled at his hotel.

Casey: I'm here. I sat next to a guy who smelled like a Bob Marley concert. Now, I just want to go to a Bob Marley concert. LOL

I could still hear him laugh.

Me: Ha Puff. Puff. Pass.

Casey: Thanks for having me over. I like sleepovers at your place.

Me: I liked having you here. I'm already in bed. You wore me out.

Casey: Good. Sleep well. I'll call you tomorrow. Miss me.

Me: Miss me too. Goodnight.

Casey: Always.

I fell asleep and dreamed of Casey with dreadlocks. They didn't look that bad, but I think he could probably pull off any look. I reveled in the notion that I might be around for all of the rest of them.

TWENTY-THREE

Casey

Monday, March 29, 2010

EVEN THOUGH WE WEREN'T close in proximity, it was like we were. I got off on talking to her through every mood she possessed. I was quickly learning all of them. A few I was afraid of. I thought I knew her, but in those days apart, I learned so much more.

Having the elephant in the room for so long, it was incredible how many other things we had to talk about with him gone.

In those few weeks, I was busy. Really busy. My Texas meeting ended up being the biggest contract we'd ever got and they didn't want to wait for anything. Marc and I discussed with more frequency buying a second brewery to keep up with demand and also make shipping easier. By then, we had a small fleet of trucks and we'd also hired three new salesmen.

"Marc, I think we should look for a building in Seattle," I told him on the phone one night from my hotel room in Austin.

"We do have a lot of accounts in the PNW, which would free up a lot of production so the San Francisco branch could accommodate Texas and the south. And even though it's a good idea, you're not fooling me. I know what you're trying to do."

"Who? Me?" I played innocent. It was obvious why I thought Seattle was the best location for the second Bay Brew location. Ask me if I gave a fuck. It made sense from every angle.

"Yeah, you. Do you think you'll move there, Casey?" Really, it didn't matter where I lived as long as Blake was close and we were both happy. You could stick my ass in Siberia if she was there, too.

"I don't know. It just made sense. And if she wants to be there instead of San Francisco, in the future, that could be my home base."

I'd known him a long time. He was my partner, my mentor, and a just a good dude. I could talk to him.

"Well, I hate to say it, but you are pulling more than your share of the weight. If being there keeps you happy, and keeps the contracts coming in, then I'll make a trip up there and find us a warehouse." I always knew I'd made the right decision working for that man. He was a no bullshit kind of guy. Marc was a straight shooter and if you approached him the same way, he appreciated the hell out of it. He said, "Actually, I've got some time. I'll try to set something up in the next day or two. No use dicking around."

"Exactly, and maybe in a year or so we could branch out again. I think looking somewhere on the central east coast would be smart. Maybe even Nashville? It's not on the coast, but it's in the middle of everywhere on that side of the country." Go big or go home. Bay Brewing was my life. I only imagined it growing and claiming more of the market nationwide.

"I'll have Aly look into it. She can crunch numbers and figure out something."

I hadn't seen Aly for weeks. I'd only been back to my house three times in the month of March. I hadn't seen anyone for that matter, and it looked like the next time I'd have a few days off would be around Foster's first birthday.

If I'd learned anything about traveling so much, it was as long as you make an effort, it doesn't matter where you are. I still talked to someone in my family every day. And I talked to Blake—in some way—every few hours. But by the end of April, I would need a few days to call my own.

I finished up the call with Marc, when I saw Blake's call coming in.

"Hello," I said.

"So check this out. There was another showing for the duplex this afternoon. I ran home to get my mom a pair of shoes and a purse I told her she could borrow after work, because I was coming here for dinner with them . . . Anyway, I'm in my closet when I hear my front door open. The showing wasn't until six, but you're supposed to be out *way* before that. Casey, it was Grant. He just walked right into my apartment." She was speaking fast, like she often did when she was riled up about something—and with good reason.

"He did what?"

"He just came right in. I yelled for Dad, thinking it had to be him. Because he's the only other person with a key. When I looked down my hall, Grant was standing there. It freaked me the fuck out."

"He can't just come into your apartment like that." The fucking bastard was really beginning to get on my nerves.

First, after it was his idea to go to couples counseling, as a condition for him to sign the divorce papers—and after Dr. Rex finally got back—he didn't even show up to the first few appointments, always with the excuse he was busy and he'd try to make it to the next one.

He was stalling was what he was doing. *That fucker.*

"Well as it turns out, he can. I knew his dad was my landlord's agent, but since you have to be gone during showings, I just figured I'd never have to see them."

"What did you say?" My pulse was racing. This cocksucker was grating on my last nerve. Even Blake admitted he wasn't the same guy she'd met and dated. But she blamed herself and felt so guilty, feeling she was responsible for the change in his demeanor. My sympathy for him was fast dissolving.

"I asked him what he was doing there and he told me he was showing the place for his dad today. And that since my car was there he thought he'd come on in," she shrieked.

"And then?" I needed to know everything. And as my mind listened to her re-tell what had happened, the other half of my mind was thinking of a solution.

"I told him he shouldn't have let himself in. He can't just come in when he wants. That's so messed up, Casey."

I didn't think she was afraid of Grant, but I was starting to wonder if maybe she should be, at least, a little concerned. I'd only seen them together the one time. And no matter how deep down I tried to bury the image of him grabbing her by the arm, it floated right back up every time the conversation turned to him. I saw—with my own eyes—his lack of care for her that night.

I refused to ignore her safety and it was time for me to do something.

"You're right. He can't just come in. Are you at your mom and dad's now? What did you do after that?" I couldn't get enough information.

"Yeah, I'm at Mom and Dad's now. Okay. So, I got my shoes and purse and I asked him to wait outside until the people came to look at it. He said he wanted to talk, but I told him I had somewhere to be. That if he wanted to talk, he could show up at our appointments—that he asked for."

That's my fucking girl.

I looked at the clock, it was barely after six. I needed to call my banker. That fucking building was mine or she was moving. And since I couldn't make that decision for her, I made the only one I could.

"Honeybee, I'll call you back. Okay? I need to call my dad really quick."

"Okay, I'm here anyway. I just wanted to call and tell you. That's messed up, isn't it? I'm not out of line, am I?" She still wanted to vent and I was glad she wasn't alone. She was livid.

"You are nowhere near out of line, Blake. He *can't* do that. He *won't* do it again."

I paced back and forth in my hotel room feeling helpless.

True, Grant didn't really do anything threatening, but my hackles were rising. He was going to start realizing really quickly that she was mine and I didn't give a shit how he felt about it anymore.

"Okay. I'll talk to you later," she said.

"I love you," I told her quickly, before she could hang up.

We still didn't say those words all that often, and sometimes I thought I needed to tell her more than I did. But at that moment, alone and kind of freaking the fuck out, *I* needed to hear them back. I hated feeling so far from her. I was just thankful she was at her parents' house, even if it was just for dinner.

"I love you back," she said.

We hung up and I dialed my father. It wasn't typical for me to call him for help, but I needed him. I'd never bought a property. And certainly not on a whim. I'd inherited my house. And truthfully, he'd handled a lot of that for me, too.

"I was just thinking about calling you, Casey. How's Texas?" he asked when he picked up.

"It's far from Washington. That's how Texas is right now, Dad. Listen I need your help. I want to buy a duplex in Seattle. Like right now." I wasn't even sure if it was possible.

"What? I don't understand," he said.

"I have to buy the place where Blake lives." I didn't have time to explain it all. I needed him making a call, or pulling some strings, or whatever the hell he did. I needed *that*.

He was concerned. "Is everything all right?"

"I think so. The short story is, Blake's ex is the agent who's selling her duplex and the motherfucker is using his key to let himself in. I want to make an offer on it tonight."

He went over a few things with me, but since my mother's passing, he was a signatory on all of my accounts. He told me he didn't know what he could do at that time of night, but he'd try his best.

I gave him the address and the number to call Grant's agency. I didn't care if Grant found out. I hoped he did.

I wanted those locks changed tomorrow.

If I couldn't be there with her, I had to know she was safe. She'd always said he'd never been violent with her, but there was an undeniable feeling in my gut telling me that he wasn't the same guy now. Evidently, this new guy was someone she didn't know, and certainly someone I didn't trust.

My dad called back a short time later, telling me we'd made a cash offer with the help of his good friend who was in real-estate. Dad explained to him it needed to happen fast. So we offered over asking, with only a small window of time for the sellers to accept.

By nine o'clock, the apartment block was under contract. The best part was, as part of the deal, all of the locks had to be changed by morning and I was assured it would be done. As detailed in the contract, their real-estate brokerage wouldn't have access to the new keys. They'd be handled solely by the locksmith that our realtor arranged.

My honeybee was safe.

It was as if an albatross of stress had been lifted from my shoulders. Knee-jerk reaction? Perhaps. But my girl meant everything to me, and I *needed* her safe. Even if I couldn't protect her with my physical presence, at least I could do this.

It was an impulsive move, but I had the means to do it. What was money worth to me if I couldn't use it when I needed to?

My dad called me crazy, but he didn't give me too much shit. I didn't expect him to, he knew first-hand I'd saved every cent I'd ever made. He laughed when he told me he was going to suggest I purchase property soon, but I'd just beaten him to it. And in a big way.

The sale didn't hurt me and I could re-sell it later if I wanted. It wasn't a bad move. It was just a fast one.

I needed to talk to Blake. I was nervous she'd see it differently, but I prayed she would understand. I couldn't allow that guy to waltz the fuck in on her whenever he wanted. End of discussion.

She called me first.

"Hey there," I answered.

"Hey," she said, sounding less wound up than she had before. "Are you sleeping? I'm sorry time got away from me over here."

No, I hadn't been sleeping. I'd been making the biggest purchase of my life thus far and kind of in a weird and twisted way, buying our first home. Sort of. Okay, that was a stretch, but I owned it and she lived there, so why split hairs? I just had to tell her I'd be her new landlord, shortly after banks opened up the next day and the papers were signed.

"Are you still at your parents' house?" She'd said *here,* so I hoped she was.

"Yeah, it's funny. I thought you were going to flip-out about Grant. But I wasn't expecting my dad to lose his shit when I told them what happened. He was not a happy camper."

I already liked her dad, now I loved him. And little did she know that under my calm exterior, I had lost *all* my shit, too. Then managed to best that dickhead, almost ex-husband of hers, all from the comfort of my hotel room.

"Really, he didn't like that too much either, huh?"

"No, he called *Mr.* Kelly, Grant's dad, and let him know about it, too. Then, Mr. Kelly called him back and said someone bought the place tonight and that the locks were being changed. I didn't realize things happened so fast."

They do when you're a motivated buyer and I had a shit-load of motivation.

"Yeah, we need to talk about that," I coaxed as I sat on the small balcony and sipped the bourbon I'd ordered up. "I bought it."

There was a pause. A long, notable pause.

"Blake?" I asked when she didn't answer after thirty seconds or so. "Are you there?"

"You did what?" She was calm, but I could hear anxiety in her voice.

"Hear me out. When you called and I thought about him being able to walk his happy ass through your door, whenever he damn well pleased, I reacted." It might seem insane to her. But could I keep my sanity worrying if he'd stop in sometime—if he were mad or drunk like he was in San Francisco—trying to get his way? I couldn't bear the thought of it.

What if the fucker came during the night when she was asleep?

And had I not jumped on the opportunity, that exact thought would have consumed me. "When you called you were obviously shaken by him letting himself in and the easiest way for me to make sure that didn't happen again was to buy the building."

"You bought my apartment?" she reiterated.

"I bought your apartment. Well, I'm buying the apartment—with conditions."

"Conditions?"

"Yes, one being every lock will be changed in the morning and the sale moves through closing in the next few days."

"You can do that?"

"Technically, yes. I can do that, but my dad helped me." I owed my old man huge for what he'd got accomplished on my behalf and so quickly. I'd think of something, but at that moment, I needed to make sure Blake and I were on the same page.

"How did you do that?"

"Money talks, honeybee. I paid cash." I wasn't ashamed of my money, but I wasn't in the business of advertising it either.

"You have cash?" she asked and she chuckled a little, taken aback.

"You have *enough cash* to just buy a duplex on a whim?"

"I guess so."

We were both silent. I gave her time to process it, and I suppose I was still letting it sink in, too. Seeing the number on your bank account balance is one thing, but seeing the power it gave you, when you needed it, was a whole different ballgame.

"Will you stay at your parents' house tonight?" I finally asked knowing that it might be the straw that broke the camel's back. If Grant were, like how I was making him out to be in my mind, he wouldn't be too thrilled to learn what I'd done. And I was pretty sure he already knew.

"You're really worried about this, aren't you?" she asked.

"Maybe. I don't know. I've never been through a divorce, Blake. I mean, my parents' divorce—sure. I don't know how this is supposed to go. Or what my role is supposed to be. What I *do* know is—that aside—you're my girlfriend and if I feel like there's even the slightest chance someone might wrong you or hurt you or even trouble you, then I want to deal with it myself."

How was that for a reformed one-night stand guy? I had catapulted right into possessive alpha Neanderthal, but I was powerless to stop it. I didn't want it to stop; it felt pretty fucking cool.

"What are you thinking?" I asked after she didn't reply.

"Well, it was a bold move, but I get why you did it. I should probably be a little pissed you didn't tell me what you were doing, for some unknown reason. Only because it just seems like what I'm supposed to think. But, Casey, I just feel so . . . so . . . loved."

And she was and I'd show her every day.

Bullseye. Point for Lou.

TWENTY-FOUR

Blake

Saturday, April 24, 2010

EVERY DAY HE PROVED how much he loved me. Sometimes he had strange ways of doing it, but the message was clear.

If it was just age, and we were always going to be aging and evolving, then I couldn't wait to see what Casey would be like in five years. Ten years. My heart felt full and I felt content from the thought of a future with him. *Our* future.

He freaking bought my apartment building, all because Grant came in without permission. It went against every slightly feminist fiber in my body to be okay with what he'd done, but I understood it. He'd been powerless for so long. How was I to know, if I'd just gone to him, if I'd just let him know I needed him in the past—that he'd be there for me in every single way that I'd let him?

It wasn't unknown to me anymore.

He was becoming more than just a friend, more than just a lover. He was what living felt like. Having someone who would argue with you over things, then blindly go into battle with you, *for* you, even when you were as wrong as I'd been so many damn times.

I talked to Micah on the phone the night before I flew to San Francisco for Foster's party. His birthday was actually Monday, but they were having his party on Saturday because it was easier. It was hard to believe he was already a year old.

"What brought all of this change on, Blake?" She laughed as she questioned me about everything that had happened since her wedding. "Cory and I were talking about this the other day. We don't get it. You guys chased each other in circles for so long. And then it was like boom. Everything just flipped."

She was right, but there wasn't just *one* moment. There were many that led me to finally admit—and not just to myself—what I wanted. What I needed.

"On my honeymoon, I knew I'd made a mistake. A *huge* mistake. One morning, I was alone on the beach and wrote a letter to him. Micah, I messed up. You don't know how badly I wanted to tell him. To take it all back. Do it all over. But there I was. Before the wedding, he came to my mom and dad's. Did you know that?"

"He did? We knew he went to the wedding, but we didn't know he saw you first."

"He did. He told me he loved me and I told him to leave. I was angry that it had taken him that long, and I was scared. Because it was my wedding day and it felt like it was out of my control. So I thought I'd just wait, then I'd leave Grant. Isn't it sad I started planning my divorce two days after my wedding?" My voice was starting to shake. Even with weeks of seeing Dr. Rex, I still struggled with forgiving myself.

"Oh, Blake," she consoled.

"Then, when I went to see him, after his mother passed away, I knew it wasn't fair to trail him along until I was brave enough. It wasn't fair to have him wait for me, when I didn't even deserve him. At your wedding, when everything came out, I didn't have to worry about telling or confessing anymore. It was out and it was like my eyes had been opened. That was my chance." It had only been four months, but so much had happened. I was taking ownership of my choices. Truthfully, it started with me making the first right one. Not going back to Grant's.

I sat there on my bed, my suitcase open and almost totally packed, talking to my friend. A friend who Casey and I had managed to put in the middle of our mess so many times.

"I owe you an apology for your wedding."

"You've apologized a million times. Stop."

"Well, I'm sorry it happened there, but I'm thankful it happened."

"I'm glad, too. I want you to be happy. The bonus is, we like seeing how happy Casey is, too."

"Good. Now how's the birthday boy?" The world didn't revolve around us. Even though Micah and Cory were always there for us both, in some way, we'd stolen focus from them on more than one occasion. And tomorrow was all about that sweet little boy.

"Into everything. Wait until you see his chubby little waddle. He's a mess." She giggled and then spoke to Foster, who was no doubt at her ankles. "Yes, you are. You're a mess."

She told me about how he was saying "mama" and "duh-duh" and how he laughed at just about everything. She confessed that every evening, while Cory was putting Foster into his pajamas, they'd have a man-to-man talk. And while she was supposed to be making his bottle, she'd secretly listen and swoon her ass off—her words, not mine—every single night.

She sided with me about needing to tell Grant I didn't want to go to couples counseling, for the same reasons. The main one being—it was a waste of time. He never showed up, always having something urgent pop up. And ultimately, it wasn't going to change a damn thing. But Casey had insisted I keep my end of the deal, and I continued to invite him anyway, until May. If he had ever showed up that would have been the six sessions we agreed to.

I was happy he never showed up. And Dr. Rex and I—even though it probably wasn't professional on her part—decided if he ever did, she'd just tell him it wasn't going to work out. She'd explain couples therapy wasn't a good solution for our marriage.

Our *marriage*. What a joke that turned out to be.

Micah and I hung up, excited we'd get to see each other the next day.

Before I fell asleep, I sent Casey a message. He was out to dinner with a new customer, but telling him goodnight was a routine I liked. I slept better after sending him even the most trivial of texts. Knowing I probably wouldn't get his reply until morning, it still left me feeling sound and like things were as they should be.

Me: I'm crashing out. I hope they loved you and they buy all the beers. LOL. I'll see you tomorrow. I love you.

I rolled over and was surprised when my phone chimed right after.

Casey: Bad meeting. Aly showed up. I'll call you in the morning to wake you up? Six thirty?

Aly.

As much as I hated her, simply because she wanted my man, I was surprised how much she'd backed off Casey after New Year's. At least, to my knowledge she had. There was no reason for me to think otherwise. He told me everything.

Besides, his text told me he wasn't pleased about her being there.

Me: Yeah, six thirty is good, but I'm still up if you want to talk now.

Casey: No. She's drunk. I'm going to put her to bed.

I took a calming breath. She was drunk, but—according to the lack of typos—he wasn't.

I trusted Casey.

I trusted Casey.

I trusted Casey.

I chanted that to myself thirty times. He'd never given me any reason not to. And I think he trusted me, too. Even though, my track record showed I shouldn't be trusted with a ten-foot pole.

Me: All right.

Casey: All right . . . and . . . ?

Me: And I love you.

Casey: I can't wait to see you tomorrow. We're not going this long again without seeing each other. It sucks too much.

Casey: . . . and I love you too.

He was right. We hadn't seen each other since Valentine's Day and it really was too long. Casey was spending a lot of time in Austin and I'd kept very busy out of town with work, too.

That was another reason the therapist appointments with Grant weren't going as planned. Working around my schedule was a challenge. But I still thought he wasn't signing the papers just to be difficult. I was really close to saying fuck it and having him served.

I didn't want to be that person, but he wasn't leaving me with many options. The sooner my divorce was final, the sooner I'd feel more comfortable making plans for Casey and me.

Or landlord and me—which I now thought was kind of hot.

After he bought my building, and had all of the locks changed, he also put up a fence. The apartment next to mine became empty and Casey was holding it for Audrey. She wanted to move out of the dorms and he thought it was the perfect solution having me right next door.

I reminded him she was an adult.

He reminded me she was still his little sister living in a big city where he didn't know many people.

Audrey was great. I was ecstatic to have someone I knew living next door. I knew he wouldn't charge her rent, because he hadn't cashed either of my checks. Casey liked the idea of being able to see her more when he had the time to visit in the future—when work for the both of us slowed down a little.

After spring semester ended, she'd move in.

Secretly, I loved spending time with her. She and Casey were so much alike, in a free spirit sort of way. And the hair. Although lighter, it was curly and even if it was a small thing, it made me smile. We were meeting up about once a week for coffee, and we were flying together for the birthday party. Being around her made me miss him less.

I hoped soon I wouldn't have to miss him at all.

Although we both traveled for work, how I would love it if we had a home base. *Our* home base. I would still miss him, but it wouldn't feel as though my heart only partially beat all the time.

Sleep didn't come easily that night, which was nothing new. Between excitement, thinking about how it would go with Casey's family, how would we act, what Casey was doing with Aly, mulling over my divorce, and staying at Casey's house for the weekend—I was an over-inflated ball of nerves.

Why did staying at his house feel so strange? Was it because I'd left him there? I found that hard to believe. I'd left him, or he'd left me in lots of places. Was it because I knew I couldn't stay? That might be a better answer.

I loved that house. The property. The layout. The kitchen. The view. *The owner.*

In my heart, that was where I really wanted to be. Going there, then having to leave all over again, was going to be a challenge. But maybe this time it wouldn't feel like leaving as much. I hoped this time it would feel like a visit and a place I was looking forward to returning to.

Thank God I packed the night before, because I totally overslept.

I didn't fall asleep until around three and I didn't wake up for my alarm. I didn't wake up until I heard knocking on my front door.

I shot out of bed and ran to the door, knowing it was Audrey. She was picking me up like we'd planned.

"Shit. I overslept!" I shouted at her in greeting, as I swung the door open and immediately turned around to start damage control.

"Chill, I'm a little early. You're fine. It's only eight," she said. That helped a little. Our flight wasn't until ten fifteen.

I jumped into the shower and washed quickly, bringing my toothbrush in with me to save time. I shaved the basics and decided it would have to do.

I was ready in ten minutes. I could put on a little makeup in flight and I decided to let my hair air-dry. Do the wavy thing. Casey had said he'd liked it like that when we were in Costa Rica anyway. I managed the front parts, so I didn't look too out of control, and called it good. I wore a pale blue skirt, a plain white top, a tan cardigan, and flats.

After a quick review of myself in the mirror, I was categorically nerdy.

We made it on time and our flight seemed to go by really quickly. On the plane, I thought I'd be the only one nervous or fidgety, I was still anxious about everything that was happening. But the closer we got to San Francisco, the more nervous Audrey got.

"Are you okay?" I asked, as we were instructed to fasten out seat belts for our final descent.

"Yeah," she said and waved me off. "I'm fine." But she didn't look fine. She looked uneasy.

"Are you sure?"

She appeared like she wanted to tell me something, but then just smiled and said, "Sometimes going home isn't easy."

"Why not?"

From what I knew of their family, they all got along great. What could she possibly have to worry about? She was doing *really* well in school. Earlier that week, when we were at coffee, she'd even told me she might start looking for a boyfriend. Which was something I'd never heard her say before. In all of the times we'd ever talked, and when I'd asked her, she'd always said she was too focused on her art and wasn't looking for a relationship. Maybe she was feeling lonely in Seattle, but it also could have been she was a nineteen-year-old wanting to fall in love. Whatever it was, it surely shouldn't make her nervous to go home.

Then, when we'd landed and I powered up my phone, my focus changed.

Casey hadn't called me that morning.

TWENTY-FIVE

Casey

Saturday, April 24, 2010

I T WASN'T UNTIL I was on the plane when I remembered, I hadn't fucking called Blake.

Damn it.

The previous night—hell, the whole day before—was a major clusterfuck. First, with Aly showing up to the meeting, and being her normal number-crunching, buzz-kill self, she brought the energy level down a little too far.

Then later in the afternoon, when I thought I could do damage control, she followed.

Then she drank.

Then she hit on the customer.

Then the customer hit on her and kept pumping her full of shots. It wasn't my place to put an end to it, so all I could do was watch. I wasn't upset that she and the guy were hitting it off. If I'd thought that was what it really was. Clearly, it was something else.

When she did shots, she'd look at me as if trying to make me jealous. Which wasn't happening. She sat on his lap, giving me coy, two-can-play-your-game smiles. She wasn't interested in him at all. So when he tried to go back to her room with her, that's where I had to step in.

He'd been handsy. She'd been handsy. Both of them had too much to drink. But I wasn't about to let some stranger go up to her room, not when she honestly expected me to step in and put an end to it. Which I would do—only not for the reasons she thought. The fact was, he didn't strike me as a gentlemanly type if she changed her mind.

So when I told him she was going to her room alone, he didn't take it very well.

"Who's gonna stop me? You're not 'er dad? She can do what she wants," he slurred.

"Well, I work for *her dad* and I'm telling you, you're not going up."

Then he shoved me.

He was a customer, so I let it go. I told Aly to get her things and that I'd walk her up. When she saw him shove me, and me turn around to ignore it, I saw realization of what her behavior had caused flash in her eyes. She knew it had gone too far.

So much fun. Not.

Thankfully, we walked out of the bar without it escalating further. Well, with the guy—my never to be, new customer—anyway. Things with Aly escalated rather fast. In the elevator, she was all over me. She smelled like a bar rag as she tried to put her arms around my neck. All I could do was continually remove them, *and* tell her to knock it off.

Just as I got her into her room, that's when I got the text from Blake. God, I'd missed her and I was lucky that Blake—through all of our drama—was never that big of a drinker. And when she was drunk, she was sweet and silly. Not sloppy and pathetic.

While I messaged Blake, I listened to Aly vomit. That was actually the highlight of the night. At least, if she threw it all up, I didn't have to worry about her choking on it in her sleep and I could, with good conscience, leave.

Helping her into bed, fully clothed, I told her, "If you ever show up at one of my meetings again, I'll sell my shares and leave Bay Brewing. And if you don't get it through your head that I don't want to be anything more than friends and coworkers with you, I'll leave anyway. I mean it."

"You won't do that," she mumbled, as she rolled over.

I turned off the light next to her bed and assured her, "Just watch me, Aly."

Then I left.

I woke up late, and since Aly was a big girl and not at all my responsibility, I didn't contact her in the morning. After a quick shower, I headed straight for the airport. For the first time in months, I wanted to get home so damn bad. Mostly because Blake was going to be there, too.

I was serious though. If Aly kept pulling shit like she had the day before, she wouldn't have to worry about me only quitting Bay Brewing—a place I fucking loved. She'd have to worry about me being her competition. It was a decision I didn't want to make, and one I would hate telling Marc, but the facts were: I loved my job, but I didn't love his daughter. Whether I did my job with them or against them, I'd be fine. The last thing I needed was another hurdle to jump with Blake.

Her dumbass husband wasn't following through with their arrangements. By him not seeing Dr. Rex, which was his ridiculous idea in the first place, my patience was running thin. Every bone in my body wanted to tell Blake to call it off when she'd asked me if she should. But I just kept thinking, I didn't want her to doubt her decision to leave her marriage. She was doing what she'd said she would, and when the time was up, she wouldn't have to carry that guilt around too. She had a surplus of guilt already.

Thankfully, he never showed up. Not one time so far. He was stalling. He may have dumbly underestimated how patient we were. We'd waited a long time to be together. His feeble attempt at drawing out their divorce was soon going to be for nothing.

I was tense on the flight, but I felt better knowing that by the end of that night we'd be sleeping in the same bed. *My bed.*

I just hoped I didn't have that fucking dream again.

When I finally pulled up to my brother's house, my shitty attitude began to lighten. You'd have to be a cold-hearted prick to show up at a first birthday party with a chip on your shoulder. Besides, today I was going to be with the people I loved most. My family and Blake, at the same time.

No false pretenses.

No hiding.

And I wasn't about to let a shitty work issue put a damper on how long I'd been waiting for that day to happen. Both the real Bay Area fog and the metaphorical kind had lifted, and it was going to be a beautiful day.

Walking up, I followed the trail of blue balloons and the sound of music that led around back. I opened the door on their backyard gate and heard, "There he is," come from Audrey. It was a full-fucking-circle moment as I walked around the side of their brick house. There was my family. My nephew and godson. And the girl I'd dreamed of sharing with my family. They all sat around watching a toddler throw a ball.

Everything else faded away. I ran my hand over my mouth and took a minute to memorize it.

My family always knew there was something out of my control with her. It finally happened. Sometimes they would quietly watch. A few times they told me I should just get over it. But whatever their opinions were at the time, they were always there. Seeing her with them, laughing and talking, undid a lot of pain and hurt we'd been through.

It was different. We had nothing to hide. We could show people our love and not keep it stowed away like we were ashamed of it. It was as if my resolution to stick by Blake was justified. *Validated. Worth the agony and effort.*

I loved her. She loved me. We were an *us*.

She stood up from the picnic table, which was covered in a safari animal plastic thing, and walked straight to me. It was kind of swift and she kind of bounced. Then she kissed me in front of all of them and I *more* than kissed her back. She didn't pull away or try to stop me. As I eased up on her, recovering from the overwhelming moment, she took my hand. I was home.

I don't know if I've *ever* felt that brand of pride.

"I've missed you," she said into my shoulder and kissed my shirt.

I kissed the top of her pretty hair and told her, "I'm sick of missing you."

Then she smiled up at me and said, "We've got this." And again it really felt like we did.

As we sat at the picnic table, where she'd been sitting when I came in, I announced to all watching us, which was everyone, "This is my girlfriend, Blake."

My dad sat back in his folding chair and wrapped an arm around Carmen, smiling. "We've met Blake, but it's nice of you to finally introduce us," he said. I wondered if he could see how much it meant to us.

I wished my mom were there, too. She would have loved seeing how big Foster was getting and how great Cory was at being a dad and husband.

He had his shit together and I really looked up to him for that. Even though he was only twenty minutes older, he'd always been the older brother I needed.

Later Blake and I played on the blanket with the birthday boy, while everyone talked and listened to Troy strum on his guitar.

We watched Foster eat cake like a maniac.

Everything was right.

As the party died down, I wondered if that would be how our lives looked in the future. Then realized, maybe some of what I was waiting for was already there. Out in the open for everyone to see.

While Blake told Foster happy birthday one last time, and helped Micah put him down for a nap, I put her bags in the back of my car with mine. I fucking loved it. When she came out of the nursery, with a finger over her mouth telling me to hush, I quietly asked, "Do you want to get out of here?"

"Yeah," she whispered back.

After we told everyone we were headed out, Micah and Cory

walked us to their front door and told us goodbye. My brother wrapped an arm around his wife's shoulder as they stood at the door watching us go. I could only imagine what they were saying to each other. I liked to think they were cheering and happy for us, but they were probably just calling us dumbasses for how long it had taken us to get where we were.

Dumbasses we had been.

Regardless, we were dumbasses leaving our godson's first birthday *together.* I hoped we left the second, third, and all of his birthdays the same way. Together. In the future, I hoped we'd get one invitation, arrive in the same car, and bring one gift. I looked forward to some weird shit.

The car ride was comfortably quiet until she asked, "Where are we going?" I didn't have any plan or destination. I'd simply been driving, enjoying the warm spring day with the windows down and her beside me.

"I don't know yet. Where *are* we going?" I asked, repeating her question and being ornery. My hand lightly squeezed her bare leg.

She covered my hand with hers and said, "Somewhere you love. Somewhere I've never been."

I knew just the place.

The brewery.

In all of the time we'd known each other, I'd never taken her there. She'd never seen one of the places I was most proud of. Plus, the brewery was just fucking cool.

"I'll buy you a beer."

She looked confused, but smiled. It was early afternoon, and after having cake and ice cream, the look on her face said beer wasn't exactly what she'd wanted.

"Beer? I don't know," she admitted. "I don't feel like going to a bar, Casey."

"We're not going to a bar," I shot back.

She looked at me, eyebrow cocked, and shook her head. "Okay."

She turned on the radio and scanned the stations for something that caught her attention. If you would have told me what song was going to come on, I would have told you to fuck off, but chance is like that.

Sometimes songs pick you.

When I heard the intro's opening drum beats, I immediately knew what song it was she'd stopped on. That damn Led Zeppelin song haunted us.

She looked up and then at me and guffawed. The laugh that bellowed out of her was almost delirious. Her head fell back onto the headrest, and she wrapped her arms around her stomach as she giggled without care of how she sounded or what she looked like. It turned into a coughing fit, finally catching her breath, somewhere around the first chorus.

"Oh my God. This fucking song," she exclaimed, as she looked at me, face red, eyes wet from crying through her laughing fit. "It's never going to leave us alone."

A breeze flowing through the car filled my nose with her scent. Then she began singing at the top of her lungs, laughing and looking carefree and dazzling.

As I went back and forth, looking at the road then back to her, I couldn't wait to get to the brewery to kiss her. Really kiss her.

Then I couldn't wait. I pulled over into the first parking spot I found on a downtown street lined with shops and offices.

Her eyes darted around looking for where it might be that I was taking her, but nothing caught her attention. Perplexed, she looked me.

I turned the key toward myself and killed the engine, turning to face her.

"Hi," I said.

"Hi there," she replied. She looked so much like the first time I'd listened to that song with her. Hair perfectly wavy and untouched after being wet, mischievous and sexy as anything I'd ever laid eyes on. It took my breath away. She was back. I couldn't see guilt or shame in her eyes. She looked like first-night Blake. Come-up-to-my-room Blake and there she was, back with me, after all that time waiting for her.

A moment passed where she realized it too. We were going to be okay.

We unclicked our seat belts at the same time and lunged for each other.

There was no kissing. No flirt in our touch. My arms wrapped around her center, and hers around my neck, and we hugged.

We sat like that, squeezing the hell out of each other forever.

"Would you do it all again?" she asked into my neck, and then giggled like it was a huge joke.

"Do hobby horses have wooden dicks?"

She pulled away and ran her hands across my cheeks and held my face merely inches from hers.

"When are you going to get new material?"

"When it stops working."

Then I kissed her beautiful fucking face off.

I made a mental note to write those old rockers a thank you. That song *was* magic and it worked every damn time.

TWENTY-SIX

Blake

Saturday, April 24, 2010

I HAD TO ADMIT, that song had some sort of power over us. Like an old friend, one you'd fought and forgiven, it was always there when we needed it.

After he kissed me, and he got us back on the road, I studied him.

Watching him drive was such a turn on. He looked both completely focused and totally relaxed. The muscles in his forearm, tight, as he held the wheel. His hair had grown out more. Even I could admit it needed a trim as it blew around in the spring air. He looked sexy, wearing mirrored aviator sunglasses as he drove. I could have gazed at him all day.

"Take the wheel for a second," he requested.

Cautiously, I gripped it from my side.

He glanced at me and asked, "Ready?" Then he leaned up from his seat, which was way too reclined for me to ever drive comfortably, and I found myself steering. He watched me and the road, back and forth, the windshield and then back to me.

Casey lifted his left leg and helped guide the wheel, as it was clear, and instead of watching traffic, I was watching him.

"You got this?" he asked and chuckled.

I shifted my focus from him and watched where we were going, as I smiled to myself.

Had anyone ever loved someone as much as I love him?

My eyes scanned the street and cars around us, then to him quickly going down his buttons, starting at the top of the lavender dress shirt he wore. Lavender isn't a color most men can pull off, but it only stood to contrast his beautiful eyes. It somehow made him all the more masculine for having the bravado to put it on. His long fingers pushed the plastic buttons through their respective holes. And when he was finished with the light work of releasing them, he shook out of the shirt, wadded it up and threw it in the back seat. Leaving him in only a tight, white V-neck T-shirt.

Could he really be mine?

I saw the sign on the massive warehouse as we grew closer.

Bay Brewing was a much larger operation than I'd realized. We drove around to a lot nestled in an alley. The fenced area was closed and locked, so when we approached, Casey had to punch in a code for it to let us in.

The large gates swung in and he drove onto the private parking lot. There were a few delivery trucks, but other than those it was empty. He whipped the car into the spot nearest the door.

"It's a lot bigger than I imagined," I confessed.

"Imagined?" he asked, and then snickered. "You've seen it before. And I'm a little—no, a lot—offended that you can't remember. That said, I'm really happy about how big you think it is." He stretched an arm over my headrest, as he leaned back in the driver's seat to taunt me.

He looked like a classic bad boy. Jeans. New Converse. Fresh white T-shirt. He pulled the glasses up over the front of his hair and left them there.

I wasn't sure what kind of cologne he had on. Hell, it was possible the scent was just his deodorant. But whatever it was, to my body, it was like waving a steak in front of a tiger. I breathed him in, in every way I could. Absorbed him into my mind. My senses. My everything.

The sight of him, sun shining through his hair, the way his chest pulled against the front of his shirt. How his legs were parted. My mouth watered thinking about what was just beyond that denim.

He watched me as I let myself get drunk on him.

"You know what I meant," I accused, but I didn't really correct him. He was, after all, right. I played dumb. "So where are we?"

"This is where the magic happens, honeybee. Remember that." He was still as cocky as the night we'd met, and I loved it.

He showed me around the brewery and told me about how they'd expanded. They were looking at buildings in other cities for logistical reasons, having grown out of the one current facility.

We stopped by what looked like a break room. He opened the refrigerator and brought out two beers. Like he'd done it every day, he found a magnetic bottle opener on the side of the old Maytag and popped the tops off, handing me one.

He lifted his and I followed his lead, like we were toasting.

"To trouble and Led Zeppelin," he said.

"To trouble and bait," I repeated. He kissed me for that.

Then, he proclaimed, "Now, taste the nectar of the gods." Casey was so dramatic.

He showed me around the rest of massive building. When we went upstairs, where the offices were, I saw Aly's name on a door as we walked past.

It reminded me.

"You didn't call me this morning. Was everything okay?"

He shook his head, and swallowed his drink, before apologizing. "I'm sorry, I woke up late."

That didn't help me feel any better. Last I'd known, he was putting

Aly to bed. My face must have shown how I didn't like the thoughts in my head. I knew they weren't true, and that I had nothing to worry about, but I still thought about it.

"I wasn't with her. She was drunk and making a fool out of herself—and, therefore, the company. I didn't stay with her last night."

"I know you didn't."

"You do?" He appeared shocked and relieved at the same time. He stopped walking as we approached the door that read "Casey Moore, V P of Sales." I was impressed.

"How do you know that?" he asked.

"Because I know you. You wouldn't do that to me."

"That's right, I wouldn't."

My stomach cramped thinking about how I'd made him feel in the past. How in the hell did he not give up on me?

"I'm sorry I've done that to you. I'm sorry you've had to fall asleep knowing I was next to someone else." That guilt might always live inside me. The excuse of, "He knew what he was getting into" never really took away the sting of it. I'd done that to him. I hated it. "That will never, *ever* be the case again. I hope, someday, you'll be able to trust me like I trust you."

His brow furrowed. He'd never liked it when I talked like that, but sometimes things needed to be said. Something I'd learned in therapy. It didn't undo what I'd done, but it relieved something inside me to own up to it. Shitty as it was.

"And I know Aly loves you. She told me she does. But I hope she knows I'll fight for you—if it comes to it."

"It won't," he stated definitively, jaw tight and eyes set on mine. "She knows I only want you. I'll only *ever* want you."

We were bound to have those moments, but they were getting easier. Tossing out old habits of building walls between us and hiding what we felt, were becoming things of the past. Our new way of communication—even if it wasn't easy—was proving much more rewarding.

Deciding that was all that needed to be said on the topic, I stated, "Well, show me this office then, Mr. President."

"*Vice* President," he corrected with a chuckle. "I like it better when you call me Lord Casey." Lord Casey was a product of my living arrangements after he bought the building. Landlord didn't suit him, so we improvised.

His office wasn't massive, but it was more than big enough for one person. Especially, since he was rarely there.

He had pictures and awards framed, which sat on a built-in, dark wooden bookcase. Empty bottles lined the top shelf. I raised a questioning eyebrow to Casey behind me, asking silently what they meant.

"Those are all of the brews we've offered here since the day I started," he explained. He was sitting on the edge of his almost bare desk. Legs and arms crossed, as he watched me investigate, he held his beer bottle to his side with just one finger wrapped around its neck.

I smiled at the sentiment. I wondered if he saved them the entire time, or if it was an afterthought. Knowing him, he'd kept the first bottle he'd ever drunk. It's funny how, and when, things become sentimental. Sentimental like our two ships that sat on the other end of his desk. He had them facing each other and it warmed my heart.

"Are they in order?" I asked, looking up at them.

"Yeah, I think so. Some have gone out and then come back, but for the most part they're in order from when I started."

"Which is your favorite?"

He chortled. "The one I'm drinking."

Smart ass.

"I'm serious."

"I'm serious, too." He finished the last of his beer and set the bottle in the trash can next to his desk. I peered back up at the bottles to see if it was up there for examining.

He moved behind me and wrapped his arms around my waist. He kissed my head and said into my hair, "It's my favorite for two reasons. One, it's the first I've had with you here. And two, hopefully, it's the one I finished drinking the first time I had sex with you in my office."

My breath caught. He'd always had a way of catching me off guard. My head rolled on its own accord and my eyes slowly closed.

"What if someone shows up?"

His hands worked my shoulders. With a firm grip, he sought out each muscle and gave it personal attention before moving to the next. He moved my hair over one shoulder so it wasn't in his way.

"No one will," he cajoled, his low tenor voice tightening my insides. "Sometimes, I'm here on Sunday evenings. I've never seen anyone. Besides, I don't care if they do. I have a lock on my door."

Well, didn't he have an answer for everything?

His hands moved to my upper arms and squeezed, pulling me nearer to his chest. Then I felt his mouth on my skin. His tongue danced over the nape of my neck. One of his hands found my hair and wrapped it around his hand, pulling my head to the side as he passionately kissed my neck.

I moaned. *Loudly.*

It was an embarrassing sound. He was no stranger to my embarrassments.

Casey pressed into my back. He was hard and I wanted all of him. My hands found his thighs, pulling his even closer. Would there ever be a time when he didn't control my body at this range?

He was the master and I his puppet. *Willingly.*

TWENTY-SEVEN

Casey

Saturday, April 24, 2010

HE-MAN DIDN'T HAVE SHIT on me. I was back to being the Master of the Fucking Universe. My thoughts and desires led her body. What I wanted, it did. Without being told.

I turned her around in my arms.

Where was I to begin?

Her mouth.

Her neck.

My lips were hungry for her and my greedy hands filled with her breasts, my lungs with her scent.

She rocked into my hip. She wanted me just as bad.

"Not yet, honeybee. Sometimes it feels like touching you only happens on leap years. I have lots of time to make up for." A coaxing leg hitched up my waist. She moaned, a desperate sound, when I picked her up carried her to the top of my desk.

"What's my name?" I crooned in her ear.

"Casey Moore."

"Good. Now, where are we?"

She panted against my shoulder. "Where the magic happens." *She remembered.*

"What day is it, honeybee?"

"April twenty-fourth."

"What did we just do?"

"Tasted the nectar of the gods." The vixen mocked me, but I wasn't fooled. I knew this Blake. She loved my games. Loved to be teased right out of her sanity. And Christ I'd missed her.

"And what do I want to do right now?"

"You want to kiss me," she said. Our language of asking for kisses welcomed me home, as she tried to press her lips to mine, but I was faster and she wasn't getting off that easy.

"Close. What do I want?" I repeated in her ear.

She moaned and rocked into my hand, which was under her skirt and between her legs. A place it always seemed to go on its own.

"You want to fuck me in your office?"

"That sounds like a question," I chastised, then spread her legs wider with the weight of my hips. I stilled my hand. She leaned into it, displaying her frustration with my pause.

"It's not, Casey. You do. You want me."

"If you only knew how much."

I moved the hair away from her neck and her body shivered as my fingers ran scribbled lines over her humming skin. All of the negative space within my body filled with Blake-scented air and my dick begged for its freedom, but patiently waited. I had the Nelson Mandela of dicks.

"I'm right here. I'm all yours."

My knees released. Thank goodness I was leaning against the desk or I would have folded like a piece-of-shit lawn chair.

"Good, now let's see how long it takes you to forget all that other shit."

Her mouth opened to mine on contact, and our teeth bumped with our haste. Both of our efforts aggressive, her need kissed mine with a lick and a sigh.

Reality and joy kicked me in the balls. She *was* mine.

It's hard to kiss when you're trying to hold your shit together, between not wanting to laugh from the joy I felt and wanting to swallow her whole, I picked her up under her ass. Her bare legs bent like pretzels around me and I sat on the desk, switching her places.

I fucking loved it when she wore skirts.

My hand slid over her bare ass.

I fucking loved when she wore those kinds of underwear. She wasted no time undoing the button and unzipping my jeans. I lifted to let her pull them down just enough so my cock could spring free. All the while, her mouth never left mine.

With my dick in one hand, she moved her panties aside and lowered herself onto me. And she rode me with long slow strides, as our kissing turned urgent.

I wanted deeper.

It wasn't enough.

"I need more, Casey," she begged. "I need you to fuck me." We agreed.

I picked her up again and began walking us to the other side of the room. She continued grinding on me as I walked. She fit perfectly in my hands and a carnal need inside me flashed thoughts of smacking her beautiful ass until my handprint stamped her peach of a backside.

Something about her body made mine a king.

Long live the queen.

I sat her down on the couch, and pulled out and away. Lust stained her cheeks and her nose was gloriously pink. I turned her around and lifted her hands above her head. Then I pulled her sweater and shirt off together. She shimmied when I tugged them over her shoulders, inside out. I ran my hand between her shoulder blades. I couldn't help myself, and kissed her back as I unclasped her bra. I slid the straps down and she lifted her arms allowing me to pull it away from her. She relaxed on her knees and bent forward to the back of the couch.

My hands ran up the long ridge of her spine and I pushed my pants the rest of the way down. They bunched together at the top of my feet and shoes.

I licked my fingers and slid them under the strap of fabric between her legs. Then like a savage who knew it wasn't a time play with his food, I put my fingers back into my mouth and wrapped a fist around my dick as I guided past her panties and straight into her.

I pushed in deep. She fell forward, and with a side-to-side rock of her hips, her body said, "Go."

She moved with me, my every action mirrored with hers. When I pushed inside, she pushed back. Full long strokes.

Blake. Air.

Blake. Air.

Once again, she yielded to me. It was intoxicating.

I bent toward her and reached around to her breast, gaining leverage and a new angle. I held tight and held myself inside her as she ground down on my dick, rocking into me, finding her own pleasure with me as the vehicle.

My arm reached for the back of the couch and her hand found mine. She laced them together. It was like I was wrapped around her and it was decidedly my new favorite way to spend April twenty-fourth.

Her head pressed against my chest and I bit her ear.

"Casey," she whimpered, "yes."

I replied with gibberish sounds that translated to, "I found your superpower and it's this right here."

I pressed my cheek against the top of her head and my eyes squeezed shut as I felt my orgasm run full speed toward the end of my cock.

She tightened down around me and said, "I'm coming. Don't stop. Please, don't stop."

There was no stopping.

Even if I could stop, why in the fuck would I want to?

Between the white noise in my ears and the sound of her saying my name, over and over, I left myself inside of her. I panted, fighting to catch my breath. After we were both finished, she buckled, falling flat onto the sofa. I rested against her back.

When everything tamed down and the air around us began to cool, I rolled to the side and pulled my pants up. She curled into the now warm leather and looked at me.

"Are you satisfied?"

"Satisfied, honeybee?" I asked her in turn. "I won't be satisfied until your head sleeps on my pillow every night. Until we're fighting over stupid shit like taking out the trash or sorting the laundry properly—like normal people. I won't be satisfied until we're having quickies while the coffee brews and we can't agree on what movie to watch. When all of our problems can be solved with a kiss and a good night's sleep. That's when I'll be satisfied.

She smiled and kissed my cheek.

Then I added, "Or were you just talking about sex?"

"I was just talking about sex." She laughed under her breath and said, "I'm hungry." Sex did that to her every time. My girl was ravenous, in more ways than one, when it came to good sex.

"What do you want?"

"Nine cheeseburgers."

"That's all?"

"I'm watching my weight."

It was almost dark when we finally pulled into my driveway after grabbing a bite to eat. I hadn't been home in over a week, so I sidled up to the mail box first. I pulled out the contents, handing them to her. Again, it hit me how these mundane tasks we were doing together made me feel like I was dreaming.

Then I thought of the dream I'd had so many nights—or nightmare if I considered the end of it—and it killed my moment.

I was sick of thinking about it. I wouldn't let some figment of my imagination ruin her being in my home. It was only a dream. It wasn't real.

I opened the garage and pulled into my spot. I glanced over at the empty one, where I had half-started projects. Then I wondered if one day, she'd be parked next to me.

I'd live wherever she wanted, but I loved this home and knew I'd always keep it.

"When was the last time you were here?"

"A little over a week, I think. And it was only for a night." I quickly tried to remember if I'd left the place in good condition. Had I cleaned everything up? I prayed there wasn't anything disgusting growing inside. "Before we go in, I don't think I knew I wasn't going to be here before you came over. So, just know that. Okay?"

She needed to be warned.

"Got it," she confirmed, as she opened her car door gently to make sure it didn't bump into my bike. "Do you still get to ride much?"

As I walked around to the back of the car to get our bags, I thought back on when had been the last time I'd taken a ride.

"I haven't ridden since New Year's Day." My last time was with Troy.

"That's a long time. How often did you ride before you were working so much?" she asked, as she picked up one of her bags and one of mine.

"Here, let me get those," I admonished, reaching to take them, but she refused.

"I've got them. You get the door and the lights."

I opened the door for her that led into the laundry room. "What did you ask me?" I asked, quickly scanning for dirty underwear and socks.

It was clean.

Actually, it was really clean. Someone had been there. There were folded towels on the drier. I didn't do that.

"How much did you ride before you started traveling so much?" she repeated.

"Not every day, but probably three or four times a week. You can put those down there."

I was curious. Who had been there?

I walked into the kitchen and turned on the light. There were fresh flowers and fruit on the counter. The place was spotless.

"What's wrong? Oh, those are pretty," said Blake from behind me.

"Someone cleaned my house." I laughed as I picked up the folded paper on the kitchen counter.

Casey,

I came by the other day to check on things and saw that this place was a mess. I cleaned it for you. You can repay me by making a charitable donation to the homeless shelter where I should have been volunteering, instead of picking up after my gross older brother.

I knew Blake was coming, so I thought I would help out. Women like a man with a clean house. You're welcome. Have a good time. I love you.

Morgan

I passed the note to Blake for her to read and she cackled.

"I think I like her," she admitted. It didn't get past me they'd talked some at the party, and for Morgan, my straight-laced baby sister, that was a big step. "I wish I had a sister who cleaned *my* apartment," she teased. "My brothers never clean-up for me."

"You're funny," I retorted.

We looked at each other over the island; it was kind of like the moment of truth.

"Does it feel strange having me here?" she asked, looking at the flowers and waiting for me to answer.

Having her there after my mom died, and then having her leave again, was tough after I was forced to be there alone—without either of them. I remember her telling me she couldn't come back until she was really mine, because it wasn't fair to me.

However, there she was, in my kitchen, after only six months, and having her there felt so fucking good. There were no stipulations. There was no dread of her running off. It felt right. Complete. Like home again.

Then again, it had to be weird for her, too. Knowing the one time I'd been with another woman—at least, since we'd met—was there. We didn't talk about it much. Really, not at all. She didn't bring it up, and I never wanted to either. It wasn't something I was proud of.

I answered, "I thought it would, but it doesn't." She smiled hopefully. "How about you?"

She walked around and looked outside through the big window that hosted a view of the garden, the sun almost completely gone to bed. I went to her and put her hand in mine.

She faced me. That was another thing she was becoming so good at. Facing me. Eyes on mine, and talking. It was rewarding. She was showing me more of the real her. It felt like a gift.

"I thought it would remind me of all the things I did. But really, it just reminds me of all the things I'm working *for.* Working toward. And now, all of that other stuff seems so far away and everything keeps getting better. I don't want to ruin it with thoughts of then. I want to make new memories. Here. With you."

What she said rang true and she was right. We had to start kicking out all of the old bad memories if we ever had a chance at replacing them. She looked peaceful and maybe a little tired. It had been a really long day.

Then she said, "If you want to talk about the past and our mistakes, we can. But talking about our scars over and over won't heal them, Casey. The only thing we can do is be more careful and give them time."

I more than fucking loved her at that moment. There were times when she'd said the wrong things, done the wrong things, but she'd changed so much over the past few months. We had changed. And she was right.

It was time for us to start letting shit go.

"I think you're smart."

My heart stopped a little when she beamed up at me, shining in my compliment.

"And . . ." The ornery little shit was fishing and lightening up the mood. I was thankful.

"And beautiful." I placed a quick kiss on her lips. "And sweet." I gave her another. "And a good cook."

"The best cook," she corrected.

"Yes. And you look good naked."

"Keep going."

"And you can eat your weight in cheeseburgers after office sex."

"And . . ." She was waiting for me to say something, but I wasn't sure. I shook my head. "I can't think of anything else. That's pretty much it."

She lifted up on her toes and pressed her sweet lips to mine.

"And I'm all yours."

I'm glad I didn't guess that, because I'd never tire of hearing *her* say it.

She was right about all of it too. But, that had to be the very best part.

Her. All. Mine.

TWENTY-EIGHT

Blake

Sunday, April 25, 2010

HEARING HIM TELL ME he loved me, as he claimed me in the very most intimate way a man can claim a woman, would never get old. We made love slowly and quietly, a contrast to our earlier passionate frenzy during my tour of the brewery. But taking our time didn't make it any less intense, or the words that we whispered to each other any less meaningful.

I peered up at him; he was perfect. He blinked lazily, lust and tenderness in his eyes, as he looked between us where we were joined. He held his weight above me and his chest expanded and contracted with each breath as they became labored, both of us getting closer to our climax.

"I've loved you for so long."

"I love you, too, Casey," I breathed, but I felt my words more than I heard them.

"Don't leave me," he said, and though he didn't mean to hurt me, knowing that he felt he had to ask, burned. He was so vulnerable, different from his office.

"I won't leave you," I promised. "I'll never leave you." No sooner were the words out of my mouth, he was off me. His face was pale and he was looking around the room. I wasn't sure what was happening.

"Casey, what's wrong?" I asked. My body feeling bereft with him having so abruptly disconnected.

There was a cold sweat on this face and I clambered down the bed to him. He was breathing much harder now, and his eyes were hazy as he looked off into the dark side of the room.

"Hey, talk to me," I said softly, not understanding. I moved his cheek gently, so we were eye to eye. He'd never acted like that before, and he wasn't saying anything. He finally moved back, closer to me, and ran his hands over his face. We sat in his bed in the dark, with only the twilight to see.

"So I have this dream sometimes," he began, and then stopped. He shook his head and took a large breath. I gave him time. Finally, he started again. "In the dream we're here. Together, like we just were. I have it all the time."

I smiled. I'd had dreams of him like that, too. What didn't make sense was why he would stop like he did. Like he was panicked.

"I love when I dream about you," I confessed.

He pulled me to his lap and I sat facing him. He brushed the hair out of my face and continued, "Well, in this dream, we say those exact same words we were just saying."

"I still mean them."

"Thank you," he said thoughtfully. "But, in the dream, you say Grant's name and he's here. Everyone's here. He tells you to hurry up, so he can take you home." His face was solemn; the dream had really messed with him. Immediately, my heart reached out to his.

I smoothed my hands over his tattoo and I kissed him. His chest. His neck. His shoulders. Before I said anything, I needed to love him. I wanted him to feel how much I cared, not just hear it.

"No. It's only a dream."

"It's not *only* a dream, Blake. I know that you love me. I do, but God, what would I do . . ."

Was that still something he worried about? Even if it was only in his dreams, the notion of him being terrorized, by me and Grant, ached.

"You don't have to worry about that anymore. I'm tired of waiting for it to be over with him. I'm in love with you. Not just for right now, Casey. Forever. Do you think that's what it is, that we're constantly waiting and dealing with him?" It seemed like a good reason. Grant wasn't in my life day-to-day, but he was still so present in everything.

"I don't know."

"I want to have him served with the divorce papers. Then he'll have to sign them." I kissed his neck again. "I want us to be together. I want to be where you are."

"Where is that?" It was dark, but my eyes had adjusted to the dim light. His handsome face was etched with apprehension. So many things were still up in the air.

"You know how you told me we're like the fish and the hook?" I asked, but I knew he'd remember.

"Yeah."

"Well, I've been thinking about it. And I think maybe we're those and maybe we're something else, too." He held me tighter and his thumbs drew lazy circles on my back as we talked.

"You're telling me there might be a flaw in the pickup line I was trying to feed you two years ago?" My heart finally started beating again when I saw a small grin break the tension in his face.

"Maybe." Although, what he fed me might have just been a pick-up line, but there was more truth in that little line about bait than in anything else in my life. We did have some crazy force that pulled us together. That was unmistakably true. I added, "But maybe we're like the wind and a sail, too."

"Our boats. Did you see them in my office?"

"I did. Stop interrupting me. I'm onto something here," I teased. "When I bought those ships, I was thinking about that old saying. The one how two ships pass in the night. But that wasn't right. I think we're more like the wind and a sail."

He looked skeptical, but said, "Go on."

"You're like the wind, and I'm like the sail. When I go against you, it's rough, almost impossible to find my path. But when my mind finally submitted to my heart, everything was easier. And the best part was, I got you."

"Listen to you," he doted.

"I was just a sail flapping in the breeze until I met you." What I'd began saying, as just something to lighten the mood, started to hit home. It was exactly how I felt. "You fill me up with so much happiness and you move me forward. Now, I go where you go. Because that's where I belong."

He leaned forward and kissed me with such force, we toppled backward onto the bed where we'd been before. Before our words had reminded him of his messed-up dream. Almost like nothing happened, almost like the whole episode was something I'd imagined, we fit back together.

And that time, when I told him I loved him and I'd never *really* leave him ever again, he said he knew. As we finally reached the high that only our bodies gave each other, I knew he was my only future and our pasts didn't matter anymore.

"Do you think we need anything else?" I asked.

He pushed the shopping cart, one foot on the ground and one foot pushing him forward—like the big kid he was—at the garden store we'd stopped at after breakfast. After an inspection of his mother's garden, we both decided it needed some help. And by help, I mean the whole thing needed replanting. He agreed.

"Gloves?" he suggested. "We don't need you getting any blisters. I have plans for those hands later on." Then he winked and I swooned, as was customary.

"Yeah, we better get gloves."

We paid for our supplies and drove back to his house.

Since there wasn't anything needing tended to inside, after his sister's way-more-thorough-than-even-my-cleaning job, we got to spend the day playing outside. We strolled down to the red shed and retrieved a few of the bigger tools we'd need. I smiled remembering what was painted on the back of the building.

"Do you think you'll ever paint over my handy art work on the other side of the shed?" I asked, carrying the hoe and rakes he handed me back up to the house. He pushed the small tiller, which looked like it had never been used.

"Nah. It's part of the shed now."

It was beautiful outside and Casey wore long cut off shorts and a loose black and white striped tank top. With his red bandanna, I'd teased him about looking like a pirate pretty much the whole day.

I laughed to myself. "Rrrr," I replied.

"Oh my god. Would you shut up? I'm gonna go change," he said, getting tired of my shit. But the smile on his face told me he liked my shit. A lot.

"What are you going to do? Make me walk the plank?"

He stopped dead, in his sexy, pirate tracks.

I was in trouble.

"Come here," he cried. Letting go of the tiller, he stalked toward me.

"No," I said, dropping the tools and busting ass to get away. "Don't. I was just kidding!" I shouted in my own defense. "Don't touch me you loose-livered sea monkey!" I was really on a roll.

He gained on me. "You think you're really funny," he accused.

Then I was in the air, tucked under his arm like a football. He spun us around and I was the one getting sea sick from the sudden motion.

"Whoa. I'm gonna puke. Put me down," I begged. "No more spinning. I'll stop."

"No more pirate jokes?"

"No more-Rrrr," I said, knowing there'd be a repercussion, but I couldn't help myself. "That was the last one. I swear-Rrrr." All right, I had a problem. I couldn't stop.

He dropped me. I rolled over on my back in the grass, out of breath. Still laughing. And still very dizzy. He stood high above me with his hands on his hips.

"I didn't know you were so sensitive about your fashion choices."

"Just keep it up, honeybee."

"Gonna spank me?"

His eyes lit up with delight, taking my comment out of context. Well, maybe not completely. It was still a spanking, just a different kind.

Instantly, my blood ran hot thinking about the times he'd done it. I was nowhere near being into whips and chains, but in the heat of the moment, when he'd swatted my ass—it had been so damn hot. I couldn't even lie to myself about it. I'd loved every second of him that way.

The idea excited him, too. He had an I'm-gonna-pink-your-ass-later look written all over his face. I loved finding new buttons to push with him. Every day was something new.

We worked on the garden for many hours. But to my disappointment, it wasn't ready for all of the veggies, fruit, and flowers we'd bought to replace the ones that didn't survive the winter and neglect.

"We got a lot done though," he told me as we cleaned up our mess and put the tools away.

"I know. I just thought we'd finish."

"Do you have to leave tomorrow?"

I did.

I wasn't even flying home. I was headed straight to Cleveland for the soft opening of one of my latest clients. "Yeah, I have to go."

He kissed me on the forehead, as he often did, and said, "Well, then let's wash up and find something to eat. I'm starving and you need some dick."

How poetic. It wasn't Shakespeare or Keats, but it did the trick.

Tuesday, April 27, 2010

The opening went great. The staff was amazing and the restaurant worked like a well-oiled machine. The chefs were comfortable and happy with the new menus, and dinner service was one of the smoothest I'd been witness to for a complete renovation.

Since it was apparent they didn't need me, after all, I called and had my flight for Tuesday moved up to an earlier time. On my way to the airport that morning, I called Dr. Rex expecting to get her voicemail. But when she answered, telling me she was between classes, it was even better.

"So how was the weekend? How'd the party go?" she asked. I'd confided so much in her recently. She felt more like a friend than my doctor. However, she always found a way to bring me back around to the answers I'd had about myself, my relationships, and what I really wanted. I owed her a lot for making me so much stronger over the past few months. Or, rather, showing me how strong I was.

She didn't like when we had to do it, but as work had become busier, we'd adapted by talking on the phone if I was out of town on a night when we'd usually meet. After I filled her in briefly about the weekend, and stated there was more I wanted to talk about, I was happy to tell her I'd be back in town—if she wanted to keep our session for that night.

"Of course. What time will you get in?"

"I can be there about seven. Will that work?"

"Sure," she said. I told her I'd see her later when my cab pulled into the airport.

All of my flights were on time, and I was back in Seattle with enough time to swing by my place, drop my things off and get my car. I pulled into the university at seven sharp.

What I hadn't expected to see was Grant's truck parked in my dad's spot. I kept driving and pulled around the building. I'd forgotten to email him to cancel when I thought I'd be out of town. It was luck I'd been able to leave early.

I was nervous. My hands shook as I gripped the steering wheel.

We hadn't spoken verbally since the day he was in my house. Other than that, it was only emails to keep him informed of when I was seeing Dr. Rex. Usually, he'd either email back he was busy or just not show up. Since I decided to move forward with having him served the divorce papers officially, I hadn't planned on seeing him until our court date.

I didn't know what to do.

Me: I got that earlier flight so I could see Dr. Rex. Grant's parked outside her building.

My phone rang.

"Hi," I said.

"Hi. Are you going in?" Casey wasn't alarmed, but he certainly sounded concerned. "If you don't want to, just call her and tell her. You don't have to go in. I think it's funny he chose today to finally show up. I didn't think he ever would." Casey was more mature than I ever gave him credit for. Through everything, he'd only acted with my best interests in mind. He never complained, putting my feelings first.

"Me, either. I don't know. Maybe I can ask him to sign them while he's here." I'd given him a copy, but I had a spare in my briefcase, which was with me in the car. "What do you think?"

"I think, if you want to do that, wait until you're both inside. Don't do it in the parking lot." He spoke calmly, but I could hear what he wasn't saying. He was concerned.

But he had a good point; I didn't want Grant getting irate. And as volatile as his personality had been over the whole thing, Casey's idea was smart.

"I think that's what I'll do. I'm gonna let you go and pull back around front."

"Please call me when you're home?"

"Okay. I will."

"Are you scared?" he asked. That was a good question. I'd never feared Grant before, and it wasn't as if I feared him physically, I just didn't want any more drama. I was tired of it dragging out for so long. Hopefully, tonight would be another stepping stone to the future I wanted with Casey and I'd do whatever it was I had to do to get there.

"No. I'm not scared. I'm a little anxious, but I'm okay," I reassured.

"Okay. Remember. We've got this."

"We've got this." It was becoming a bit of a creed between us.

"Okay, bye."

"Call me later. Bye," he said as I hung up.

Slipping my phone into my purse, I reached behind my seat to my briefcase. I found the papers quickly, put them in the passenger seat, and drove around to the other side of the building.

When I pulled in, Grant was standing outside of his truck leaning against it.

"I thought that was you," he said as I got out.

"Yeah, my phone rang so I took a call really quick."

He looked fine, calm. I felt some of my apprehension leave from those few words we'd spoken.

"I'm surprised you came," I said and headed toward the door. He followed.

I needed to be polite, but I didn't want him thinking the appointment was something it most certainly was not.

"Sorry about that. I've been busy," he said and held the door open for me as I passed through.

"That's good. I've been busy too."

Since he didn't know where we were going, I moved us in the direction of Dr. Rex's office. He figured it out when the door opened. But he stopped, and said, "Wait."

I halted and my head rolled to the side as I looked at him.

"What, Grant?"

He fidgeted, looking more like the Grant I was becoming used to.

"I'm glad you want to try to work this out, Blake. I've really missed you."

Was he kidding? *Work it out?* We hadn't spoken in months.

"Grant, there isn't anything to work out. I only kept inviting you because Casey said I needed to keep the arrangement I'd made with you." Then I thought better of what I'd said, having been so used to just telling the truth, it was hard to filter myself. Even with Grant.

"You're still with him?" he asked. Where did he get off?

"Yes, I'm still with him. I love him, Grant."

"You know he bought your apartment building and changed all the locks, right?"

"So?" I replied hastily. What I really wanted to say was, "Yeah, so you wouldn't just walk in whenever you pleased." But I didn't. That time, I watched my mouth.

"So . . . it doesn't even bother you that he'd try to control you like that?"

There was no controlling the raw laugh that propelled from me.

"First of all," I stated, "thanks for being so concerned that you didn't bother to mention it for months. And second, Casey wasn't trying to control me. He was *helping* me."

"Is that what he's telling you, Blake?" Grant was becoming agitated. But hell, so was I.

"Hello," Dr. Rex interjected from her doorway. "Grant?" She

questioned with her eyes, and I gave her a nod. "Blake, do you want to come in?" I did want to go in, but I didn't see any point in him coming in at all.

"I do," I answered her. Then I looked at Grant and said, "But I think you should leave." I wasn't sure where it came from, but I said it. It was what I wanted.

The look he gave me was priceless. It said, "I just got here."

So I put on a look that said, "I don't give a fuck," and walked my ass into Dr. Rex's office and shut the door.

There comes a time when a woman has to be a bitch. And in all the years past, when I should have just been the bitch and got shit over with, I'd tried to be nice. I'd tried to do what I thought was expected of me. But that wasn't who I was anymore. And the new Blake, as it turns out, is sometimes a real bitch.

TWENTY-NINE

Casey

Thursday, June 3, 2010

WORK WAS A BITCH. A busy, slave-driving bitch. We both stayed really fucking busy through May. But we met in Atlanta, and she let me pretend we got a do over—at the club. That time, I didn't leave her alone in the closet.

After we reenacted the sex we'd had in the closet that one hot night—on her recommendation—she giggled and asked where her fifty bucks was. To tell you the truth, I didn't think doing it again in there could top the first time, but was I ever wrong.

It was a wonder how Blake started looking at our old mistakes. She so easily decided we could either laugh or cry about them. And since we now made the rules, she chose laughing.

She'd just met with her lawyer the week before, having been gone so much, and now they were moving forward with having Grant served. He had to sign the papers and he was supposed to get them on Monday.

The phone rang. I smiled. It never got old. *My honeybee.*

After thinking back to where we were at the same time the year before—when days turned to weeks, and then to nothing—it was really fucking cool that I'd just got off the phone with her and there she was. Calling again.

I still felt the same electricity and luck as when my phone lit up inside of Hook, Line and Sinker that first night. I'd never forget.

Honeybee: Rm 315

Then after a few long weeks—that looking back weren't really that long at all—we would text all day and chat whenever the mood struck us—which tended to be a fucking lot. In those first few months after we'd met, I'd send her texts about anything. She must have thought I was crazy. I'd send her any useless bit of fucking knowledge I could find, just to have something to say. All along I should have been telling her I missed her. And how I wanted to know what all of her yearbook pictures looked like and what she did on Thanksgiving. I'd wanted to discover everything I could about her.

I still did.

But I didn't think to do that. I'd played the game as much as she had. I wasn't honest with her either.

Somewhere between my phone ringing one and three times, I realized I didn't even know when her birthday was.

What kind of guy, who claimed they loved someone, didn't know something as trivial as that? And I was trying to convince her how much I really loved her, when I'd never thought to learn everything I could?

I didn't want to be another Grant to her. I never wanted to take Blake for granted.

No wonder she never believed I was serious in the past. And what an incredible amount of faith on her part, to trust I was worth all the chaos now. I hadn't known how to be the man she deserved me to be, but it was starting to come together for me. And by buying the Seattle building, on my own, after thinking about it and talking to Marc about what had gone down again with Aly, I knew it was the right move to have a franchise that was all me.

I loved being so close to her and having her finally calling my phone—more than just once in a day. It felt like everything was going to be fucking okay—for real this time. I kept feeling that, little by little, we actually were getting there.

I answered the call. "You know if you're not careful, you'll be dangerously close to being called my stalker. And when is your birthday?"

"April 24th, two days before Foster's. And stalker?"

Two days before Foster's birthday? I'd had no idea.

We were together on April 24th. The day of his party *was* her birthday. She never mentioned it. Fuck. Again, I'd disconnected myself from her real life, when I was trying to make a whole new life for us. I wasn't seeing the goddamned forest for the trees.

"I'm sorry I missed your birthday."

"You didn't. Not this year." She laughed when she said it, like I was absurd for feeling bad.

"I didn't know it was your birthday. I didn't get to tell you."

"I saw you on my birthday. *You* were my wish. The only present I wanted."

What a sweet fucking human. Another side effect of never telling her things, and the worst side effect if I were being honest, was that she never felt like she could tell me either, like those parts didn't matter, because I was too stupid to ask. I had to be better for her too. For us. Shit, for everyone.

"I should have known your birthday."

"It just never came up since I've been your official girlfriend, and you've been my official . . . landlord. And why would I tell you back then, when we were just . . ." She paused there. I could hear her tapping the side of the phone and the thumping ticked a steady beat as she looked for the right word.

"Together," I offered.

"Were we? Were we ever together then?"

She made a good point. It was a lonely fucking affair, but that word didn't seem to taste right.

"Involved?"

She laughed. "That sounds like something my mom would say about a Lifetime movie. *They were involved, Blake,*" she said in what I guessed was a mocking impression of her mother's recount of said movie.

"I don't know. I've still never even picked you up and taken you out on a date or anything, so it isn't like I've been the best . . . landlord." I didn't even buy her a fucking birthday card. I was the worst, but I'd get better.

"You've taken me on dates, Casey," she argued. "Plenty of times. Roller skating. You took me to Costa Rica for goodness sake. And way before that. Maybe they weren't dates for you, but they were for me. You picked me up at Reggie's," she paused in thought, "I think of that night as our first date."

"You do? That wasn't a very good date." I had to admit, I loved the memory of that night, but it was *no* first date. Not one I should have given her. Yet another time I reinforced the idea of how casual my feelings were. I took her to my fucking hotel room for fuck's sake. Then expected her to leave me for a guy who bought her a house? I'd been out of my damn mind.

How in the hell was she still even talking to me? How was I worth the effort?

Yes, I loved her and since things had changed over the holidays I'd been better, but calling her my girlfriend and treating her like one were two completely different things. I didn't want to mess this up.

"And all of those times you waited for me down in the lobby. It was like being picked up for a date. Those count, Casey. Even if we didn't treat them like they did. They counted." It relieved me hearing her re-tell it like that—jaded and skewed as I thought it was. She was sentimental. More than she ever knew.

"Were you this smart the whole time?"

I laughed at her laughing and sat down in my office chair. She didn't sound too bent out of shape about the fit I was having. She just let me have it.

"Come see me," she said, and the hint of a whine in her voice was so damn cute. She missed me.

"When?" I wanted to go to her that very second. And if my body was capable of teleporting it would have done it automatically on her command.

"My mom and dad's anniversary party."

"Are you serious?" We'd talked about me meeting her family, it just never seemed like it was ever going to happen. Something so small. So insignificant to everyone else on the planet. But after hearing about them for the past two years, I felt like I already knew them. And I remembered how I felt being open with our relationship in front of my clan. I wanted to give that to her.

"Of course I am. It's time and I want you to meet them," she said proudly and my dick got hard. Yeah. It wasn't the right moment, but fuck if it was the totally right fucking moment, too.

"It's about *damn* time." I thought how long we'd known each other.

Last week was two years ago since we'd met. Since Hook, Line and Sinker. Since the first night, I was sucked into the crazy world, where Blake meant everything.

One year since her wedding and I thought all hope for a future with her was lost. It was only fitting I was meeting her parents around the same date.

"Yeah, that's what my dad said, too."

"I think he and I will get along great if we really finally get to meet." I knew she hadn't been hiding me or anything. We'd both been working, and she'd been coming to San Francisco instead of home, nearly every other weekend.

"Then come with me to their party. It's Saturday. Thirty years married." Did she really think she had to convince me? To be with her? Still?

Foster's birthday aside, we didn't have a great track record with big events. Births. Weddings. Most of our major turning points occurred during those. I loved that she was inviting me, but let's face it, Blake and I had a fading tendency to pack drama on every trip—and paid more to check the extra baggage.

I didn't want their first impression of me to be a man who'd show up at their event, knowing they couldn't really react to me being there like they would if we were meeting privately.

Okay, maybe I was expecting the worst, even though she'd told me lots of times they'd love me. If she felt it was a good time to cross that milestone, I wouldn't miss it for the world. I just needed to improvise a little—just to be safe.

"No, Blake. Not like that. I don't want to pull a fast one on them. It's not right. I don't want them to be polite because someone might overhear what they're saying. I want them comfortable enough to let us—me—have it if they want. I want to meet *them*. I want them to meet *me*." I deserved a bit of scrutiny.

She didn't hesitate. No sooner were my words out of my mouth, before she added, "Then come early. Come tomorrow. Reggie will be here tomorrow night. And we'll all have dinner. Oh my God." She didn't say anything for a few seconds. I think it was starting to sink in for her, too. "This is really happening. Isn't it?"

"I think so, honeybee."

Her joyful excitement then changed to something sounding much more somber.

Was she crying? She was. And having heard how excited she was only seconds before, I knew they were happy tears. Tears of relief. Tears for our newest, small victory.

She sniffled, then I heard her blow her nose. It wasn't hot at all, but I didn't have her on speakerphone and my hard-as-hell dick didn't hear it. I was beginning to love the moments when pages finally felt turned.

She continued, her voice covered in emotion, "You don't know how long I've wanted you to meet my family." Then she sniffed again.

"You're ready for this?" I hoped she was, because I was ready.

"Yes, and Casey, I want *them* to meet *you,* too. You're so right about that."

"Okay then. This is happening."

"I'll do whatever it takes to be with you. Full-time. And this, it feels like one of the last steps."

I wanted that, too. Hell, it was starting to feel necessary. Lot of couples work odd shifts or out of town, but I was quickly realizing I couldn't do without her. I wanted to be near her, more than not. And soon.

"I miss you so fucking much. Do you know that?" She had to know, but I wasn't going to be the fool who let it go without being said. As much of a pussy as it made me sound. She was worth being a pussy for. I'd done that to us too many times—not telling her what she needed to hear. I wasn't going to assume she knew anything, and I'd pledge to her how I felt as often as I had to. It felt like one of those times.

"I know that in the past I've confused you, or didn't say everything outright. I know for a long time I was playing along. But that game is over now. I love you. I want you. Every day. As soon as fucking possible, honeybee. I. Love. You."

It only made it that much worse because we were having the conversation on the phone.

"I love you too," she said. "I've tried to do this on my own, Casey. And I failed us each time, because I'm stronger *with* you. When you're near me, I can do anything. I tried to do everything my way, or some delusional version of the right way or whatever. But I was wrong. This *is* the right way, because it's *our* way. And I'm proud of our way."

I let her words settle in. And I'll be a son of a bitch if she hadn't really understood where I was coming from. She knew. She knew *me.* She knew what we needed.

We really have got this.

"Now, book a flight for tomorrow. Text me goodnight. Then call and harass me in the morning."

I looked at our ships that sat on my desk. I had originally positioned them facing each other, because I just wanted to get where she was. But now, that was all wrong. The wind was never blowing us in the same direction until that moment. We weren't passing each other by this time. She was right with her analogy. This time the wind would blow the both of us together. In the same direction. I moved them, side by side. Now, they'd both face forward.

Before hanging up, she told me she loved me again and asked that I let her know when I'd be in town the next day.

I was going to meet her family. And in front of all of them, I'd announce I was opening my own branch of Bay Brewing Company—in Seattle.

We wouldn't have to choose one place or the other. We could have both. We could have everything.

She'd realize when I said I wanted to be where she was, that I'd meant it.

Me: Do you want me to pick you up? I've got a rental.

Honeybee: Don't be silly. I can pick you up at the airport. I just have something to do at five. When do you get in?

Me: About 4:15. What do you have to do?

Honeybee: Nosy, are we?

Me: Not we, just me. Now tell me. Secrets don't make friends.

Honeybee: We're already friends. I was going to tell you when

I saw you, but Grant agreed to sign the papers tomorrow after work. I'm picking them up after he gets off.

I stood up out of my chair and read the message.
Papers.
Signed divorce papers.
This *was* real.

Me: Do you want me to go with you?

Honeybee: No. It'll be fine. I'm only stopping by to pick them up.

I couldn't argue with her, even though I wanted to. I had to concentrate and trust she knew it was all right to go alone. If she was worried, she would have told me. But something felt off.

Maybe, it was just me not believing it was real.

Me: I'll meet you at your parents' then. I'll wait in the car until you get there.

Honeybee: Okay. I won't be long. Meet about 5:30? We'll go in together. You're really coming?

Me: You can bet your sweet ass I'll be there.

Honeybee: I'll see you tomorrow.

Me: Tomorrow. Goodnight.

We were going to have a happy life. I didn't have to wish for it any longer. We were still going to fuck up. There were going to be days when we didn't get along and things wouldn't always be perfect.

But we'd figure it out. Our bond was strong and only getting stronger. It was going to be a great ride.

THIRTY

Blake

Thursday, June 3, 2010

THE ROAD TO WHERE we were had been bumpy. That was an understatement. But maybe good things don't just come to those who wait. Maybe good things also come to those strong enough to fight when it looked like a losing battle. Those who never gave up.

And when I missed him, all I had to do was remind myself that.

Talking to him on the phone always made me feel better, even though we were miles apart. There was something so amazing about telling him I wanted to see him, and him saying that he'd come. Just like that.

It was surreal how things were lining up the way I'd dreamed they would.

By this time the next night, I'd have signed divorce papers. It wasn't that I was excited about getting a divorce. It wasn't like that at all. I never should have married Grant to begin with. I still felt guilty about doing that to him. To our families. And to Casey. It wasn't until recently when I'd realized I'd been hurting myself just as much.

Seeing Dr. Rex helped tremendously. I finally sensed I was doing things for the sole purpose of making *me* happy. And all along, those were the same things that made Casey happy too. How much time had

I wasted trying to make Grant happy when he wasn't making me feel the same way?

I was a coward, but not anymore.

Me: Tell me you love me and I'll go to sleep.

Casey: I fucking love you.

I giggled.

Me: You have a way with words. I fucking love you too. I can't wait to see you tomorrow.

Casey: Go to sleep and it will get here faster.

I yawned and looked at the time on my phone. It was after eleven and I had a big day on my horizon. I'd taken the next day off work to help my mom get things ready for the party, but I still had a long day of running here and there picking things up for her. Which was perfect. The day would fly fast and I would be counting down the minutes.

As my eyes grew heavy I sent him one final message.

Me: We've so fucking got this.

The next morning I felt like I was on top of the world. Casey called early telling me he had to get a move on, but he wanted to say good morning first. We were kind of making me a little sick.

It was awesome.

I had to pick up Reggie from the airport and while I waited by baggage claim, I kept imagining Casey walking down the path from the arrival gates instead of my brother. While I was there, I called the caterers and confirmed everything for the next day and added a few more servers. Now that Casey was coming, I didn't feel like spending the entire night in the kitchen.

It was a small party of only about sixty, but that was a lot when they were all in a few small rooms.

The movers had already come, packed, and moved a lot of their furniture. My parents had a nice-sized home, but there was just too much stuff in there for it to be a functional space for a party. My mom finally agreed to my idea of having them moved out for the night, when I told her the furniture would be safer in storage for the weekend. Much safer than in everyone's way. And since she had a penchant for red wine, she'd agreed.

We had some small tables brought in and removing everything worked perfectly for having a band out on their deck. We'd leave the French doors open, allowing both music and guests to float in and out.

According to my list, as soon as I dropped Reggie off at Mom and Dad's, I'd have just enough time to go back to my apartment and take a quick shower before going to Grant's.

It was odd, that just out of the blue he decided he would sign, but I wasn't about to argue.

I wanted it over. The sooner the better.

"There's my brat," Reggie said as he hugged me. "So lover-boy is coming over tonight, huh?"

I'd told him on the phone earlier about Grant signing the papers and how Casey was flying in to come to the party. But only after he changed the subject when I asked if he'd seen anything of Nora. I was unrelenting. Call it sister's intuition, but I knew there was something there.

"Yeah, I'm a little nervous."

"I would be, too. Did you tell Mom and Dad he was coming over?"

"No. I didn't know what to say and they're busy with this party. I figured I'd just see how it goes when I bring him tonight first."

"All right. So where is he? Are we picking him up, too?"

"No. He's getting a car and meeting me there after I finish up with Grant. Where's your date, beefcake?" I teased, knowing he didn't have one. But I was in a great mood and teasing him was fun.

Turns out my joke wasn't funny. His face got serious and he started walking toward the exit.

"Chicago," he mumbled. He kept talking as he walked, but I

couldn't make out what he was saying under his breath. It sounded like he was chanting something. I guess everyone has their own complicated stuff.

I'd leave him alone. I understood *complicated.* I was fluent.

On the way to Mom and Dad's, I told him about the difference we'd witnessed in Shane over the past few months. The working out. The new apartment. He finally moved out last month. Reggie and Shane didn't talk a whole lot after Shane married Kari, but I think they emailed some. And I hoped they'd get closer again.

After Shane's divorce—and frankly for some time before that—he'd changed from a fun-loving guy into a quiet introvert. I think Reggie felt bad for not being there for him and I'd had my own problems taking center stage.

Shane and I had spent a lot of time together last fall after I left Casey but not as much in the past six months. Then it was more of a buddy system than anything. We were both miserable and it was nice having someone to be with without having to explain everything.

I was surprised when Reggie said he'd noticed a shift too, saying that Shane was thinking about starting up a small business and had asked him for advice. Neither of us knew what the catalyst for it was, but Shane was looking and acting like a man with a mission. We agreed that whatever the shift had been, we weren't going to question it.

I dropped Reggie off and headed straight to my apartment.

There were so many things going through my mind as I showered.

I walked myself through the next few hours and how I saw them going.

I'd go to Grant's house—it was always Grant's house—and in my imagination he was civil and polite, but brief. He would sign and we'd have an awkward hug and pledge to be friends. Of course, I had at one time cared for him, but in reality, I don't know if I'd ever miss him after the divorce.

Looking back, I never missed him. *Ever.*

I never thought about calling him. I never wondered what he was doing. I never wished he was with me. But before Casey, I didn't even know those types of thoughts existed. Thoughts that were so consuming. So intoxicating.

It took falling in love with another man to make me see I didn't even know what love was to begin with. It definitely wasn't what I had with Grant.

As I shaved my legs, I thought about how surreal it was to be having dinner with Casey, my brothers, and my parents. True enough, I was giddy with the thoughts of bringing him back to my apartment—after the impromptu meet-my-parents' dinner. But I was elated he wanted to meet my family and I wanted to show him off.

It felt so right.

I toweled off and smiled at myself in the mirror. I'd done it. I wasn't sure what *it* was, but a feeling of peace cleaned away every last knot of anxiety that had set up residence in my stomach over the past few years.

I fantasized about Casey shaking my dad's hand. My dad looking at me and seeing me smile. Then he'd say to Casey, "It's nice to finally meet you." Happy tears sprang to my eyes as I imagined my mother telling me how handsome she thought he was. Because, of course, she'd be just as smitten as I.

And it wasn't like it was the first time he'd ever been to my apartment—hell, he owned the damn thing—but with all the weekend's excitement, it felt like a miracle I'd be spending it with him. Sharing it with him. Making new memories where we laughed and smiled.

No fighting.

No worrying.

No struggle.

No leaving and crying.

My current dreams were coming true and it was time to start making new ones.

I knew how Casey felt about marriage. However, I had kind of a bad run as a wife, but considering he was the man I was bad *with,* maybe he was cutting me some slack.

Dinner wasn't going to be anything fancy, but on more than one phone call that week, Casey mentioned me wearing a skirt the next time we saw each other. That was an easy enough wish to grant. I knew what he was thinking and I'd be reaping the benefits later.

I decided on a maxi dress. That counted as a skirt in my book. I let my hair dry naturally, only fixing the stubborn front pieces. I applied only blush and some mascara. The best part about summer was the tan. And thankfully, so far, I'd been outside more. A lot of my color came from being in San Francisco where I'd visited him every few weekends.

I sprayed a little perfume on my neck and gave myself one last look. My reflection proved that happy looked good on me and I felt beautiful.

With my purse and my extra set of divorce papers, I was ready. In the event Grant either didn't have them or wanted to keep his copy, I had a spare. I was a little behind schedule, but it would be fine.

I drove to the house I'd lived in so briefly and wondered how long I would have lived there had I never met Casey. Would I be happily married—or at least what I knew of happy—to Grant? Would we have been planning children? Would we have ended in a divorce anyway? The more I thought about it, the more I believed yes, eventually our marriage would have failed. Maybe Casey was just a catalyst, one that thankfully opened my eyes so much sooner.

I felt jittery, like I'd had too much coffee, but attributed it to nerves. I took a few deep breaths and walked up the sidewalk, stopping outside the door to knock.

It wasn't my home.

I waited.

Then I heard Grant come down the stairs near the door.

"Hello, Blake," he greeted and stepped back for me to come in. I stopped only feet inside the door. I wasn't staying long. "Welcome home," he said and shut the door.

If that was supposed to be a joke, it wasn't funny. I fought the urge to roll my eyes and let it roll off my back. I didn't have time to get into a pissing match, I had a dinner to get to, and Casey would be showing up at my parents' any minute.

"Hi, Grant. Thanks for agreeing to sign the papers," I said doing my part, for polite and civility's sake.

"I haven't signed them yet. They're upstairs." He probably had them in the room I'd been using as an office. His office now, I presumed.

"That's fine. I can wait down here while you get them," I said.

His face went from almost friendly to annoyed.

"You can't stay a little while?" It was a question, but sounded like an accusation.

I looked around and then noticed a wine glass on the table, an empty tumbler and candles lit. My muscles tensed, but I remained calm.

"I thought we could have a drink. For old time's sake," he said motioning for me to follow him to the dining area.

"No, thanks. I'm going to my parents'."

He stepped closer and something inside me regretted not bringing in my phone. I left it in the car. He took another step closer and I wished I'd let Casey come with me.

His hand came up to move my hair and I moved out of his reach. What was he thinking?

"Don't. I just want the papers and I want to leave. Please."

"Was I *bad* to you?" He'd been drinking. In his nearness, I could smell it. I didn't even know who he was anymore. The Grant I dated rarely drank, especially at home.

I slowly took a step back, needing some distance. My heart rate was beginning to beat overtime. Nervousness was turning to fear. I just needed to stay long enough to get what I came for.

"No, you weren't bad to me," I affirmed. I would say anything I needed, if it meant he'd sign the damn papers and I could go. I'd already been there longer than I wanted.

"Was I bad in bed?" he said and, again, leaned into my space. "I didn't *please* you?"

My stomach rolled. Fuck the papers. He was getting served Monday. To hell with this.

"I think I'm going to go. This was a mistake." I didn't need it. I probably deserved it, but I had better things to do.

Casey was waiting for me. He was meeting my mom and dad.

"No. I think you're going to stay and tell me what I did that was *so* bad you had to fuck another guy the whole time we were married." That was the moment I started getting really scared. Not uncomfortable. Scared. My instincts screamed to go. And it felt like my body was ready to run at any moment. And because of that, I was leaving.

I didn't say anything else. I simply turned on my heels for the door. But before my hand found the knob, he had my arm.

"You can't leave without your precious papers, Blake. Your divorce papers."

His hand squeezed around my arm. My eyes filled with tears, less from the pain he was inflicting and more for the sadness I felt having made him that way.

My voice shook as I said, "I'm sorry. I don't need the papers."

I needed Casey. I needed to leave.

"Oh, you changed your mind? That's even better. We'll rip them up."

I peered into his eyes and saw a total stranger. Though the things he said were from anger, his voice still sounded eerily complacent, like a robot. And now it wasn't a joke. It was scaring the fuck out of me.

"Please, just let me go," I asked and brought my free hand up to where he was holding me and tried to pull him off. That sentence spoke to so much more than just my arm, and he heard it too.

"I'm not sure if I'm ready to let you leave just yet. Let's go get those papers." He pulled and my instincts told me to pull back, and my body acted like it was trying to sit. My legs locked and yanked, but he held me tighter.

Then he began to pull me up the stairs.

"Stop. Please, just stop. Please. I want to go. Why are you acting like this? This isn't like you," I pleaded.

"You want to go? This isn't like me? I gave you everything. You didn't have to work and travel like you were. You could have had a good life here with me. We could have had a family." He aggressively wrenched my arm, but I still resisted, trying to hold my footing below the first step. "But, no. I wasn't good enough, so you fucked someone else. So this is the new me, Blake. Maybe you'll like me better this way."

He'd managed to pull me up two steps. The skin on my arm throbbed as he pressed flesh against bone.

I had to stop crying and figure out what to do. I couldn't concentrate on my arm. I needed to get away. He was crazy.

Step after step, he went backward, jerking me as he went, his force only waning when I struggled against his hold. I fought and pulled back, almost bringing us both down. He stopped, grabbed a fistful of my hair, and heaved me up toward him.

I silently screamed and surrendered a little ground. He trudged me up a little farther by the head.

"Does he pull your hair? Maybe that's what women want these days. Is that it?"

I couldn't suppress my sobs and my focus began to blur. I just wanted to go to my mom and dad's. I should never have come. I didn't know he would be like this. I didn't see it coming.

Casey is waiting for me. What if he thinks I changed my mind? What if he leaves?

True horror gripped me with that thought.

My mind scrambled.

I went a little easier. Grant was actually pulling some of my hair out and it hurt like hell. I could feel it tear from my scalp lock by lock. It burned as it ripped from me.

"See? That's better. I think you like it. Maybe when we get up here we'll just call your parents and tell them you're not coming to dinner. Then, you'll be free to have a drink with me. After we rip up those papers we don't need," he said as we topped the flight of stairs.

"I'm not staying here," I defiantly squeaked out. "Just let me go. Please." I tried to pull back again, but his grip was unrelenting.

"Oh, I think you'll do what I want to do for a change tonight, Blake."

I needed to hit him. I'd known that the whole time. I was just afraid he'd hit back. *Would he really hit me?* But I didn't have a choice. Something told me if he got me to the very top of the stairs it would only get worse. I swung up at him and only hit him weakly in the arm.

"You like to hit, too?" He jerked my head up so he was staring into my eyes. The venom inside his was terrifying.

He wasn't concerned for me.

He wasn't worried about me.

He only cared about proving a point and making me pay for what I'd done.

This was about his pride, not his love for me.

There was no love for me.

Then I felt his fist across my cheek and it blinded me. I saw stars as every nerve in my cheek roared in agony. I'd never been hit before. And since he held my head with a fist of my hair, the force of the blow also sent searing pain through my scalp. I felt skin rip away from skin. I'd never been in pain like that and my senses all at once began to shut down.

He was yelling, but I couldn't hear.

He was so close, but I couldn't smell the vile liquor anymore.

He was a monster, but he was fading.

I was going to pass out.

Casey is going to think I'm not coming. He's going to leave me.

A fleeting surge of adrenaline spiked through my system. I had one more shot. I didn't overthink it, there wasn't time. I lunged forward, taking him off guard since he was pulling me. Head first into his thigh—which was the closest part of him I could reach and I bit him. I bit through his jeans until I felt his skin break in my mouth. Until I tasted blood. Metallic and salty.

"You fucking bitch!" he screamed, as I twisted my head back and forth.

He had to let me go.

In my attack, he'd released my hair and arm to smack and hit my head and face. I let up.

I was free, but too quickly, to urgent to get away, I leaned back. My feet slipped and went backward.

And then there was nothing.

THIRTY-ONE

Casey

Friday, June 4, 2010

NOTHING.

She hadn't called me all afternoon. She'd been busy, and I didn't want to bother her. I tried to be cool and not let my overactive imagination wander. But it was getting to me.

I sat in her parents' driveway, watching the minutes tick by on the clock in my rental car.

She was only five fucking minutes late. No reason for alarm.

Then it was ten.

I stirred uncomfortably. Looked at my phone. It read the same time as the dashboard and I saw I had not erroneously missed any calls from her.

What is it about time, and waiting for someone that causes minutes to stretch into years? I stayed calm, but my senses were watching for her in every capacity. A call. Headlights on the street. The sound of her voice.

Her family's party wasn't until the next day, but the wide, paved driveway to their house was full of vehicles.

Fifteen minutes.

Twenty minutes.

If anyone saw me sitting out there, I feared they'd wonder who I was and what I was doing.

I checked my fucking phone again, then said, "Fuck it," and decided to text.

Me: Everything okay? I'm in front of your parents' house.

I waited five more minutes. Still nothing.

I did a search on my phone to find Grant's address. When I found it and was just about to turn over the ignition, I saw the front porch light turn on and their door open.

Reggie stepped outside so I got out of the car, thankfully having already met that brother before. I was glad it was him. We met halfway up the cement sidewalk.

"Hey, Casey. It's good to see you," he said in greeting, holding a hand out for me to shake. I extended mine to him, noticing the tremble in my fingers. My body felt weird, but I pushed it aside. I was being foolish.

He smiled and seemed friendly enough.

Was I expecting them to hate me? In some ways, maybe I was. I was the other man. The home-wrecker. I just hoped they also saw me as the man Blake loved and someone who she deemed worthy of this whole mess.

"Hi, it's good to see you, too."

He looked past me to the car and asked, "Are you here with Blake? I don't see her."

"I was meeting her here. I think she's running late." I looked at my watch.

Thirty-six motherfucking minutes.

"Actually, she's about a half hour late and she's not replying to my messages."

He pulled his phone out of his jeans pocket and swiped it open. "Let me see if I can get her to answer," he said.

I liked Reggie.

He was definitely a dude I didn't want to piss off. He was even bigger, more bulked up than the first times we'd met. That one warning look he'd given me at the airport in Chicago, was enough for me to make sure I stayed on his good side.

I watched as he held the phone to his ear and waited. My heart began to race even more. Faintly, hearing her phone ring though the speaker on his phone.

Something wasn't right.

She would have called.

I was going to Grant's. *Now.*

"You know what, I think I'm gonna go look for her. Make sure she's okay."

As soon as I said that, the expression on his face asked me a million questions, but he only spoke two. "Why wouldn't she be okay? Do you know where she is?" Her older brother's voice changed from the casual friendly tone he'd just used, to one that wasn't friendly at all.

"She told me she was running by Grant's place. She said that he finally agreed to sign the divorce papers." I didn't feel like sticking around any longer. I needed to get to her. My instincts were unmistakably telling me, fast wasn't fast enough. "I'm going over there."

"Wait," Reggie said. But I wasn't going to. Hopefully, he saw it as me being concerned and not crazy, but at that moment I didn't really care. And I was kind of crazy.

"Sorry, Reggie, I'm not waiting. I won't cause any trouble, I just need to know she's all right." I was already headed back to the car. The beginning symptoms of panic and adrenaline setting alight my system.

"I'm going, too," I heard from right behind me. And when I got to the driver's side and opened the door, it was almost like déjà vu—looking at the stern brotherly face over the roof of the car.

"If you're concerned, then I'm concerned. She's my sister." That was all he needed to say.

As I drove, Reggie instructed where to turn. Of course, I already knew, but I let him continue telling me anyway. It was too much of an effort to tell him to stop and my mind was elsewhere, running through the many nightmarish possibilities I hoped were just an overreaction on my part.

The car handled well as I easily broke every speed limit on the way.

When we pulled up, nothing looked off. Her car was parked out front just as I suspected. Reggie wasted no time getting out of the car and didn't bother waiting for me, though I was right behind him. Maybe he was feeding off my anxiety, but his pace told me he, too, was worried at that point.

A sound I never wanted to hear again leaked through the walls of the house, "Get up, you bitch!" Flashes of neon red lit my vision.

Reggie, being in front of me, saw what I'd feared through the window first.

Grant had hurt Blake, but I didn't know how badly or what he'd done. And, honestly, that was just semantics. It was simple. He hurt *her* and I was about to kill *him*.

"You motherfucker!" Reggie roared, as he barged in through the thankfully unlocked door.

"What did you do?" Reggie yelled as he went to Blake on the ground close to the stairs. I couldn't stop to look. I wanted to and everything in my body told me to, but since Reggie went to her first, I decided I'd deal with Grant.

I felt violent. Enraged. I wanted to hurt him. Needed to hurt him.

If it was bad, and since I couldn't hear her say anything, I knew it was, I'd lose control. If I actually saw it, I wouldn't stop until I killed him.

Why didn't I come with her?

I hadn't bothered looking in the window and therefore hadn't seen what Reggie had seen. Upon entering the house and quickly scanning for information, I saw the table with candles and two empty glasses. A bottle of wine. Grant backing away from where I knew Blake was when Reggie came through the door. She was on the ground and she wasn't making any sounds.

Don't fucking look.

Reggie was already on the phone. "I need the police and an ambulance at 9335 Aloha St. Now!" The urgency with which he spoke said what I needed to know. He was with her and he'd take care of her. I needed to take care of the bastard who hurt her.

"What's he doing?" mumbled Grant as he continued to back away. I stalked forward, trying to control myself. All the while, he was in my sights. My target.

Rage. I'd never experienced blinding rage, but hearing Reggie frantically call for help on Blake's behalf . . . I pursued a retreating

Grant. The spineless fucking coward.

"She fell," he explained. His hands up in defense.

"She tripped on her dress. You can't just barge in here," he complained, taking more steps backward into the dining room. I saw blood seeping through his pants.

I refused to focus on the details Reggie was telling the emergency dispatcher.

I only saw Grant.

"What happened to your leg, Grant?" asked my voice, but I hadn't planned to say anything. My thoughts and processes split, dividing into different roles. My mind controlled my mouth, while anger controlled my body.

He looked down at the side of his thigh and then back up at me. I was close enough to smell the alcohol on his breath.

"Goddammit!" screamed Reggie. "What the fuck did you do to my sister?"

"She's *my* wife," Grant said, with a hardened jaw. The cornered dog that he was began showing his teeth.

He had a lot of fucking nerve. I asked, even toned, "Your wife?" The motherfucker was about to get a lesson. "That's where you're wrong. She might have shared a wedding day with you, but she's mine." I was a flame-ready fuse and he was the match. If he struck me the wrong way, I was prepared to burn him to the fucking ground.

The distance between us closed and he leaned back over the table set for two. I pressed into him. Before I beat him to a pulp, I needed to know one thing.

"Where. Are. The. Divorce. Papers?" I demanded slowly and plainly, so the bastard would understand me. I wasn't leaving until they were signed and he wasn't leaving until I had them.

That was what *she* wanted. What she came for.

Then, he'd be going one of two places: Jail or the hospital. *Preferably both.*

Grant sneered at me with smugness and defiance. That didn't suit me. My clenched hand met his gut. And then again in quick succession. The power coursing through me wasn't even driving my swings full force. I'd held back. *For now.*

He tried to swing back, but I caught him with a left to his other side causing him to take a knee.

"Maybe you didn't fucking hear me. Where are the goddamned papers you told her you'd sign?" I shouted in his ear as he hunched over. I grabbed his neck to bring him back up.

I heard sirens.

He still didn't talk. I was done with his bullshit.

My fist met his face with a force I hadn't known I possessed. I felt his nose break, and immediately there was blood pouring from it.

It felt good.

You hurt her. I hurt you.

I still hadn't allowed myself to look at Blake's prone body on the floor. If I looked I'd kill him for sure.

"Where are they?" I repeated. He was bent at the waist holding his face.

"They're in a drawer upstairs. I'll get them. I'll get them," he wailed.

The sirens grew louder. If he didn't sign them before the police arrived, then everything she came there for was for nothing. All she went through was for nothing.

Not on my watch, fucker.

I seized the back of his neck and squeezed with all my might. "I'm going up there with you and you're *not* coming down unless they're signed. Do you understand me?" I pulled him toward me and I turned around, with hopes of avoiding seeing what I knew was there.

But I failed.

My honeybee. My everything.

Reggie was hunched over her, rubbing her cheek. Her eyes were closed. Her tear-stained face looked like she was sleeping, but her legs were sprawled out and one of her arms was under her. There was blood under her head.

I staved off the urge to vomit from seeing her like that.

My precious fucking honeybee.

There wasn't a thing I could do for her except finish what she'd come for. The ambulance was close. They would help her. I would help her too. I'd finish this fucking mess for us.

The sirens got closer.

"You're okay," he said softly to her. As we went to walk past, Reggie sprung so fast I thought he was going to hit me. In an instant he was in Grant's face, one which I held straight ahead by his neck.

Reggie cocked an arm to swing and I yelled, "Reggie!" A hit like that from him would ensure Grant would be out cold and I needed him to make good on what he'd told her he would do. He saw it in my eyes. This was my fight. "Not yet."

Reggie backed down, but latched onto the front of his shirt and said, almost savagely, "If she tells me you hurt her like this on purpose, I'm going to ruin you. And I'm going to love doing it."

I thought I'd seen his business face, but I was way off. A vein throbbed in his forehead. Then he let him go, mumbling to himself, and we walked past them and up the stairs. There was blood on the wall and again, my gut lurched imagining what she'd been through.

I pointed at her brother as we climbed. "Don't fucking leave her."

No longer was I worried about him, he didn't scare me nearly as bad as seeing her on the ground.

I surged forward, roughly pushing Grant up the stairs.

The sirens screamed through the air.

"Which room, asshole?"

When he didn't answer me fast enough, I put applied more pressure to his neck. My white-knuckled fingers ached and my nails dug into his skin.

"There! On the right. Let me go and I'll get them."

The sirens stopped.

I rushed into the room and released him, shoving his worthless ass inside. I flipped on the switch. An office.

He wobbled over to his desk and opened the top drawer.

From downstairs I heard Reggie yell, "Hurry up!" to whoever had arrived. I saw red and blue lights reflecting off the houses from the office's second-story window.

"You think you can just take whatever you want from people?" Grant sneered. "We were going to have a life. A good life." I don't know if the pussy bastard was crying, or if the punch to his nose made his eyes look like that. Red and crazy.

But when he lifted his arm from the drawer, there was no mistaking what I saw. A gun.

Little did he know, my give-a-fuck was downstairs with my girl.

"Fucking shoot me!" I yelled. "Do you think that's going to fix anything? Go ahead. You're pissed that your wife loves me? Go ahead. Do it." I'd lost all rational thought.

"I want those papers, Grant. So you've got two fucking choices." I wasn't backing down. Gun or no gun. "Sign the fucking papers or shoot me. Because, you know what, either fucking way you lose, Grant. *You* lose. You don't get her back. Just. Fucking. Do. Something!"

The revolver shook in his hand and I heard it click as he pulled the hammer back.

"Seattle PD. Drop. Your. Weapon!" boomed a man from behind me.

Grant's eyes closed and his head fell back a little, an eerie smile spread across his face.

"You lose too, Casey."

Then the gun fired.

THIRTY-TWO

Blake

Saturday, June 5, 2010

PAIN. AGONIZING PAIN. MY head hurt. There was more aching, but in no specific locations.

There was a ringing in my ears and I could faintly hear its vibrato singing through my body. It amplified the more I focused on it. The sound was shrill and distracted me from my ghostly thoughts.

My muscles were tense and contracted. They tightened, almost pulsing in time with a faint beeping.

It was maddening.

I felt inverted. All of my organs doing their jobs outside of me. And my external senses were buried deep within. My brain had thoughts separate from my limbs. My eyes remained closed, but my mind wasn't processing things in three dimensions anyway.

Beep. Pulse.

It was too warm. I considered kicking my legs, but I was caught. Panic hit me.

My safety felt like a popped blister. I was exposed and raw.

My leg moved without request, kicking lightly at first. It was more like a twitch. Then the other one jostled and pain shot up my thigh and hip. It was physical pain, something that felt both missed and remembered at the same time through my haze.

Then my foot slowly unscrambled the sheet, kicking free. The air was cold outside the fabric, my feet were covered, but my leg was bare and it absorbed the feeling of exposure.

Through the ringing in my ears, I thought I heard a voice.

My legs stopped moving, but my eyes wouldn't open. I felt like I was underwater and my senses were diluted.

The sound was louder. Closer.

My fist squeezed again and a potent surge of adrenaline raced through my detached body.

Beep. Pulse.

I wasn't alone. A sense of nearness to another person tiptoed into my dark awareness.

My senses worked collectively trying to unravel the mystery of who was there. My ears rang constantly and I could feel the vibration of a voice, but the words didn't register clearly enough to listen.

My silent body screamed, each cell waving a flag.

Help.

A bitterness blanketed my tongue and there was something in my throat that made it itch. My lips didn't move, except to bunch and pinch when the beeping and pulsing refrained.

The stinging underneath my dry eyelids was fiery hot and they watered to dowse the burn. They were heavy, yet they flinched in time to the routine the rest of my body aligned itself with.

My nose worked overtime. Looked for clues and taking stock of my surroundings. It wasn't that my other senses were lazy; they were simply busy finding their places. Metallic air registered through my nose and my left lung ached each time I asked it to do more.

Inhale, pain. Exhale, more pain.

Beep. Pulse.

Where is he? Where was I? Why do I feel burglarized? What's missing? Someone is in here. I need to say something.

My fingers felt like melting ice, liquid and light, yet cold and stiff.

Someone was talking. Their voice sounded muffled . . . like through a pillow.

A felt a touch on my leg. It was warm and gentle. It was him.

Casey, I was trying to get to you. You didn't leave me. I'm trying to get to you.

Then the darkness came back.

THIRTY-THREE

Casey

Tuesday, June 8, 2010

*C*OME BACK TO ME, *Blake.*

"She still has a lot of swelling and we're going to keep her unconscious for another day to let it subside. She has some fluid lingering right here," the doctor said and motioned with his hand right behind his ears. "We don't think that there will be any permanent damage, but we'll have to wait to be sure."

Wait.

I knew waiting.

I'd say I was good at waiting, but who wasn't when they didn't have a choice. The talent of waiting was like the ability to change a tire. Most people can do it if they have to, but if someone will do it for you, that's the way to go. I was just practiced at sucking it up and changing the tire myself.

She'd been asleep for three days. That's a long time if you've ever watched someone just sleep. I knew she was asleep—for real—because when no one was around, I told her jokes. The dirty ones she said she hated, but laughed at every time.

I hadn't heard her laugh for three fucking, long-ass, never-ending days.

Waiting for her laugh was the biggest, flattest, most off-the-rim blow-out of my life.

But I was hanging in there.

Most of the time.

Sometimes.

Sometimes I wasn't. In those moments, when nobody was around—when her mom was getting coffee—I wasn't okay. It's not a manly thing to say, but you go fucking nuts just sitting there, thinking. And not knowing what happened. What he'd said to her. What he'd done to her. It was killing me.

That sweet fucking woman who never wanted to hurt anyone, least of all that selfish prick, was always the one getting the lion's share of the pain.

But also, I really missed her laugh. Maybe I mentioned that.

When you're in a hospital, thinking the worst things imaginable, and no one is there to tell you you're wrong, you lose a little bit of control at a time. The things you can usually think about without becoming a wadded-up fool, become things that make you wish you looked as put together as the wadded-up fool. Because that would be better.

I thought about my mom a lot. It was hard not to when the last time I'd been in a hospital was with her. Then one day, we went home without her. And that's a feeling you don't soon forget.

But I wouldn't be leaving without Blake.

I thought about how her dad apologized to me a few nights before, when he was having—what some might call—a weak moment. When he'd become pretty upset. It was a weird first time meeting her parents.

"I'm sorry I gave her away to him," he'd said, as he'd sat in the coveted comfy chair, his hands praying in front of weepy eyes while he spoke to me. His daughter lay there with six fractured ribs, four on one side and two on the other. A herniated disc in her back, that would probably give her trouble again later in life—we were told. Thirteen stitches in her head, which the doctor said looked like a tear, and therefore, not likely sustained in the fall. A bruised arm, with definable fingers marks wrapping all the way around her small tricep. A fat lip and a bruised cheek. More bruises on her back, arms, and legs. And a goddamned concussion, bad enough they were keeping her asleep until the swelling subsided.

So I could see where her dad was coming from; I felt much the same. I knew she was going over there and I didn't go with her, even when something said I should.

But at that moment, when her dad said that to me, I went back in time to where Blake's dad thought giving her away to Grant had been the best option. And I felt the massive weight of that with him.

"I'm sorry I wasn't man enough to prove you wrong back then," I'd admitted.

That night, her dad and I talked about a lot of things and I told him, rather than asked him, that when she was ready, I wanted her to be my wife, for no other reason than I wanted to be *her* husband.

I wanted to prove I woke up every day for her and my every decision bore her in mind. I wanted to be her best friend and know I was the one she counted on.

I told her dad how I'd bought the new building in Seattle—mostly on my own—and if Blake wanted to stay there, I'd never pressure her to leave. But if she wanted to move, I had a house big enough for us to make it our home.

It didn't matter to me either way anymore. There was only one thing I knew for certain. I wanted to be where she was, because those days were my favorites. Days without her I simply existed. My days with Blake were the ones I truly *lived*.

Her mom stayed every night with Blake and me.

They never asked me to leave or give them privacy. I wouldn't even if they had. I only left for about an hour the other afternoon after the doctors came in, to take a shower. Audrey had gotten some things together for me to take back to her place and made me eat a sandwich.

It was so weird going into Blake's place—my building—alone. Her sweet smell lived in that apartment and if I had to leave her side to go anywhere, it was there.

I didn't stay gone long, even though I knew they were keeping her medicated. I needed to be there when she woke up or if, God forbid, anything happened.

Grant sustained a gunshot wound to the shoulder and was released from the hospital into custody about twenty-four hours later. The police don't like it when you don't put your gun down.

Then Grant's family's lawyer put enough pressure on him that he signed the divorce papers on Monday, before he saw a judge regarding his other offenses. His lawyer thought it looked better if he was compliant with the papers, since Blake's father had their lawyer officially serve Grant while he was in jail.

Then the motherfucker posted bail.

Blake's dad didn't mess around though, and we all got orders of protection against Grant. Because Phil, Blake's dad, insisted. The only person who needed protection was Grant if he ever thought he'd step foot near Blake again.

I got to meet Dr. Rex when she came by on the fourth and last day Blake was asleep.

"Thanks for being there for her," I told the doctor, who was more like a friend to my honeybee. "She really likes talking to you."

"I really like listening," she replied, as she looked her over and held her hand. "I never thought this would happen. She never said he was violent." I saw guilt in her eyes as she quietly examined Blake's many injuries.

"I don't think she ever thought he'd go this far either." She would have told me, or I would have been able to tell if she'd honestly been scared of him. I'd thought his behavior was awful over those past months, but even I never saw it coming. It's crazy what can send a person over the edge.

Dr. Rex didn't stay long, and as the drugs faded out of her system, I could see signs of Blake returning. Almost piece by piece.

They took out the breathing tube, since she was breathing well on her own, and the medicine didn't have her so bogged down.

Her hands would move and her face would tick as if she were dreaming. Her mom and dad went down to the cafeteria for dinner, and it was just us.

"Open your eyes, Blake. Come on," I said softly. I'd said it hundreds of times that day, but that time I'd said it out loud. "I'm waiting for you and I really miss you." I sat in the comfy chair that had become permanently located next to her bed. Someone was always in it and it was finally my turn.

I held her hand in both of mine and kissed each of her fingers. They were warm, and every so often they'd twitch.

"Do you know how much I love you? Have I told you enough?" I asked her. "Did I ever tell you that I rigged it so our booths were across from each other at the first show we did in Atlanta? The organizer must have thought I was crazy. I even bribed her with free beer for her husband." I looked up at her peaceful face. "Why didn't I tell you I loved you *then*? Why didn't I tell you in Chicago that you were it for me? Because I think I knew then, too. Please be okay, honeybee. I'll do anything. I'll never cut my hair again. I'll never be gone for more than one night at a time. I'll never let you wonder how perfect you are. Your perfect heart? It's perfect for mine."

"Don't cut your hair," I heard her rasp.

Her eyes were still closed, but I knew I hadn't imagined it. I stood to lean over her and I smoothed my hand across the side of her face.

"I won't. Blake, are you okay?" I thought maybe I should get a nurse. The swelling had gone down in her head, but they assured us she'd probably have a major headache when she finally woke up. They'd gauge how to treat it when she could tell them how bad it was.

"I'm sore," she mumbled. Her sweet voice was the most gravely, hoarse, but wonderful music to my ears.

"I know you are. You're pretty banged up."

The police would want to come and talk to her. I didn't want to be around for that. Still, I had to. I wouldn't let her go through any of it alone.

"I'm in the hospital?" she asked. "I'm thirsty."

I grabbed the Styrofoam cup, which Jackie, the nice nurse, kept fresh for her for when she finally came to, and bent the straw so she could sip.

"Here," I told her, bringing the plastic to her mouth. Her eyes still didn't open, they were closed tightly, but her mouth did and she took a small drink. "Do your eyes hurt?"

She shook her head no and then winced, no doubt feeling the contusion and bruising she had on the back of her scalp. Her stitches were up higher.

"I'm tired," she said after she swallowed. "I'm so tired."

"I know. Just sleep, I'll be here."

"Don't leave," she whispered and her fingers stretched out like they wanted mine. I gave them to her and she held them loosely, but inside it felt so tight. "Please don't go. I was trying to get to you so you wouldn't leave me." Then she nodded back off.

Her mom and dad came back in, and Blake woke up again—just enough for them to see she was going to be okay. So they went home.

I stayed.

That was a long night.

I slept in the chair by her bed and laid my head on the mattress next to our linked hands. Whenever she'd stir, I'd wake up. The nurses came in almost every hour to check her IV and monitors, but they were used to me by then.

"Casey, let me get you another pillow. You know the comfy chair reclines, right? You can't be getting any sleep like that," said Jackie—did I mention Jackie was our favorite? She was. She brought me coffee every morning, too. And not just the shit from down the hall. She got me the better stuff from downstairs and brought it to me in a mug.

Good nurses make all the difference.

I didn't take her up on the pillow; I wasn't that uncomfortable.

I fell asleep around the time of the early morning shift change and didn't wake up until I felt Blake's hand in my hair, lazily spinning a curl around her fingers.

I opened my eyes to find her watching me. My eyes burned, having missed looking into hers.

"Hi," she said.

"Good morning." I stood and kissed her lips and for the first time in too damn long; they finally fucking kissed me back. "I missed you."

"I missed you, too. How long have I been here?" she asked. She still looked tired and weak, but color rose into her face and I could already see a world of difference.

"It's Wednesday," I said.

The look on her face, realizing just how long it had been made her lip quiver. "Wednesday?" she said as she teared up.

"It's okay. You're okay," I reassured her. "You were just sleeping."

"I'm okay," she said back, but she didn't sound very confident.

"The police want me to call them when you wake up. They want to talk to you about what happened."

Her head fell to the side and a tear slid down her cheek. "I don't want to talk about it. I don't remember." Not wanting to talk about it first and not remembering second wasn't very believable.

"You can tell them that. It's okay. I promise."

"Where is he?" she asked, but didn't look back up at me. Her gaze was directed somewhere out the window.

"I don't know. The police shot him. He was in the hospital for a little while and then he went to jail. Monday he had a hearing and bailed out."

"They shot him?"

"He had a gun upstairs."

She turned on her side away from me. So I walked around the bed.

"You don't have to talk about it right now. All you have to do is rest and feel better. Okay?" I moved the hair from her wet face. It was eating me alive to see how she'd reacted. When I'd woken up she'd looked fine.

"I should have gone with you," I said and kissed her temple. "I'm so fucking sorry."

"I'm okay," she said. Then sniffled a little and started to lean up.

"Are they going to serve him the papers?"

I hoped this part would bring her some sort of relief.

"They're signed, honeybee. They served him with a new set. When you sign those, it's done. Your lawyer said he'd have them processed in just a few days."

"I want to sign them now."

"I can have your dad bring them when he comes."

"You met my dad?" she asked and her lips started to shake again. "I missed it? And my mom?"

Realization came over her again. I didn't like seeing her feeling robbed of the memory, but she looked so unbearably cute.

"I missed their party?"

I wasn't sure I was handling things the way I should have. All I could do was tell her the truth.

"They just postponed it. You didn't miss it, honeybee." I sat next to her so we were level. "And I met your parents, yes. But everything is good." I smiled. "I think they like me."

She finally smiled back. "I knew they would."

"What's not to like?"

She was quiet for a few minutes and she seemed to study me. She gazed at me so intensely, with so much love. I could feel it.

"Casey, I need something."

"Anything."

"As soon as those papers go through," she said so tenderly, "will you marry me?"

I didn't know her reasons. And I didn't want to say no. But it wasn't the way she deserved. The way we deserved.

She was awake. She was all right. And she wanted to be *my* wife.

I'd say she still had a lot of medicine in her system, but all three of those things made my fucking life better in every single way.

. . . The Sail.

EPILOGUE

H E WAS THERE. HE didn't leave. And I wanted *him* to be my husband.

I'd heard bits and pieces of conversations while asleep. I thought I'd remembered Casey saying he wanted to marry me. But everything was still a little foggy. Things were still connecting and slowly beginning to make sense.

It was weird. I'd known Casey was there and I'd known my family had been there, too.

So when it hit me that it was the first time they'd met, it was like I knew it, but was just finding out all at the same time.

Events and reality from dreaming, were still hard to trust. I was processing what had happened, against the things I'd been fantasizing about.

I relived going to Grant's over and over.

But other times, I was with Casey and I was safe and loved. That was what I wanted.

I didn't know how I'd deal with all of it. I still didn't know the whole story, but I knew one thing. I needed Casey.

"Did you just propose to me?" he asked with a smirk and a curious brow. "Those drugs must be good," he said and chuckled a little, not taking me seriously. "There's a chapel downstairs."

That sounded fine to me. I wanted to be his and I wasn't willing to wait any longer than I had to. We'd wasted so much time. We'd made so many mistakes in not telling each other what we wanted. What we needed.

I knew it was a long shot. And I wasn't the best of brides. But in the history of wives, if I was his, I'd be the best there ever was.

"I'm serious," I said, emotion swelling from deep inside. "I want to be your wife. I want to be yours. I don't want to be Blake Kelly anymore, Casey. Please?" I wept, but I couldn't help it when I finally admitted such a fundamental truth.

He scooted closer and wrapped his arms around me. My head found his shoulder and he spoke into my ear.

"You beautiful, precious woman, yes. I will marry you. I'll marry you right now, but *I* want to ask *you*. Okay? I won't ask you to wait long. And I don't want a long engagement. But, Blake, I've been dreaming about asking you to marry me for a long, long time. So just give me a little bit here. You won't have to wait long. I love you more than this. Let me show you."

I turned my head into his face. "I hate waiting for you."

I trusted his heart, my heart's other half, but I needed to be his. Needed him to be mine.

"The best things are worth waiting a little for, honeybee. Otherwise, fairy tales would start with happily ever after."

ACKNOWLEDGEMENTS

My cup hasn't just runneth over, it has flooded my world. Support from family, friends, authors, bloggers and readers has more than once left me speechless. To readers who've cried and laughed and hung-on with these two characters, I'm forever indebted to you. You've felt what they felt and been through what they have. Consequently, you've changed my life. Thank you.

I'd like to acknowledge my beta team Megan, Bianca, Wendy, Michelle P., Jessica, Michelle T., Toski and Natasha. They are so supportive and can see through my crazy ramblings to the story I'm trying to tell. Then they help me organize those thoughts into *almost* coherent pieces. They ask, "Mo, you can make this better?" I can. So, I revise.

Then Marion (Marion Making Manuscripts) my wonderful editor, in turn, takes those pieces and says, "No. You can do much better here and here. I think you're trying to say . . ." She's right. I revise.

Then my manuscript goes off to my second editor, Claire (Bare Naked Words, Author Services) who says, "Make this better. Stronger. Clearer. You don't need this." Again, I revise.

Then I sent it to my proofreaders. Candy, Jordan, Sandra, Rachel, Jackie, Michelle and Laura tell me, "All of these things can be better. Fix them." One more time, I revise.

It's because of all of you, Sail is *infinitesimally* better than what I'm capable of on my own. My team needs no revision.

Thank you to Ari at Cover It! Designs and Stacey at Champagne Formatting for making Sail look exactly how I imagined it.

To my friends in the Mo Stash and the honeybees in Take the Bait who keep me laughing, happy and moving forward. I love you.

Wendy, you're such a blessing to me. I'm so happy to work with you.

To Chelle, Aly and Erin, I'm proud to call you friends. You're classy, smart and talented women who know everything!

To DS, you're becoming one of my favorite writing partners. I can't wait to see what you do.

To Nat, you're still mine. Forever. It's not up for discussion.

Because it felt wrong not saying something about Laurel, I'd like to note she's cool, too.

Danny, I love you. Thank you for putting up with me. And Blake and Casey. (And Chelle and Aly. And Natasha. And Kelly.) I can only write about love because you give me so much of it. So much that I have love to spare. *Fifty-five cents* worth.

ABOUT THE AUTHOR

M. Mabie lives in Illinois with her husband. She loves reading and writing romance. She cares about politics but will not discuss them in public. She uses the same fork at every meal, watches Wayne's World while cleaning, and lets her dog sleep on her head. M. Mabie has never been accused of being tight lipped or shy. In fact, if you listen very closely, you can probably hear her flapping her gums. You're encouraged to contact M. Mabie about her future works, as well as this one.

Website: http://www.mmabie.com
FaceBook: http://www.facebook.com/AuthorMMabie
Twitter: http://www.twitter.com/AuthorMMabie

CPSIA information can be obtained
at www.ICGtesting.com
Printed in the USA
LVOW10s1138020417

529322LV00009B/562/P